S
Y
2 x
P9-BXZ-907

## She should be afraid . . .

. . . Tess realized drowsily, as she opened her eyes and first saw the huge dark silhouette framed against the blood-red sky beyond the slit of window. In his billowing cloak he reminded her of a fierce hawk limned in fire. Galen.

She wasn't afraid. There was something supremely natural in waking and seeing Galen watching her. She was glad the waiting was over. The years had passed so slowly, the loneliness had gone on too long. "Galen . . ." She inhaled sharply as he turned his face toward her. The features were the same, but his expression made them alien to her. He looked younger, harder, his dark eyes glittering in the firelight, his lips curving in a reckless smile that held an element of cruelty. "I think it would be best if we talk," she murmured.

"I'm done with talk." He shrugged off his cloak and dropped it on the carpet in front of the hearth. "And I'm done with waiting."

Waiting. The word stirred something in her memory, a realization that had come to her in that half-waking state only a moment ago. "You're not yourself. Let's go back to the palace and we'll—"

"On the contrary, you've never seen me more myself than I am at this moment." He unbuttoned his shirt, took it off, and dropped it carelessly on the floor. His tone was soft, easy, almost carefree, and yet Tess found herself tensing as if confronted by a wild animal. The comparison was apt because in this moment Galen seemed a magnificent cat-like creature, lithe, silken, completely sensual.

**Bantam Books by Iris Johansen**

LONG AFTER MIDNIGHT
THE UGLY DUCKLING
LION'S BRIDE
DARK RIDER
MIDNIGHT WARRIOR
THE BELOVED SCOUNDREL
THE MAGNIFICENT ROGUE
THE TIGER PRINCE
THE DELANEY CHRISTMAS CAROL
LAST BRIDGE HOME
THE GOLDEN BARBARIAN
REAP THE WIND
STORM WINDS
THE WIND DANCER

# THE

# Golden

# Barbarian

## *Iris Johansen*

*Bantam Books*

New York • Toronto • London • Sydney • Auckland

*This edition contains the complete text
of the original hardcover edition.*
NOT ONE WORD HAS BEEN OMITTED.

THE GOLDEN BARBARIAN
*A Bantam Book*

*PUBLISHING HISTORY*
*Doubleday edition published 1991*
*Bantam edition / April 1992*

*All rights reserved.*
*Copyright © 1991 by Iris Johansen.*
*Cover art copyright © 1992 by Alan Ayers.*

*No part of this book may be reproduced or transmitted in any form
or by any means, electronic or mechanical, including photocopying, recording,
or by any information storage and retrieval system, without permission in
writing
from the publisher.*
*For information address: Doubleday, 1540 Broadway, New York, NY 10036.*

> *If you purchased this book without a cover you should be aware that this
> book is stolen property. It was reported as "unsold and destroyed" to the
> publisher and neither the author nor the publisher has received any
> payment for this "stripped book."*

ISBN 0-553-29604-3

*Published simultaneously in the United States and Canada*

Bantam Books are published by Bantam Books, a division of Bantam Doubleday Dell Publishing Group, Inc. Its trademark, consisting of the words "Bantam Books" and the portrayal of a rooster, is Registered in U.S. Patent and
Trademark Office and in other countries. Marca Registrada. Bantam Books,
1540 Broadway, New York, New York 10036.

PRINTED IN THE UNITED STATES OF AMERICA

OPM   19   18   17   16   15   14   13   12   11

# Prologue

Belajo, Tamrovia
April 8, 1797

She was going to die!

Tess could feel herself sinking deeper and deeper into the quicksand as each second passed. The muck was already up to her shoulders and creeping higher. Sweet Mary, she didn't want to die, to slip beneath that slimy surface and never come up again.

It had all happened so fast. . . .

Apollo whimpered and started struggling once more against the insidious suction.

No, she couldn't die. If she died, Apollo would also die and this would have been for nothing.

Tess drew the wolfhound closer and stroked

his long muzzle. "Shh. It's all right, boy. I'll think of something."

"It will be interesting to discover what that will be."

Dizzying relief poured through her as she glanced over her shoulder to see her cousin Sacha, sitting his horse a few yards away. Luck was with her today. Not only were she and Apollo not going to die, but she might get out of this without even a beating. Sacha Rubinoff wasn't like any other grown-up she knew. Though he was almost twenty-five to her twelve, he never ignored her, and was more apt to laugh than frown at her misdemeanors. "I can't get out, Sacha. The vine broke and I—"

"What the devil do we have here?"

Sacha had been joined by another rider, and Tess glanced impatiently at the man. Couldn't he see she had no time for conversation? It was Sacha's new friend, the barbarian from that outlandish country across the border. "Sacha's golden barbarian" she had heard her father call him, and she had wondered why. After all, with an olive complexion and dark hair and eyes, he was more bronze than golden. She looked again at her cousin and demanded, "Get us out of here, Sacha."

Sacha grinned. "Presently." He turned to the man who had reined in beside him. "I don't believe you've been introduced to my young cousin, Galen. Sheikh Galen Ben Raschid, permit me to present Her Highness Theresa Christina Maria

Rubinoff. I assure you she's not usually so filthy." His brow drew together as he ruminated on his assertion. "Though now that I think upon it—"

"Sacha!" The mud was up to her throat, and she was having trouble keeping Apollo's muzzle above the thick ooze. "Stop teasing me!"

"Oh, very well." He swung off his gray mare and began looking around for a branch. "I must remember to reprimand your governess, Cousin." He turned to Galen. "She's all of twelve years old and apparently can't read that large Danger sign by the tree."

"I can read," Tess said indignantly. "And I know this forest better than you. It was Apollo. He ran ahead of me, and when he got stuck, he began thrashing and sank deeper, and I held onto the vine from that tree and—"

"Had to go in after him." Sacha sighed as he picked up a long branch and tested it for sturdiness. "Not clever, Tess."

"I couldn't let him die." The mud was almost up to her chin, and fear tightened her throat. "Can you . . . hurry?"

Sacha extended the branch out over the mud pool. It lacked a foot of reaching her. "You can make it. Let go of the dog and move slowly across and grab hold. I'll pull you in."

The branch appeared to be sturdy enough, and she knew how strong Sacha was. In a moment she could be on safe ground. She looked longingly at the branch.

Then she shook her head. "I can't leave

Apollo. He'd start thrashing and go under. You'll have to think of something else."

Sacha's grin disappeared. "There's no time, Tess. Don't be stupid. He's just a hound. You'll go under yourself in a few minutes."

Panic soared through her, and she could feel the tears sting her eyes. She was going to die, after all. "I *can't* leave him."

Sacha began cursing beneath his breath.

"You must be very still." It was the other man speaking to her. Galen Ben Raschid removed his elegant dark blue brocade coat and laid it over the pommel before slipping from the saddle. "Try not to move at all until I tell you." He jerked off his gleaming black boots and tossed them aside.

"You're going in after the stubborn chit?" Sacha shook his head. "That's my task, friend."

Galen smiled. "A prince of the realm up to his ears in mud? Leave it to me. A little dirt and an uncivilized brigand are nothing out of the ordinary. Do keep that branch handy, though."

He stepped onto the quicksand. He was a big man, his weight far greater than Tess's, and he immediately sank to his knees. By the time he reached her, the mud was up to his waist.

"Hold tight to the hound," Galen said as he searched beneath the surface, found and grasped her waist. "Don't try to help me." He lifted her head and called, "The branch, Sacha."

Tess murmured soothingly to Apollo before shifting her grip from his neck to his middle.

"What if his nose goes under? He won't be able to breathe."

"We'll be out of here in a moment. You might start worrying about breathing yourself."

"Apollo is my responsibility." She added absently, "You'll take care of me."

"I will?"

"Yes." She had no doubt that she was safe now. From the moment he had slipped his arms about her waist and started pulling her toward firm ground, she had felt a strange sense of boundless security. She glanced around and met his gaze. "I know you won't let me go."

His arm instinctively tightened on her waist. "No, I won't let you go." He looked away from her. "I've gone to far too much trouble to lose you now. Another few inches and I'll be able to grab the branch, and then we'll let Sacha do the work."

"Better than getting filthy in that muck," Sacha called cheerfully. "I have no fondness for playing in the mud. I've thought it over, and I believe I'm actually doing you a favor, Galen. You might never have had this experience in Sedikhan. Of course, you have sand dunes, but what about—"

"The branch."

Sacha extended the branch a little farther, and Galen grabbed it with his free hand.

Sacha backed away, working the branch hand over hand to pull them through the mud. In a moment he was reaching down and jerking Galen out of the quicksand.

"Dear Lord!" Sacha exclaimed. Galen was

coated with gray-brown mud from his chin to his stockinged feet, and Sacha began to roar with laughter. "*Merde*. This is wonderful. I wish your *chères amies* could see you now. Perhaps they wouldn't be so eager to come to your bed."

"Or perhaps they'd be more eager," Galen said dryly as he turned and lifted Tess onto solid ground. "It's not my fine looks that make them open their thighs."

"What a cynic you are. You have no faith at all in the fair sex."

Galen glanced meaningfully at Tess. "This is no talk for children to hear."

"Tess?" Sacha shook his head. "She may be a child, but she's not ignorant. She grew up at court and knows the way of things." He turned to Tess. "Don't you, brat?"

"Talk later." Tess was struggling, tugging at Apollo, trying to get him out of the mud. "Help me."

Galen pushed her aside, grabbed the wolfhound by the shoulders, and lifted him from the muck onto safe ground.

The borzoi immediately repaid him by shaking his lean body, sending mud flying in all directions.

"Ungrateful wretch." Galen wiped a splotch of mud from his cheek.

"He couldn't help it," Tess defended the animal fiercely. "Dogs do that. You can't expect—" She rounded on Sacha fiercely. "Stop laughing at him. My lord Ben Raschid was very brave and does not deserve this from you."

Sacha's blue eyes gleamed with mischief. "Another conquest, Galen. A little young, but in a few years she'll blossom into—"

"Pay no attention to him," Tess told Galen in disgust.

"Have no fear." Galen cast Sacha a disparaging glance. "I do not."

"Where is Pauline, Tess?" Sacha asked. "I trust you're not wandering in the forest alone?"

"Of course not." Tess didn't look at him as she knelt by Apollo and tried futilely to scrape some of the mud off his long hair. "But she and Mandle are busy. They stopped as soon as we entered the forest and won't miss me for a while."

"Busy?"

"Fornicating."

Sacha chuckled as he saw the faint ripple of shock cross Galen's face. "That certainly should keep her busy enough. Once is never enough for Pauline."

"Who is this Pauline?" Galen asked.

"Pauline Calbren is Tess's loyal and virtuous nurse," Sacha said. "And Mandle is one of my dear uncle's grooms."

"This is doing no good." Tess gave up on Apollo's coat, stood, and slipped her hand into Galen's. "Come with me. There's a lake beyond that hill where we can bathe off this mud." She turned toward his horse and stopped short, her eyes widening in delight. "Sweet Mary, he's beautiful." She dropped Galen's hand and took a step closer to the stallion, who shied away from her. "Why didn't I notice how lovely he was?"

"It's understandable. You were a tad busy trying to stay alive," Sacha said.

Tess ignored his flippancy. "What's his name?"

"Telzan," Galen answered.

"I'm not going to hurt you, Telzan," she crooned softly as she took another step forward. The horse gazed at her uncertainly and then stood still under her hand as she touched the white diamond on his muzzle.

"Amazing," the young sheikh murmured. "He doesn't usually let strangers touch him."

"He knows I like him." She rubbed the spot between the horse's eyes that was particularly sensitive. "He wouldn't have shied away from me in the first place if I didn't smell so foul from that bog."

"Now that you've brought it to my attention . . ." Sacha wrinkled his nose. "I believe I would shy away from you too."

Galen smiled quizzically. "You're very good with horses."

"When she's not falling into bogs, the brat spends most of her time sneaking away to the palace stables," Sacha said.

"This horse wasn't in the stables." Tess's tone was positive as she turned to glance at Galen. "I would have noticed him."

"I've been keeping him near my lodging in town. I arrived at the palace today."

"Is he from Sedikhan?"

"Yes."

"I've never seen a horse that has so much power and grace. Are there other horses like this in—"

"Tess." Sacha wrinkled his nose again. "Now!"

Tess nodded. "We'll walk to the lake. You won't want to mount your horse and get him all muddy."

"Yes, heaven forbid you should get your horse muddy, Galen," Sacha said solemnly.

"I believe you're enjoying this a little too much," Galen said silkily. "I may have to toss you into that bog to even matters out." He lifted Tess easily in his arms and set her on his horse, then mounted behind her. "But not until I can get clean enough to feel properly superior."

"I'm dripping that funny green slime on your saddle," Tess protested. "I told you we should walk."

He kicked the horse into a gallop and headed toward the hill she had indicated. Apollo skittered after them, barking joyously. "A little mud on his withers? That's as nothing to Telzan. He's accustomed to far rougher treatment."

She looked disapprovingly at him over her shoulder. "You don't use spurs?"

"No, and I don't make it a practice to listen to the commands of children."

"I didn't command you. I simply told you it would be better."

"It's much the same thing." Galen rounded the

hill and a moment later stopped before the small lake bordered by stands of tall pines. "Is the water deep here?"

"No."

"Good." He scooped her from the horse and dropped her into the lake.

The cold took her breath as she fought her way to the surface.

He was still sitting his horse, watching her with a faint expectant smile on his face.

"Oh, that's good." She gasped. "Thank you."

His smile faded, and he looked at her speculatively. "It appears you have more gratitude than your hound. I expected you to be outraged."

Apollo jumped into the lake after her, splattering mud and water in her face. She laughed and ducked her face and head in the water again. Then, shaking water from her hair, she asked, "Why?" She gazed at him, the water running down her cheeks, her face alight with laughter. "I was muddy, and you took care of the matter. Why should I mind?"

"Let's just say I haven't found the ladies of the Tamrovian court to have your lack of sensibility."

"But I'm not a lady of the court." She ducked her head into the water again and then briskly wrung out her mop of auburn curls. "And I won't have to worry about being one for at least four years. I'm still in the schoolroom."

"I see." He swung off the black stallion. "Then you won't be offended if I bathe with you." He jumped into the lake and waded out farther into the water until it crested his chin. "Lord, it's cold."

"It's only April." She scrubbed her hair thoroughly and then ducked her head again. "Are the lakes not still cold in your country?"

"Not this cold. Tamrovia is in the Balkans, and Sedikhan is principally desert country." He dipped his head into the water and scrubbed it as vigorously as Tess had hers. "Though the lakes in the hills near Zalandan are not overwarm."

His wet hair shone ebony in the sunlight, and his face was ruddy with cold beneath a rich tan. The strong rays burnished his bronze skin to a shade nearer to gold, and Tess found herself staring at him in fascination. The sheikh's features were not comely as Sacha's were. His high cheekbones seemed carved with the same boldness as the granite of the rocks scattered around the lake's edge, and his dark eyes were deep-set and heavy lidded. He looked as different from the other courtiers as the wolves her father hunted were different from her gentle Apollo: harder, stronger, fiercer. Galen's actions also set him apart. He had not hesitated to plunge into the smelly bog to save her, any more than she had hesitated going in after Apollo. Even Sacha, who was fond of her, had tried to find a way of avoiding the quicksand.

Galen startled her by asking suddenly, "Why are you gazing so intently at me, *kilen?*"

"*Kilen?*"

"It means 'little one' or 'little girl' in my language."

"Oh." She looked away. "I was wondering if they called you 'golden' because of the color of your skin.

He didn't answer for a moment, only smiling sardonically. "Do they whisper about me in the schoolrooms too? No, they call me 'golden' because of the color of the gold in my purse, and the quantities of lucre therein."

She glanced back at him. "You're very rich?"

"As Midas. My hills near Zalandan are filled with gold." His lips twisted. "I'm so rich, my barbarian presence is tolerated and even occasionally sought out here in your august court."

He was hurting. She could feel it, and instinctively moved to soothe his pain. "Barbarian means wild, doesn't it? I would not think it so bad to be wild. The forest is full of beautiful wild things."

"But they are not invited to the most fashionable salons."

"Then they should be," she said staunchly.

"You won't say that in five years' time."

"Yes, I will." She waded out of the water and plopped down onto the bank, and Apollo clambered after her. She had lost both shoes, and her brown velvet gown was ruined. She would most certainly get a whipping for her misadventure. However, she would not worry about that now. She was not often allowed to talk to grown-ups, and Galen Ben Raschid was quite the most interesting one she had ever met. "I won't change."

"We shall see." Galen waded to the bank and then levered himself down beside her. "It will surprise me if you don't. Your enchanting mother is not one of my advocates."

"She's afraid of my father, and I don't think he likes you."

"Why is she afraid of your father?"

She looked at him in surprise. "Because he beats her when he's displeased."

"Really?" Galen tilted his head to look at her. "And does he whip you when you displease him?"

"Of course," she said matter-of-factly. "My mother says it is the way of all fathers with their children. Do you not whip your children?"

"I have no children," Galen said. "And it's not the way of the El Zalan to beat the women of our families. There are better ways of chastising them."

"What ways?"

"Never mind."

"You probably beat them but do not wish to admit it. My mother says some men don't like it known, but all of them beat their wives and children."

"I do not have a wife either." He frowned. "And I do not beat helpless women."

"Don't be angry. I won't speak of it again." She reached out and stroked Apollo's sopping coat. "I didn't mean to displease you. Actually, I believe I like you."

"I'm honored." He smiled crookedly and inclined his head.

She flushed. "No, truly. I mean it. I do not like many people, but I think I like you." She added awkwardly, "I thank you for not letting me die in the bog. It was most generous of you to go to the trouble."

"I was only being selfish. I have an appointment with His Majesty, and it would have ruined all my plans, even spoiled my entire day, if I'd had to stand by to watch the bog being scoured for your lifeless body."

"You're joking." She smiled uncertainly. "And you saved Apollo too."

"Why do you call him 'Apollo'? Because he's so handsome?"

She shook her head. "Because of Daphne."

"Daphne?"

"Those aren't really their names. About a year ago my father bought Apollo and Daphne from a Russian count who called them 'Wolf' and 'Sheba.' My father wanted them to have babies and raise a whole pack of hunters." She sighed. "But Daphne won't have anything to do with Apollo."

Galen burst into laughter. "And you named her Daphne after the nymph who turned herself into a tree to avoid Apollo's amorous advances?"

She nodded. "But perhaps Apollo will be able to change her mind soon." She frowned worriedly. "My father is becoming very angry with them both."

"And he will be angrier still if you do not get back to your maidservant soon."

They turned at the sound of an approaching horse. Sacha rode at a leisurely pace over to them and dropped Galen's boots onto the ground. "You look little better than when I last saw the two of you."

"We look *much* better," Tess protested indignantly. "We're clean, and we don't stink anymore." She reluctantly got to her feet. "But I must go." She hesitated. She did not want to leave them. Sacha always made her laugh, and as for his friend . . . She did not quite know how he made her feel. Most people were easy to put in nooks, but the sheikh puzzled her. He was . . . dark inside. Not black, as in evil. He was night dark. But Tess had always liked the night far better than the day. When darkness fell, the boringly obvious was deliciously transformed, shrouded in mystery, exciting. She dropped a curtsy and smiled tentatively at Galen. "Good-bye, my lord."

A flashing white smile lit up his face. "It's been an interesting experience meeting you, *kilen*."

She turned and started at a trot toward the forest.

"Wait," Sacha called. "Let me take you up on my horse and we'll—"

"No!" She shook her head adamantly. "It's better that I go alone. Pauline will say I shouldn't have troubled you. She'll be angry enough. . . ." The next moment she had disappeared into the forest, with Apollo at her heels.

"Go after her," Galen said tersely. "You can't have a child wandering around in the forest. She'll get lost or fall into another damn bog."

Sacha shook his head. "She knows the forest too well to become lost. She'll be fine."

Galen's lips thinned. "With a maid who fornicates under the child's eyes? Are you going to tell her mother?"

"No, she would dismiss Pauline."

"Good. An action much to be desired."

Sacha shook his head. "Bad. Tess, the poor imp, has little enough freedom. You've met my dear uncle Axel. His Highness has the distinction of being one of the most arrogant bastards on the face of the earth. He treats Tess little better than a chattel." He grimaced. "Worse, when she angers him. At least with a careless strumpet like Pauline as a servant, Tess gets to escape that prison of a schoolroom occasionally." He glanced curiously at Galen. "Why are you so concerned? You're not one to worry about the morals of serving wenches." He chuckled. "Unless it interferes with you having your way with them."

Galen's reaction was as much a surprise to him as to Sacha. Something about Tess Rubinoff's honesty and matter-of-fact acceptance of the world around her had oddly touched him. "Your cousin has courage. It's a quality I admire." He shrugged as he tugged on his left boot. "But it's of no concern to me. I only mentioned it because the child is your kin." He glanced at Sacha. "Though you seem to know overmuch about the lack of virtue of this Pauline."

Sacha nodded with satisfaction. "Last summer." He puffed up his chest and beamed bliss-

fully. "For four splendid weeks I gored her every
night like the bull I am, and she loved every minute of it. I had her screaming with pleasure."

"And where did this goring take place?"

"In her chamber."

Galen pulled on his other boot. "Beside the
nursery?"

Sacha frowned. "Yes. Why?"

"No special reason. Just curious." No wonder
Sacha had not been worried about talking out of
turn in front of his cousin. His presence in the
slut's bed had contributed as much as Pauline's
other partners to the child's worldly education.
Galen stood up, struggled into his silk coat, then
swung up onto Telzan's back. "Let's get back to
the palace. These wet clothes are beginning to
feel uncomfortable, and I must be ready for my
audience with your father in three hours."

Sacha nodded. "You know I would help you
more if I could?" He shook his head. "A second
son has little power in a monarchy."

Galen smiled as he urged his horse into a
trot. "You've done more than I hoped. You've introduced me at court and persuaded your father
to listen to the wild man from Sedikhan. I
wouldn't have received even that boon if you
hadn't interceded."

"I may not have done you a favor. Both my
father and older brother have little use for
me. . . . I'm much too flippant for their tastes."

But, Galen knew, beneath Sacha's flippancy
lay keen intelligence and a good heart. Soon after

making the acquaintance of Sacha Rubinoff, Galen had realized that the young prince's notorious pranks and mischief-making stemmed from boredom. The society into which he'd been born simply did not suit his volatile nature. Of late, Galen had begun to wonder what kind of man Sacha would have been if he had been raised to the sword and seasoned by battle. "You've done me a very great favor. You've given me what I came to Tamrovia to obtain."

Sacha's smile faded. "Don't count too much on this audience. It's difficult to stir my father into any decisive action these days."

"I have to try." He tried to suppress any show of desperation. "I have to make your father see that an alliance must be formed for the sake of both our countries."

Sacha pushed back his chair and stood up when Galen strode out of the audience chamber into the anteroom. "How did it—" Galen's stormy expression answered his question. "Not well."

"No alliance," Galen said curtly. "His Majesty sees no advantage in aligning himself with a primitive tribe that can offer him nothing for his protection but promises." Galen strode down the hall past the row of footmen, his every step charged with explosive energy. "Fool! Can't he see that a united Sedikhan could offer Tamrovia more than he could offer us?"

"You're speaking of my august father," Sacha

reminded him mildly as he fell into step with Galen.

"He *is* a fool."

"Yes," Sacha agreed amiably. "A very stubborn one."

"I needed this alliance to mold the tribes into a single central government. With Tamrovia as an ally the El Zalan could use the threat of a foreign invasion to rally the chieftains. There's little as powerful as a threat from an outside force to unify those who enjoy being at odds." Galen's voice vibrated harshly off the fresco-decorated domed ceilings. "Dammit, the wars *can't* go on. They're ripping Sedikhan apart. We can't go forward as long as the tribes continue to raid and kill each other."

Sacha had heard it all before and remained sympathetically silent.

"Tamrovia's forces are puny compared to the might of Sedikhan's warriors. Your father is a lunatic to believe we couldn't help defend his borders."

Sacha didn't mind this further insult to his father as he felt much the same. However, he wasn't sure he liked his country's military might impugned. He decided to change the subject. "So what do you do now?"

"Go home," Galen muttered savagely. "What else is there for me to do? Go back to warring and killing and protecting my own. It's the way of life in Sedikhan."

"You could stay here."

"Where I'm looked upon as a barbarian?" Galen shook his head. "No, my friend. I'd soon grow tired of the jokes, the innuendos, and show them how a real barbarian behaves." He glanced at Sacha. "Why don't you come to Sedikhan with me? You have no fondness for the life here at the court."

"I might do that. I hear your women are beautiful and exceedingly generous to us poor males."

"Come and find out."

Sacha's eyes gleamed with mischief. "But one can spend only so much time involved in bed play. And, since you're determined to make Sedikhan into such a boringly peaceful place . . ." He studied Galen speculatively. "I've always wondered why you chose such a path."

Galen didn't respond.

"You're matchless with a sword, a dead shot. Yet you—"

"What does it matter?"

"I'm curious. I've found that anything I do well I wish to do again."

"I . . . I like it too much," Galen said haltingly, not looking at him.

Puzzled, Sacha gazed at him. Then, suddenly, he understood. Powerful emotions seethed beneath Galen Ben Raschid's apparently calm exterior. Once allowed beyond Galen's facade, Sacha had found the sheikh possessed a recklessness and undisciplined nature that matched his own.

How would a nature so untamed respond to the unlimited opportunity for violence now existing in Sedikhan?

Galen was watching the expressions flitting across Sacha's face. "Yes," he said quietly. "I'm even more of a savage than they think I am." His lips tightened. "But I don't have to be. I have intelligence and strength of will. A man need not remain uncivilized because of his birth and perhaps even his instincts."

But it would be a lifelong battle between Galen's innate savagery and reason, Sacha thought with sympathy. "When will you leave Tamrovia?"

"Tomorrow at dawn." Galen smiled brilliantly. "Stop frowning. I haven't given up. I'm just going home to regroup my forces. If I can't get Tamrovia for an ally, perhaps I'll go to France and apply to Napoleon."

"France is a long way from Sedikhan."

"And Napoleon is very greedy. He might decide to 'protect' me out of all the gold in Zalandan." Galen shrugged. "Still, it's something to consider."

"Your mother was French, wasn't she?"

"Yes," he said curtly as he stopped at the foot of the marble staircase. "French and Tamrovian." He changed the subject. "I'm going back to my apartment and tell Said to make arrangements for the journey."

"But I'll see you this evening?"

Galen nodded, and a reckless smile lit his face. "By all means. Meet me here in the hall at eight. We'll find several accommodating ladies, and I'll show you how a warrior of the El Zalan takes his pleasure."

Before Sacha could speak, Galen was swiftly climbing the staircase.

"Several?" Sacha murmured, intrigued. He was suddenly sure it was going to prove a most interesting evening.

Someone was watching him.

Galen came wide awake in bed.

His muscles were tensed, ready to spring, but he lay quite still, his eyes slitted. His dagger was on the table by the bed, but he'd have to reach over the woman curled on his left to reach it.

"My lord Galen."

His lids flicked open. Gray eyes gazed down at him from a white, strained face surrounded by a riot of auburn curls, a child's face.

Tess Rubinoff's small hand tightened on the copper candle-holder she held. "Have you had too much wine too?" she whispered.

"What the devil are you doing here?" He jerked upright, instinctively reaching for a sheet to cover his nudity.

Tess breathed a sigh of relief. "You're not drunk. I went to Sacha's chamber first and could not make him understand. . . ." She took a step back. "I need help. I can't do it by myself. Will you—" Her glance fell on the naked woman curled up on the far side of him. "Two of them? Pauline never had more than one at a time. Why do you—"

"How did you get in here? I wasn't too drunk to lock the door."

"Through the dressing room. There's a secret

passage that leads into many rooms in the palace. I discovered it three years ago," Tess murmured absently, still studying the golden-haired woman nestled close to Galen. "That's Lady Camilla, isn't it? She looks thinner without her clothes. Who is the other one?"

"That's none of your concern." He frowned. "Said is sleeping in the dressing room."

"Your servant? I was very quiet. He didn't wake up." She shrugged dismissively. "But that's not important. I need your help." She glanced at the sheet he'd pulled over his hips. "Are you cold?" She turned and snatched his crimson velvet robe from a chair beside the bed. "Here, put this on."

"Thank you," he said dryly as he slipped his arms into the sleeves of the robe. "You're very considerate, if not overly circumspect."

Camilla turned over and moaned in her sleep.

Tess glanced casually at her. "They're both sleeping very soundly. Are they in their cups too?"

"They've had a few glasses of wine."

Tess critically studied the slumbering women. "More than a few glasses. But I suppose we don't want to chance waking them. I really shouldn't be here."

"I believe I've already made that observation."

"I'll wait for you in the dressing room." She turned and started across the chamber to the door of the antechamber.

"If Said wakes up, he'll cut your throat before I can join you. The men of our tribe do not appreciate midnight visitors."

"I've learned to move very quietly. I won't wake him."

"Then you can move right back to your chamber. I have no intention of going anyw—" The back of the child's white gown was spattered with brown-red stains. Bloodstains.

She glanced over her shoulder. "What?"

"Nothing. Go on. I'll join you in a moment."

She opened the paneled door and disappeared from view.

Galen muttered a curse as he carefully climbed over Camilla and slipped from the bed.

He didn't need this problem after several hours of roistering and sexual indulgence. His head was only a little clearer than Sacha's, and his temper was not of the best. If the child had been beaten by that brutal ox of a father, it was Sacha's concern and not Galen's. She was not his kinswoman, and he had no reason to feel such a flare of rage at the sight of blood on her gown. His emotion for the waif probably stemmed from his rescue of her from the bog. He would listen to her tale of woe and then send her back to her chamber with a promise to talk to Sacha in the morning.

He opened the door to the dressing room to find Tess sitting patiently on a chair against the far wall. Lord, she was tiny. Fine-boned and fragile, she looked closer to nine than twelve in her prim, full-skirted white gown. The candle she had set on the low console beside her chair revealed a dusting of golden freckles over her small nose and burnished her wild aureole of curls. Said slept peacefully on a cot opposite Tess, Galen noticed with exasperation. How the devil had she managed not to wake him?

Galen stepped inside the room. "Said!"

Said Abdul raised his tousled head, instantly awake. "What is—" He broke off as he saw the child sitting a few yards away. "Who—"

"That's not important." Galen could hardly blame him for being stunned. When Said had retired for the night, the females with whom Galen had been occupied had definitely not been children. "Leave us. I'll call when I need you."

Said nodded dazedly, rolled out of bed, wrapping his blanket around his naked body. In another moment he stumbled past Galen into the bedchamber.

Tess sat up straighter in the chair as Galen shut the door and leaned back against it. "I have to hurry. Father told my mother she must take more concern in my upbringing, and she may check on me tonight."

"Your back?"

She frowned uncomprehendingly. "What are— Oh, is it bleeding again? I'm glad you told me. I'll have to soak my gown in cold water when I get back to my chamber." She shook her head. "No, my mother suspects Pauline of not watching me closely enough."

"Your presence here certainly supports that supposition." His lips tightened. "I'm glad someone cares that you're not in your bed at this hour."

"Of course they care," she said, surprised. "I have value for them. They have no son, and I must make a great marriage to compensate for my mother's failing. If anything happened to me, they would have nothing."

"I see." Arranged marriages were also common in his country, but for some reason the idea that this child was treated only as a game piece filled him with anger. "And who are you to marry?"

"It will be decided later. I should really be affianced by now." She wrinkled her nose. "But my father hopes I will become more comely later and attract better offers." Her gaze went to the door of the bedchamber. "Like Lady Camilla. She had many offers before they wed her to Count Evaigne. You must be a great relief to her after fornicating with that old man."

He bowed mockingly. "I tried to make the experience memorable. She did not seem disap—" He broke off as he realized he was talking to her as if she were an experienced lady of the court instead of a girl still in the schoolroom. "We should not be talking about the lady's infidelities."

She turned her crystal-gray gaze on him. "Why not? I meant no insult. I know that this is how things are done. First, the marriage, and then a young, strong man to bed. Pauline says that every wife has a lover, sometimes two or—"

"I'm not interested in what Pauline says," he said irritably. "Why are you here?"

She drew a deep breath. "Apollo."

Whatever he had expected, it was not this. "The dog?"

Tess nodded, her small hands clutching the arms of the chair. "I was stupid. Pauline was angry about the gown, and I told her about Apollo and the bog. She told my mother, and my mother told my father, and—"

"He beat you."

She looked at him, startled. "Why should that bother me? I expected nothing else. No, it was Apollo. My father was angry, and said that this was the last straw. The bitch will not mate, and Apollo had almost cost him dear." Her enormous eyes were filled with tears that shimmered in the candlelight. "He ordered them both killed."

He felt a sudden surge of tenderness as he gazed at her. He, too, had experienced the pain of having beloved animals taken from him by death. "I'm sorry."

"I did not come to you for sympathy. I need help." She wiped her eyes with the back of her hand. "It's not done yet, and I can't let it happen. As soon as they locked me in my chamber, I came out the secret passage and across the courtyard to the kennels to see Simon, the kennel master. He's a good man. He said he could put off killing the dogs, but they must be gone before my father visits in the morning."

"And you want *me* to get rid of them?"

"No, I wanted Sacha, but he was in—"

"His cups," Galen finished. "So I'm your second choice."

"Don't you see? I have no place to take them where they'll be safe, and, in truth, you are a much better choice than Sacha," she said eagerly. "Because even if Sacha sent the dogs to one of his estates in the country, my father might still hear of it and take action, but he would never go to Sedikhan."

"True. Who would go to such a savage wasteland?"

She ignored the irony in his tone. "You saw Apollo. I know he's gentle, but he's only a little over a year old, and perhaps he could be taught to hunt or guard your home. And Daphne—"

"Refuses to breed."

"You could find another use for her." Tess's voice was shaking. "She's very good-tempered and loving. She comes when I call her and puts her head beneath my hand and her hair feels so soft and—" Her voice broke, and she had to stop for a moment. When she spoke again, her words were almost inaudible. "I love them so. I can't let them die. Please, will you take them away from here?"

He was journeying by land, and the animals would be nothing but trouble on the long road home. He would be a fool to burden himself with two animals already considered useless. Yet Galen found himself immeasurably moved by Tess's plea. She was clearly a poignantly lonely child, and the wolfhounds were probably the only things she loved in this world. Yet she was being forced to beg him to rob her of them. Galen sighed in resignation. "Where are they now?"

Her face was suddenly luminous with hope. "You'll do it?"

He nodded reluctantly. "Though how I'll manage them on the journey back to Sedikhan, I have no idea. Said and I don't travel with the same pomp and fanfare as the nobles of your court."

She collapsed back against the cushions of the chair as the tension left her. "Thank God."

"I don't mean to be blasphemous, but shouldn't your thanks include me? I'm the one who's going to be severely inconvenienced for the next several weeks."

"I do thank you." Her voice vibrated with passionate sincerity. "And I promise I'll find a way to repay you."

He looked at her quizzically. "Indeed? And just what would you do to express your gratitude?"

"Anything," she said simply. "Anything at all."

She meant it. He could almost feel the intensity of the emotion sweeping through the young girl. "Without reservations?" A curiously arrested expression crossed his face as a thought suddenly occurred to him. "Someday I may decide to take advantage of your generous offer." He came across the room and drew her to her feet. "But not now. Where is this secret passage?"

She gestured to a candelabra affixed to the wall a few feet away. "You turn the candelabra to the left."

Galen twisted the candelabra, and a recessed wooden panel swung open. "Back to your chamber now. I'll get dressed and go down to tell your

kennel master to take the dogs to the woods beyond the castle and wait for Said and me."

"What if he won't do it?"

"He'll do it. Gold has a certain persuasive
eloquence."

"You'll bribe him?"

"Your debt is increasing by leaps and bounds,
isn't it?" He handed her the copper candle-holder
and gave her a gentle push toward the waiting
darkness of the passage. "You must remember
how great your debt is when it comes time for me
to collect."

"I will." She cast a quick glance over her
shoulder. "They'll be safe? Truly?"

"Truly." He smiled. "You have my word."

The next instant she had disappeared into the
darkness.

The panel swung shut, and Galen gazed thoughtfully at it, the curious smile still lingering on his
lips.

It seemed fate had intervened on his behalf,
and he would be a fool to refuse her gift. It would
take patience, determination, and a certain amount of
planning before he could accomplish his goal, but
the unity of Sedikhan was all-important.

He turned on his heel and strode back toward
the bedchamber. He would dress and tell Said
they were leaving for Sedikhan at once.

No, not quite at once.

He must first seek out Sacha and sober him
up enough to have a long talk with him.

# Chapter 1

Port of Dinar, Tamrovia
May 3, 1803

The longboat was only a few yards from the dock
when Tess caught sight of Sacha's tall, graceful
form. He was leaning indolently against a stack of
wooden boxes.

Sacha hadn't changed a whit, Tess thought
with relief. His auburn hair so like her own,
blazed in the sunlight. As they drew close to
shore, she saw that his slim, muscular body was
garbed as it always had been, with faultless ele-
gance. Today, he wore tight cream-colored buck-
skin trousers and a gold brocade coat. An intricately
tied cravat complimented his pristine white shirt.

"Sacha!" Tess waved frantically, leaning perilously far over the side of the longboat. "Sacha, it is I!"

She heard the captain mutter something in the front of the boat, but she ignored him and continued waving. "Sacha!"

He straightened away from the boxes, and a grin lit his face.

"I warn you, if you fall into the sea, I'll let you drown," he called. "This is the first time I've worn this coat, and I like it over much."

"You look like a peacock," she called back. "In Paris they're dressing with far more simplicity."

"Brat. How would you know? You've been in a convent for six years."

"I have eyes." As the longboat drew up to the dock, she took the hand Sacha reached out to her and rose cautiously to her feet. "Besides, Pauline told me."

"Ah yes, how could I forget Pauline." Sacha's hands were on her small waist, lifting her onto the dock. He groaned and staggered back a step. "*Merde*, you weigh a ton. It must be all that learning and religion they've stuffed into you." His blue eyes gleamed with mischief as he looked her up and down. "Thank God it doesn't show, or you'd never get a husband."

Tess's happiness dimmed at his mention of marriage, then she firmly dismissed the thought. There could be no other reason for her father to send for her, but it was not her way to brood on storm clouds in the distance when the sun was shining and the world close at hand was beautiful.

"I don't weigh a ton." She had often wished she did weigh more. No matter how much she ate, she remained unimpressively tiny in height and far too slender. She scarcely came to the middle button on Sacha's fine linen shirt. She lifted her chin, a mock expression of hauteur on her face. "It's you who have grown weak and puny with dissipation and excess. I wonder my father even puts enough trust in you to escort me to Belajo."

His smile faded, and he glanced away from her. "I'd better get you to the inn. The carriage is around the corner."

"One moment." She turned to the captain, who was getting out of the longboat and held out her hand. "Good-bye, Captain. Thank you for being so kind to me. It's been a very interesting voyage. You must come to Belajo sometime soon."

The grizzled captain lifted her gloved hand to his lips. "It's been interesting for us also, Your Highness," he said dryly. "Still, I wouldn't mind sailing with you again." He paused. "In a year or two."

She nodded. "I understand." She turned back to Sacha and slipped her arm through his. "I'm ready now."

Sacha glanced curiously back over his shoulder at the captain as they strolled toward the street. "The captain doesn't appear too pleased with you. What did you do to the poor man?"

"Nothing." She noted his skeptical glance and said defensively, "Well, it was the first time I had been aboard a ship without someone peering over my shoulder and telling me what I must or must not do. When I sailed for France six years ago, Pauline was with me. She wouldn't allow me a proper exploration of the ship." Quartered in Paris after she had escorted her charge to France, Pauline had married a young baker when Tess had been in the convent of St. Marguérite only a few months. "Pauline failed to show up at the pier when this ship was about to sail, and the sisters didn't have time to make other arrangements for my chaperonage."

"And what portions of the ship did you explore?"

"Have you ever been in the crow's nest?"

"That little box on top of the mast? Good God, no. I have no head for heights."

"You can see forever," Tess said dreamily. "And the wind blows your hair, and the scent of the salt and the sea is like nothing I've ever smelled."

"May I ask how you got up to the crow's nest?"

"I climbed up the masts. I had to take off my shoes, but it was little different from climbing trees in the forest at home." She frowned. "The captain's shouting did distract me, however."

"I imagine he was a bit concerned," Sacha said solemnly.

"Well, he should have waited until I reached the top before he shouted."

"I'm sure you told him that."

She nodded. "But he was too angry to listen." She looked intently at Sacha. "Is our escort at the inn?"

"No, our party arrives tomorrow. I came on ahead." A young groom jumped down from the back of the carriage and opened the door. "I thought you'd appreciate a few days of rest before we started overland. It's a four-day journey."

"I did nothing but rest on board the ship. I tried to help the sailors, but they wouldn't let me." If the fate she suspected did await her at Belajo, she was not eager to make haste on the journey. "May we have supper at that café?" She tilted her head to indicate a café bearing a sign with a painting of a mermaid curled up on a rock. "I've never eaten in a café, Sacha. Could we please?"

He nodded indulgently. "A café, yes. But not one on the waterfront."

Her face fell in disappointment. "Why not? Sailors are most interesting. They tell such grand and glorious tales."

Sacha handed her into the carriage. "More glorious than truthful."

"I'd like to see for myself." She leaned forward, her face glowing with eagerness. "Someday I'd like to take a journey to the east and follow the route of Marco Polo. Wouldn't that be a great adventure?"

Sacha's expression softened as he looked at her. "A very great adventure." He followed her into the carriage and seated himself across from her. "But you won't find any Marco Polos at the Mermaid Café, and sailors' haunts are notoriously disreputable."

"What difference does that make? You'd be with me." She wrinkled her nose ruefully. "If you fear for my virtue, I assure you no one will pay the least notice of me. I'm too small. The sailors on the ship treated me as if I were a demented infant." She leaned back on the cushioned seats as the carriage started the bouncing journey over the cobblestones. "When the man my father has chosen as my bridegroom sees me, he will very likely back out of the arrangement." She grinned as a sudden thought came to her. "What a splendid idea. If I make myself even uglier, it may be years before he can make another match."

Sacha's lids half veiled his eyes. "You have no desire for marriage?"

"Why should I?" she said. "The convent was bad enough, but at least the sisters were kind. A husband . . ." She abruptly looked out the window. "I do not like the thought of it."

"Not every man is like your father," he said gently.

"No, but they all seek to use women for their own purposes." She straightened her shoulders and smiled with an effort. "I do not wish to speak of it. Tell me what you have been doing this long time I've been away. I received only a few letters from my mother since I left Tamrovia, and each was heavy with lectures on learning meekness and obedience. You've not wed?"

"Sweet Mary, no," Sacha said in horror.

"How have you escaped that fate? You must be all of thirty."

"By staying away from court and letting every woman there forget I exist." He frowned. "And thirty is far from ancient."

She chuckled, her eyes sparkling with mirth. "But we've already discussed how puny you are."

"And how impudent you are." He smiled. "I'm glad the nuns didn't crush the spirit out of you."

His narrowed gaze on her face held surprising keenness, and Tess realized that her first impression had been wrong. Sacha *had* changed.

When she had left Tamrovia, he had been softer, lazier, even a bit foppish. Now, in spite of the languid airs he assumed, she could sense an undefinable toughness, a greater confidence, as if the softness had been honed away by the experiences of the last years. "You didn't answer me. What have you been doing?"

The sharpness of his regard was hooded again as his lids veiled his eyes. "Oh, this and that. Traveling. Acquiring new skills."

"What new skills?"

He leaned back on the cushions. "You're a curious puss. Perhaps I should ask the same of you. What did you learn in your convent?"

"That I never wanted to return to one."

He chuckled. "What else?"

"Sewing, weaving, candlemaking. Nothing of real importance. Well, except scripture, of course." She tilted her head and studied him shrewdly. "Why don't you want to answer me?"

"All in good time." He glanced out the window. "We're about to reach the inn. I've arranged for the innkeeper's daughter to act as your maid, and your boxes should arrive—"

"Why did you arrange for a servant? You didn't know Pauline wouldn't be with me."

He hesitated before he smiled teasingly. "Perhaps I thought you needed the help of a younger, more vigorous woman. Our winsome Pauline must be all of two and thirty by now." He sighed morosely. "Even more ancient than my humble self."

She laughed. "Her husband wishes she were a little less vigorous. Married a little over five years to her and he appears worn and weary."

"Pauline was never one to accept anything but the most enthusiastic cooperation . . . even if she had to force the pace."

The carriage came to a stop, and instantly the footman opened the door. Sacha sprang to the ground and helped Tess out. "Go into the inn. The innkeeper will show you to your chamber. I'll stay here until the second coach arrives and send up your boxes."

"Surely, the innkeeper could—"

But Sacha was already striding across the flagstones toward the stable, and after hesitating a moment, Tess turned and entered the inn.

"All is well?" Galen asked as Sacha entered the stable.

Sacha waited just inside the door until his eyes adjusted to the dimness. The stable was empty except for Galen, who was kneeling beside his stallion in one of the stalls to the left of the door.

The sheikh's coat had been cast aside, and the sleeves of his white shirt were rolled past his elbow. A huge kettle of water boiled over a small fire at the back of the stable, and the air was filled with the scent of herbs mingled with hay and manure.

"No," Sacha said shortly. "All is not well. I feel like a Judas."

"There's no reason for you to feel a traitor." Galen carefully wrapped a warm, damp cloth around his stallion's delicate left front ankle. "The poison is drawing well. He should be ready to travel in a day or so."

"Why don't you let Said do that?"

"Because Selik belongs to me, and I take care of my own." He lifted his head and met Sacha's gaze, saying with soft emphasis, "Everything I own."

Sacha knew this was true, and it was the only fact that made this situation tolerable. "She's little more than a child, dammit."

"Old enough. I've waited a long time."

"I know, but—"

"I won't use force."

But he would still have his way. Sacha had learned during these last six years how strong Galen's will could be. "I like the imp. I've always liked her. She doesn't deserve to be used."

"Unless she *chooses* to let herself be used." Galen rose to his feet and patted the black's nose. "And we're all pawns in the scheme of things."

Sacha stared broodingly at him. "What would

you do if I asked you not to carry on with your scheme?"

Galen's stroking hand on the horse's muzzle stopped in midmotion. "I'd consider it. You're my friend, and the woman is your cousin."

"Consider, but not comply."

"You know how important she is to me. You've been to Sedikhan." Galen continued to stroke the horse.

Yes, Sacha knew the importance of Tess in Galen's plan; it only added to his sense of being torn between loyalties. He smiled lopsidedly. "I've often wondered if that was why you persuaded me to go to Sedikhan. Am I a pawn, too, Galen?"

Galen smiled. "Of course that's why I wanted you in my homeland. Do you expect me to deny it? But it's not a pawn you've been to me all these years." He said gently, "I have no greater friend in the world."

Yes, they were friends, companions at arms, closer often than brothers. Sacha slowly shook his head. "Hell, I don't know what to do."

"Do nothing." Galen's hand fell from the horse. He turned and picked up his black coat. "It will be her choice." He shrugged into the coat, and then started toward the door. "Suppose I go and see what she says."

"Now?"

"I thought I'd wait until after we'd supped, but I think I'll have to put you out of your misery. You'll be happier once the decision is made." He grimaced. "And since I stink of horse and herbal salve, you'll know that I'm not trying to sway her with anything but reason." He started for the door. "When that cloth cools, dip it into the bucket of hot water and apply it again. I'll rejoin you after I've talked to Tess."

The chamber wasn't overluxurious, but at least it was clean. Tess bounced experimentally on the bed and made a face. Hard as the pallet in her cell in the convent. Well, it did not matter. She refused to let anything spoil her last few days of liberty.

She smiled in satisfaction as she untied the ribbons on her bonnet, took it off and sent it sailing across the room onto the cushioned chair by the door. That was better. She had always hated hats, but Pauline had insisted on providing her with dozens of the dratted things as they assembled a wardrobe for her before leaving Paris.

She stripped off her long white gloves and ruffled her hair, sending pins and clips flying before she crossed to the washstand and poured water from the flowered pitcher into the basin.

A knock sounded on the door.

"*Entrez,*" she called as she splashed water on her face. "You've been long enough, Sacha. It will be dark soon, and I'm hungry." She reached for the towel and turned to face him. "And I do want to go back to the waterfront—" Her eyes widened in shock.

Galen Ben Raschid stood in the doorway. "May I come in?"

He didn't wait for an answer as he took a few
steps forward and closed the door. He bowed
slightly. "It's been a long time. You've grown into
a young lady, Your Highness."

"I'm only three inches taller." What a stupid
thing to blurt out, she thought in self-disgust. She
couldn't seem to form an intelligent thought.

His gaze flicked to the fullness of her bodice.
"Sometimes a few inches can make an enormous
difference."

She felt an odd heat surge through her, and
knew she must be blushing. "I'm waiting for
Sacha. I've just come from France and—" Enough
of this babbling. "But you must know. Are you
traveling with Sacha? I didn't expect to see you
again after you left Tamrovia."

"I had every intention of seeing you again."
He strolled across the room toward her, moving
with animallike grace. He was bigger than she remembered, a giant of a man, and she found herself mesmerized by the flexing of the powerful
muscles of his thighs and calves beneath his
clinging black trousers. He wore a black silk coat
but no cravat, and the top button of his white
shirt was unfastened to reveal his strong brown
throat. She was conscious of a blatant maleness
about him that was shocking in intensity. He
looked the same, but he must have changed in
some way. All those years ago she had not felt
nervous in his presence.

"In fact, I've expended a good deal of effort
to see you again." He took the towel from her.

"Your face is wet." He began to gently dab her cheek.

The action was almost servile, yet there was nothing servile about Galen Ben Raschid. He dried her face as if he had every right to touch her intimately. She was quite still as she stared up at him, unable to look away. His shining black hair was tied back in a queue, and his face appeared leaner and tanner than it had been six years before. Yet the power she had sensed still seemed to be running deep beneath his controlled expression. She began to feel an odd breathlessness, and looked hurriedly away from him. "I was washing my face." Another stupidly obvious remark. What was wrong with her?

"Yes." He dabbed lightly at her chin. "You still have the most exquisite skin. Most women lose such a silky glow after childhood."

"Do they?" He stood so close, she caught the scent of horse, leather, herbs, and soap clinging to him, and felt the warmth his body was emitting. She took the towel from him and put it on the washstand. Her hand was trembling, she noticed with no surprise. "How are Apollo and Daphne?"

"In fine health."

"Good. I've often thought of them." She took a step back and asked again, "Did you come with Sacha?"

"No." He smiled faintly. "Sacha came with me. Not very willingly, I might add. He's full of doubts and apprehensions." He moved across the chamber to the chair by the door. "May I sit down?"

"I'm expecting Sacha at any moment."

He looked curiously at her. "You're afraid of me. How odd. It's not how I remember you."

"Nonsense. I'm not afraid of you. I'm merely surprised. I wasn't expecting to see you, and I was caught off guard."

"Off guard?" He repeated the expression thoughtfully. "And are you always on guard?" His gaze searched her face. "Yes, I think perhaps you are. Not surprising, considering the life you've lived." He gestured to the chair by the window. "Please sit down. I'm no threat to you."

"Sacha will—"

"Sacha won't be here until our discussion is over."

Tess hesitated, then moved quickly across the room and sat on the edge of the chair, folding her hands in her lap.

He smiled, started to sit, and then paused. "Yours?" He reached down and picked up her feathered bonnet.

The bonnet looked exceptionally silly and frivolous in his tanned, capable hands. Beautiful hands, she noticed absently. Long, graceful fingers with a certain rhythm of movement as he turned the bit of velvet-and-feather-trimmed confection to look at it from all angles.

"It doesn't look like you."

"Pauline chose it. She said it was all the crack."

"And you believed her?"

Tess shrugged. "It didn't matter."

"No." He set the hat on a table near the chair. "You're not a woman for fuss and feathers. I'd choose something entirely different for you." He sat down and rested his hands on the arms of the chair. "If you were mine."

Her gaze flew to his face, her muscles tensing.

"That frightened you again." He smiled. "A slip of the tongue. We barbarians are regretfully primitive, and possessiveness is one of our uncivilized traits." He leaned forward. "But there's nothing to be apprehensive about. I've learned to control myself so that I'm a savage only when I choose to be."

She frowned. "I don't understand you."

"You will. It's quite simple. I have a proposition for you." His gaze held hers steadfastly. "I need to join with you in marriage."

Her eyes widened, and she could feel the muscles of her stomach go rigid as if she were warding off a blow. "What?"

"I need an irreversible bond between Tamrovia and the El Zalan. King Lionel has seen fit to refuse an alliance between us. He regards the El Zalan as just another wild tribe of Bedouins. However, in my country a marriage tie is as strong as a political agreement. Brother does not fight brother. The tribes would assume a marriage with a member of the Tamrovian royal house would also offer me military protection." His hands tightened on the cushioned arms of the chair until his knuckles turned white. "I *have* to unite the tribes of Sedikhan under one rule, and the only way I can do it is to show them that my forces are more powerful than theirs. Might is everything in Sedikhan. An alliance with Tamrovia would—"

"Stop." She shook her head dazedly. "Why do you come to me? I have no say in this. My father will choose my husband, and he—"

"Will not choose a wild sheikh from Sedikhan," he finished for her.

She nodded slowly. "I meant no offense."

"None taken. I know how the court of Tamrovia regards me, and that's why I've come to you. We will wed tomorrow." He smiled. "And we will not bother to tell your father until it's too late for him to act."

Incredulous, she laughed. "That time will never come. Do you not realize I'm his property? If I married without his will, he would only petition the pope to annul it."

"Do you wish to remain his property?"

"I have no choice."

"I'm giving you a choice, one a woman of your station seldom gets to make." Galen's voice deepened persuasively. "Freedom."

Tess felt a flutter of hope stir deep within her. "Marriage is not freedom."

"It could be. It *will* be." He smiled. "Have you ever thought how it might feel to be free? To do what you wish, when you wish?"

"No." She had not let herself think of it because it hurt too much. "It's not possible."

"I can make it happen."

She jumped to her feet and went to the window to stare blindly down at the courtyard below. "You're no different from other men. You said it yourself. You like to own things."

"I also said I could control myself. Wed me tomorrow, and in three years I'll send you to Paris or London, wherever you wish to go. I'll give you a fine house and take care of your every need. You can play the great lady and have a fashionable salon. You'll live the life you wish to live." He paused before adding, "Without the encumbrance of a husband. Naturally, I'd remain in Sedikhan."

"According to tradition, that is not at all natural."

"I don't think you care a snap of your fingers for tradition."

She turned to face him. "You'd truly do this?"

He nodded.

It was too wonderful to be true. She would not have to go back to Belajo ever again. She would not have to subdue her behavior and act the mind-less chattel as her mother did.

She began to pace back and forth, her hands clasped behind her back. "It could never work. My father would capture us before we reached the border."

Galen shook his head. "The border is only a day's ride from here."

"He would follow us to your Zalandan."

"He might be tempted," Galen agreed. "But once in Sedikhan I anticipate no problem. We're a warrior breed. Your Tamrovians are soft in comparison."

She lifted her chin defiantly. "Then why do you need us as a show of power?"

"An invisible sword is as good as a real one, if the enemy believes it's pointed at his heart."

"Wouldn't your show of force be useless if the other sheikhs realized Tamrovia was against this marriage?"

A flicker of surprise crossed his face. "Very perceptive. Yes, it would. But it won't happen. I only need six months to soothe your father's ire and make him tolerate me as a son-in-law."

"You won't have six months."

"Yes, I will. Perhaps a little longer." He paused. "It depends upon when he decides to send word to the convent that you're to come home to Tamrovia."

"But he's already brought—" Realization dawned. "Sacha?"

"He paid a visit to his uncle and took the opportunity to write a letter to the Mother Superior and affix your father's seal to the letter."

She remembered Pauline's sudden desertion at the last moment. "And Pauline?"

"She would have been in the way on the journey to Zalandan. I assure you that she was more than content with the compensation we forwarded her."

"I see. You've been very thorough."

"But eminently civilized," he said mockingly. "My father kidnapped my mother and forced her to wed him after my birth. But I'm not my father. I've always found choice is far better than force."

She gazed at him shrewdly. "As long as the choice is in your favor."

"Why should marriage not benefit both of us?"

She nibbled at her lower lip. "Why me?"

"You're the only daughter of the brother of the king of Tamrovia." He met her gaze. "And you impressed me as possessing a certain boldness and sense of purpose that would be essential to my plan."

"Three years and I'm free?"

He nodded. "You won't find your life in Zalandan intolerable. We have certain comforts."

"Could I have a horse? A wonderful, beautiful horse like Telzan?"

A tiny smile appeared on his lips. "It's just as well I have little vanity, or I might be insulted that you require a four-footed bribe to wed me."

"Could I?" she persisted.

He nodded gravely. "One beautiful horse. I have a golden palomino mare that would suit you admirably."

Excitement and fear churned within her. "I don't know. . . ."

"One more thing."

She looked warily at him.

"I'll require a child as quickly as possible."

She stared at him in uncertainty. "A child?"

"You seem surprised. I don't believe I'm being unreasonable."

"No, every man wants a son."

"It doesn't have to be a son. Just a child to strengthen the bond. Your father would have a good deal more trouble making a match for you if you were carrying another man's child." He stood up. "And in my people's eyes a child would prove the strength of the alliance."

It had been drummed into her from childhood that it would be her duty to bear her husband as many children as she was capable of bearing, but the possibility had seemed as nebulous as the man who would give them to her. "A child . . ."

"The babe would be no bother to you. I'll keep it in Sedikhan when you leave."

For some reason that thought brought a wrenching pain.

Galen's gaze narrowed on her face. "What's wrong?"

"I don't know." She spoke haltingly. "But it hurt me when you took Apollo and Daphne away. What if . . . I might want—"

"I suggest we discuss the disposition of the child when it becomes a reality." He smiled. "By 'as quickly as possible,' I didn't mean tomorrow. I will let you become accustomed to me before the marriage is consummated. I've waited a long time. I can wait a little longer. Suppose I leave you to think about my offer." He glanced over his shoulder as he walked to the door. "It's a very good bargain. Everything you could want. Would you rather Sacha took you home to Belajo?" He read the answer in her expression and added softly, "Then be bold, *kilen*."

The door shut behind him.

She whirled and looked out the window again.

*"Be bold."*

She had never lacked boldness, but these circumstances were different, and the step he wanted her to take would affect her entire future. She would be defying her father to journey to a wild land with a man who was as strange and barbaric as Sedikhan.

Yet Galen had been entirely reasonable and urbane as he had outlined his proposal to her. He had used persuasion, not force. Why was she still thinking of him as a barbarian?

She caught sight of him below, striding toward the stable. His pace was unhurried, almost leisurely, but every step held enormous power under complete control.

She suddenly realized his iron control was at the core of her fascination with him. She had sensed a deeply layered explosive violence in him as he outlined his proposition, and she had been waiting for it to surface.

She was being foolish. If he did possess a violent nature, she would probably never see it. He had given her a choice. But what if she refused his proposal? Would he still be so calm and reasonable?

Galen disappeared into the stable, and Tess felt a sudden easing, as if she had been released from bondage. Bondage? What an odd thought when he had offered her only freedom.

She turned away from the window and sat down in the chair. Resting her chin on her hand, she dreamily gazed into thin air.

Freedom. The thought was honey-sweet, and the temptation nearly irresistible. Three years and she could be free for the rest of her life. Three years was not such a long time. She had spent six at the convent, and Zalandan had to be better than that dreary place.

Freedom.

"Well?" Sacha asked as Galen came into the stable.

"I left her to mull over my proposition." Galen took off his coat and hung it over the side of the stall again. He knelt beside Sacha in the stall. "I'll carry on."

"Does she need me?"

Galen's brow rose as he glanced sidewise at Sacha. "I don't know why you persist in believing I'm victimizing your sweet cousin. I was everything gentlemanly and courteous to her."

"She's still a child. I'd hoped while she was away, she would become—"

"Convents don't contribute to worldly wisdom." Galen dipped the cloth in the hot water again. "That's why you were able to persuade her father to send her away." He applied the salve and wrapped it tight around the stallion's ankle. "She's not really a child. She may lack experience, but we both know she is anything but ignorant and naive."

Sacha remembered the luminous look on Tess's face when she had spoken of traveling the route of Marco Polo. "She has her dreams."

"So do I." Galen waited another moment, then loosened the bandage and began to unwind it. "Sedikhan."

Sacha frowned as he looked at the bandage. "How many times are you going to do that?"

Galen put the cloth in the hot water in the bucket. "As long as it takes to get the results I need."

"All night?"

"If necessary." Galen squeezed the water out of the cloth and began spreading the salve on the bandage.

Sacha felt a sudden uneasiness as he realized Galen's determination in this matter, small as it might be, was as nothing compared to his devotion to his grand plan.

"Why don't you warn her?" Galen suggested without looking at him. "It's what you want to do."

"You won't try to stop me?"

"Why should I? It will make you feel better." He wound the bandage tightly around the horse's ankle. "And it won't make any difference."

"You think you've convinced her?"

"No," Galen said softly, "I *know* I've convinced her."

"You don't have to do it." Sacha gazed at Tess's taut back as she looked out the window. "All you have to do is say you don't wish to marry Galen, and we'll set out for Belajo in the morning."

"It was you, wasn't it?" Tess asked in a low

voice. "I was surprised when my father told me I was to go to France. It was you who presented the idea and talked him into it. Why?"

"Galen decided you needed protection, and he believed the sisters would provide it."

"And do you always do what Sheikh Ben Raschid tells you to do?"

"He convinced me it was for your good."

"Yes, he can be very persuasive." She turned to face him. "But I'm surprised he can so easily get you to do as he wishes."

"He does not—" He broke off and grimaced ruefully. "It's true he had no trouble molding me to his wishes at that time. I was a thoughtless popinjay who had more concern for the cut of my coat than anything happening around me."

She studied him thoughtfully. "But you've changed."

"Sedikhan changed me. Galen changed me." Sacha glanced down at his gold brocade coat. "Though I admit I still like an occasional bit of flash and glitter."

"There's nothing wrong with flash and glitter." She smiled affectionately. "And that empty-headed popinjay was very kind to me."

"No, I wasn't. I should have done more to help you. It's not enough to care, one has to act."

"Is that what you learned in Sedikhan?"

"Yes, that and other things."

"Then it must be a very interesting country. Why are you trying to persuade me not to go?"

"I feel responsible."

"And?"

"It's a difficult situation. I don't want you hurt."

"Yet you consented to maneuver me into this position."

"Galen needed you. Sedikhan needed you. I thought it wouldn't be such a bad bargain for you."

"And now you do?"

He shrugged. "I don't know. Galen is . . . He's not always . . ." After a long pause he said softly, "In Zalandan Galen is all-powerful, and his people love him. His power is even greater than my father's."

"That cannot be so bad if his people hold him in affection."

"You don't understand. Galen's desire to have Sedikhan united is a passion that sweeps everything else away." He gazed at her soberly. "I don't want you to be swept away, Tess."

She laughed. "Why should I be affected by all that? I'd be a visitor in Sedikhan for three years, perhaps less."

He could see the excitement flushing her cheeks and had a sinking feeling his words had not swayed her. "Three years can be a long time."

"I have only one question. Do you believe I can trust Galen to keep his promise?"

"Yes."

She crossed the room to give him a fleeting kiss on the cheek. "I thank you for your concern, Sacha, but it will truly be fine." A hint of bleakness colored her voice as she continued, "I know I'm only a pawn to your friend, but when have I ever been anything else? At least I'll have a chance at independence, if I agree to his terms. No one else will offer me even that possibility. You were right, he was right: It's not a bad bargain."

"You've made up your mind?"

She nodded as she took a step back. "And I'd better tell him. Where is he?"

"In the stable. I'll go with you."

"I'll go alone." She cast him a gamine grin. "Stop frowning. Everything is going to be splendid."

# Chapter 2

"What are you doing?" Tess asked from the doorway of the stable.

Galen turned toward her. The light of the setting sun behind her sharply silhouetted her slender figure, seeming to etch her hair in dark flame. "My horse was bitten by a snake on the way to Dinar, and the wound is infected," he explained slowly.

"It's getting dark, you'll need a lantern."

"I was about to light one."

"I'll do it. Don't leave him." She moved quickly to a lantern hanging on a post near the door. On a ledge below was a flint and stone. She struck them together, flame flared, and a moment later she was carrying the lighted lantern to Galen.

He could see the shadow of her limbs through the thin blue batiste of the high-waisted gown she still wore.

She set the lantern on the ground beside the bucket and admired the horse. Her hand stroked his muzzle. "He's beautiful. What's his name?"

"Selik."

"What happened to Telzan?"

"I use him for breeding now. Selik is one of his colts."

"He's very gentle. You don't expect that quality in a stallion."

He gazed at her curiously. "And what do you know about stallions?"

"Not enough. I need to learn more." She knelt beside him. "Was the snake poisonous?"

"Yes, but it was only a glancing strike."

"What salve are you using?"

"An herbal mixture of mustard grass and rye."

"Have you tried mixing mint with it?"

"No."

"It cools the flesh, which makes the animal able to tolerate greater heat from the cloth."

"How do you know?"

"I experimented with several herbs when one of the Count's mares developed a strain." She reached past him, unwound the cloth from around Selik's ankle, and gently stroked the horse's ankle. "Just look. Have you ever seen such delicate bones?"

Her bones were far more delicate, he thought. He felt as if he could crush her with one careless caress. He could see the tracing of blue veins at her wrist, and the steady pounding of the pulse at her temple a few inches from his own. "Exceptional."

"One has to wonder how ankles such as those ever manage to support all that weight." She dipped the cloth in the bucket and squeezed out the excess moisture. "We're going to need more very hot water."

"I'll get it." He stood up, took the bucket to the door, and threw out the water, then turned and strode over to the kettle and filled the bucket again. "What count?"

"Hmm?" Her brow was knotted in concentration as she wrapped the ankle. "Oh, the Count de Sanvene. He owned the estate next to the convent. He had a fine stable of horses, but not one to compare to this boy." She sat back on her heels to look admiringly up at the stallion. "Do you have many horses like Selik?"

"No horse is like another."

"I agree."

"The sisters let you visit the Count?"

"Not at first. I had to sneak away." She grimaced. "I can't tell you how many times I was caught and sent to the Reverend Mother for discipline."

"How old was the man?"

"I don't know." She shrugged. "I never asked him."

"Guess." Galen heard the sharpness in his voice and tried to temper it as she glanced at him in surprise. "Young?"

She shook her head. "He had grandchildren, I think."

Galen felt a little of his tension melt away. He brought the bucket of steaming water to her side. "You liked him?"

"I liked his horses." She nodded. "He was quite irritable at first, but when he saw I could be useful around the stable, he became almost pleasant."

"Almost?"

"Well, he didn't shout at me anymore, and he visited the Mother Superior and convinced her to let me come twice a week."

"How did he do that?"

"He assured her he would watch over me, and he told her I had a healing talent with animals. He also said he was sure Saint Francis of Assisi would have approved of my helping the beasts." She chuckled. "It was the first time I'd ever been compared to a saint. The Reverend Mother was very surprised."

"So the good Count acquired a new stableboy?"

"I didn't mind. I loved being with the horses. They made the convent bearable." She turned to him, her face alight with eagerness. "Someday I'm going to have a fine stable and breed horses like Selik and Telzan."

He found his gaze following the graceful line of her throat down to the upper swell of her small breasts bared by the low neckline of her gown. Her fair skin possessed an incredible sheen. He wondered how soft it would feel to the touch.

"And I'll have dogs and perhaps carrier pigeons." She took the bandage from Selik's ankle. "Don't you think that would be a happy life?"

"No fashionable salon?"

Her laughter rang out. "What would I do with a salon? I cannot imagine anything more boring than sitting around reading poetry and discussing Voltaire and Rousseau."

The strong herbal smell mingled with the scent of lavender and soap that emanated from her. He bent closer, letting the fragrance invade his senses, and felt an urgent quickening in his loins. He had not expected this to happen so quickly. Dammit, he did not want it to happen yet. His body was readying itself to enter her—and she was more aware of his horse than of him.

She glanced at him. "We can't leave for Sedikhan tomorrow. Selik won't be ready."

He went still. "The next day will do as well." He waited for a moment and then asked casually, "I take it this means you agree to the arrangement?"

"Of course." She looked at him in surprise. "You knew I would."

"Let's say I thought there was a reasonable chance."

"Say what you like. You knew I wouldn't be able to resist what you offered." She dipped the cloth in the hot water. "I think the poison is drawing, but not enough. We'll have to keep bathing

it and applying fresh salve for most of the night.
I'll take the first watch. You go rest."

"I can do it alone."

"Why should you? It's better with two."

He did not argue with her. He needed to have
her powerfully united with him, and this shared
experience would be an important beginning. He
smiled and rose to his feet. "You're right, most
things are better with two." He strolled over and
sat down on the fresh hay spread in the empty
stall across from Selik's. "You take the first two
hours. I'll take the next two." He drew his knees
up and linked his arms loosely around them, his
gaze on Tess Rubinoff. She moved with a neat,
economical grace, every motion purposeful and
full of vitality. The short puffed sleeves of her
gown revealed exquisitely formed bare arms flowing into small, capable hands that were wonder-
fully gentle as she touched the horse. What a rare
blend of strength and fire lay beneath that delicate
exterior. Small women had never appealed to him,
yet he felt the muscles of his stomach clench painfully as he thought how tight she'd be around him
as he plunged in and out of her body—

He tried to rid himself of such thoughts as he
drew back into the shadows and leaned his head
against the rough wall. He did not want Tess to
become aware of his body's reaction to her at the
moment. She was filled with soaring hope and
plans for the future—precisely the emotions he
had hoped to arouse in her.

\*　　\*　　\*

She was being lifted from the straw of the stall and carried.

"Sacha?" she murmured sleepily.

"No. Shh, go back to sleep. I'm only taking you to your chamber."

Galen. Her eyelids felt too heavy to open. "Selik?"

"He'll be fine. It's almost morning."

Cool air struck her face as Galen carried her out of the stable. She roused. "You'll have to change to cold compresses now to take the swelling down."

"I started to use cold water while you were dozing."

"I didn't mean to fall asleep."

"You worked very hard. You deserve your sleep."

Her lids lifted slowly. Galen's face was only inches from hers. She stared dreamily at the sharp molding of his cheekbones, his well-shaped lips. She had not noticed his lips before because his large dark eyes so dominated his other features.

He must have become aware of her study, for he looked down at her.

He smiled. "Sleep, *kilen*. All will be well. I promise you. You can trust me."

She remembered his inflexible determination, his quiet tenderness toward Selik during the past hours. Yes, she could trust him.

She closed her eyes and willed herself to go back to sleep, safe in Galen's arms.

*     *     *

The marriage between Tess and Galen was performed by Father Francis Desleps in the Cathedral of the Holy Redeemer at three o'clock the following afternoon. Galen followed Muslim customs, but he was a Christian . . . and a man with a powerful influence over Father Desleps. Galen had succeeded in getting a very fast special dispensation for them to marry, so there would be no thrice-published banns and other preliminaries to their wedding.

Tess felt strange kneeling before the altar with Galen at her side. But surely it would have felt strange with any man, she assured herself. Marriage only occurred once in a lifetime, and it was unlikely one would get accustomed to the ceremony. She smiled.

"You have been smiling for some time now," Galen commented after they had thanked the priest and were walking back up the long aisle. "May I ask what's so amusing?"

"I was just thinking it was quite ordinary to be feeling so peculiar. After all, marriage occurs only once."

"Occurs? You make it sound like an act of nature." He took her arm and helped her down the steps to the cobbled street. "And it's not inconceivable that you should marry again. Life in Sedikhan isn't the safest existence, and wealthy widows are much sought after."

"I shall never marry again," she said positively. "Why should I submit to that trap? My life will be very pleasant without a husband getting in my way."

"Husbands have certain uses."

"Protection? I can hire servants for that."

He helped her into the carriage waiting in front of the church. "I wasn't thinking about protection. More in the nature of . . . companionship."

"Most husbands are dreadful companions. They're too busy pursuing other ladies to furnish a wife with adequate company." She leaned back in the carriage. "No, a woman is much better off with no man about to trouble her."

He leaned back on the seat and gazed at her, smiling faintly as the carriage started with a lurch. "We shall see if you continue in your opinion. There must be some reason the state of connubial bliss still exists."

She looked at him in surprise. "Practicality. A man must be sure of his heirs, and a woman cannot have the father of her children deserting her after the first flush of passion fades."

His dark eyes were watching her impassively. "Is that what happens?"

She nodded positively. "Of course. You know it yourself. I'd wager you never thought of Lady Camilla or that other woman again after you had your way with them."

"Oh, I thought of them."

She frowned. "You did? When?"

"Whenever my body needed a woman."

Her cheeks grew hot, and she looked hastily

away from him. "That isn't thinking, that's lust-
ing." She leaned forward and gazed out the
window, and was immediately rewarded with a
glimpse of a familiar sign. "Oh, there's that interesting café. I asked Sacha to take me there, but
he refused." She turned to Galen. "Will you take
me . . . tonight?" She added quickly, "Providing
Selik is doing well, of course."

"Naturally, any bridal repast would have to be
postponed if Selik isn't in the pink."

"Why are you smiling, Galen? We both know
this ceremony has no importance."

"It's of the utmost importance."

She gestured impatiently. "You know what I
mean—only the alliance is important. Will you
take me to the café?"

"Why not? I owe you a supper for your labor
with Selik last night, and it may prove an enlight-
ening experience for you."


"I like it," Tess announced, her gaze roaming the
noisy café. The boards of the wooden floor were
warped and sagging, and the torches affixed to the
walls sent out plumes of smoke that stung the eyes
and made the air blue with haze. "Isn't it exciting,
Sacha?"

"You shouldn't be here."

"Of course I should be here." She glanced mischievously over her shoulder at Galen as she sat
down on the chair he was holding for her. "I'm a
married woman, and therefore privileged to go
where I wish. Isn't that correct, my lord?"

"Within certain limits." Galen's expression was impassive as he glanced around the room. "However, I see little to recommend this establishment."

"How can you say such a thing?" Tess folded her gloved hands on the scarred table. "It's perfectly splendid, and I'm sure the food will be excellent."

"Providing there are no cockroaches in the stew." Sacha sat next to Galen and motioned to a burly servant.

"There were no cockroaches in the stew on board the ship. The food was a bit boring, but the cook was clean, and I'm sure that—Is that a strumpet?" Tess stared at a fair-haired woman in a dirty green dress who sat on a sailor's lap. "She's quite pretty, isn't she?"

"Prettier than most of her breed," Sacha said as the waiter unceremoniously plopped down three glasses and filled them with red wine from a huge leather carafe slung on a strap about her neck.

"Breed?" Tess frowned. "I don't like that word. It makes her sound like a horse or a cow."

Sacha waved the waiter away as he appraised the woman's huge breasts spilling over the neckline of her gown. "There are some similarities, you must admit."

"I do not admit to anything of the sort. She's a woman, not an animal. She obviously lets herself be used because she has no other means to support herself."

"And what about your Pauline?" Galen asked softly. "Why does she let herself be used?"

"Pauline isn't a strumpet, she's . . ." Tess hesitated, thinking about it. "She's not overly bright and has few interests. Perhaps she does it to keep from becoming bored."

Sacha choked on his wine. "Quite possible. She certainly applies herself to . . . er, entertaining herself."

Tess knew they were laughing at her, but she didn't care. The subject of physical pleasure was not really important to her except as a curiosity. This place was too interesting to waste time on trivialities. "I'm hungry. May we eat now?"

"But of course." Galen's lips quirked. "It's a husband's duty to satisfy his wife's . . . appetites."

"Stop it, Sacha." Tess giggled helplessly as Sacha swung her in a wide circle all the while moving across the courtyard toward the inn. "You've had too much to drink. We'll both end up in a heap on the ground."

"You insult me," said Sacha, looking owlishly at her. "You think I can't hold my wine. This is a felicitous occasion, and I'm merely happy. Extraordinarily happy."

"You're extraordinarily drunk." Tess smiled indulgently as she steadied him against the doorjamb. "You would think this was your wedding day by the way you're celebrating."

"I'm celebrating because it's *not* my wedding day." Sacha's smile faded, and his eyes filled with morose tears as he touched her cheek with a gentle finger. "Poor little imp."

"She seems to be doing better than you are at the moment," Galen said as he caught up with them. He threw open the door. "Come on, I'll help you up the stairs."

"Not necessary." Sacha lurched through the door toward the staircase. "I'm perfectly able to—" His foot slipped on the second step, and he pitched forward.

"Perfectly able to fall flat on your face."

"I stumbled," Sacha said with dignity. "How do they expect a man to see to get up the stairs with only one candle left burning?"

"Strange that *I* have no trouble seeing." Galen helped Sacha to his feet and slipped his arm around his waist. "I've just finished nursing Selik, and have no intention of acquiring another patient."

"Are you comparing me to a horse?"

"Only when you're sober. When drunk, your intellect bears a distinct resemblance to that of a sun-addled camel."

"Insult upon insult."

"What else can you expect from a barbarian?" Galen started up the steps, bearing at least half of Sacha's weight.

Sacha began to sing beneath his breath.

"Shall I call his servant?" Tess asked.

"Sacha no longer travels with a servant." Galen paused to shift his hold and drape Sacha's arm about his neck. "Said takes care of both of us when we travel."

"Indeed?" Tess closed the front door and watched them climb. "How odd." The Sacha she had known had always traveled with a full entourage of servants ranging from cooks and valets to grooms.

"Not so odd. Servants get in the way when traveling in the desert." Galen had reached the top of the steps and looked down at her. "Go to your chamber. I'll join you shortly."

She felt the smile freeze on her lips as shock rippled through her. "You will?"

"Of course."

"Of course," Tess muttered. What else could she have expected? This was her wedding night, wasn't it? A child was part of the bargain, and she was no ninny, ignorant of how one was conceived. Yet he had said he would give her time, and she had thought—

"Tess," Galen said softly over his shoulder. "Go to your chamber."

Tess nodded jerkily and flew up the staircase, edging around him and Sacha to get to her chamber. She should not feel so disappointed by Galen. She knew that few men kept their word to the women of their households. She slammed the door behind her and pressed back against the panels, her heart pounding wildly, her cheeks fever-hot. It would not be so terrible once she got used to it. Pauline had actually liked being mounted. Tess had often heard her beg for it.

But Tess was not Pauline.

Still, she had made a bargain and must keep her part of it.

Undress. She knew that was part of it. To ready herself for the act, she must shed her clothing. She should be unclothed when Galen came to her.

Tess drew a deep breath and pushed away from the door. Her fingers went to the delicate pearl buttons marching down the back of her spring-green gown.

Five minutes later she was completely nude and lying beneath the covers. The room was warm. There was no reason for her to be shivering. Everything would be fine. Pauline liked it, and the woman at the café had not seemed to mind when the sailor fondled her bre—

The door opened. Galen stopped just inside the door and lifted the candle he carried. He saw Tess huddled against the oak headboard and his lips tightened with displeasure. "How delightful to have such an accommodating bride. I admit I didn't expect to find you so compliant."

"I don't feel compliant." Her voice was trembling, and she forced herself to steady it. "I have no liking for this."

The grimness faded from his expression. "Then why are you being so meek?"

"It's not meekness. It's honor. We clearly cannot have a babe if I do not accept you into my body."

"I see." He closed the door behind him. "But I believe I told you I could wait for consummation."

"But you said—" Relief surged through her. "I thought you'd changed your mind."

"I keep my promises. You'll be the first to know when I change my mind." He set the pewter candle-holder down on the closest table, removed his coat, and laid it across a chair. "I have no intention of forcing you."

"It wouldn't be force. A bargain is a bargain."

"It's a quirk of mine that I prefer enthusiasm to forbearance." He untied his striped cravat and pulled it off. "You may not conceive a child at once, and I dislike the idea of you gritting your teeth every time I touch you."

"I cannot promise you enthusiasm." Her hand clutched more tightly to the blanket. "I don't think I'll care for it. Though I admit I'm a little confused by it all. Pauline likes it, but I have seen mares mounted by stallions that don't look as if they're very . . ."—she paused, searching for the correct word—"comfortable."

"Comfortable?" He smiled. "No, there's little comfort in it. And I can't promise you there will be no pain, but I believe you'll find it interesting." He unbuttoned his shirt and took it off. "When I show you the way of it."

She stared at his powerful muscles. They ridged his shoulders, grew large on his upper arms, and chest. Her gaze followed the black triangle of hair on his chest to where it disappeared into the waistband of his black trousers. His flesh looked like burnished bronze. A queer fluttery feeling started in the pit of her stomach. "If you aren't going to fornicate with me, why are you removing your clothes?"

"I'm going to bed."

"With me? Why? You have a chamber of your own."

His lips twisted. "Unlike the nobility of Tamrovia, in Zalandan husbands and wives not only sleep in the same chamber but the same bed."

"How peculiar. I should think the lack of privacy must be something of an imposition." She shrugged. "Oh well, I suppose I'll become accustomed to it."

"I trust so. Lower the cover."

She stiffened, her eyes widening. "What?"

"Sit up and drop the cover. I want to look at you."

Her cheeks began to sting. "I see no purpose in looking if you're not going to do anything."

"There's a purpose. Lower the blanket."

She forced herself to release her grasp, and the cover fell to her waist. She felt as if her flesh were ablaze as she lifted her chin defiantly to glare at him. "What rhyme or reason is there in exposing myself? I'm no beauty like Lady Camilla. You'll get no pleasure from staring at me."

"No, you're no Camilla." His gaze lingered on her shoulders before traveling down to her breasts. "But sometimes the smaller jewel has the most beautiful facets."

"And sometimes the facets are so small you can't tell whether they're beautiful or not." She couldn't breathe. Her breasts felt tight, yet they were swelling under his gaze. "May I pull up the blanket now, my lord?"

He slowly shook his head, his gaze never leaving her breasts. "I think not. I believe we're making progress."

"Toward what end?"

He smiled. "Why, to the end of becoming accustomed to each other. From now on you will sleep naked in my bed, and I will fondle and caress you whenever I am moved to do so." He sat down in the chair by the door, pulled off his left boot, and dropped it on the floor. "Kneel on the bed, facing me."

She didn't look at him as she threw aside the blanket and knelt on her haunches, facing him. "You cannot be enjoying this." She heard his other boot drop to the floor. "I believe you're doing this to shame me."

"Don't you like to have me look at you?"

"It makes me most uncomfortable."

"You shouldn't be uncomfortable. You're quite lovely."

She snorted derisively. "I have hideous red hair and eyes too big for my face and—"

"The most exquisite breasts and limbs I've ever seen."

She inhaled sharply and kept her gaze fastened on the wall behind his shoulder.

"You don't believe me?"

She swallowed. "No."

"Then I suppose I'll have to furnish proof. Look at me."

Her gaze moved reluctantly from the wall. He was naked, standing perfectly at ease, his legs slightly astride, a brawny study in sleek bronze and black.

Her eyes widened as they traveled down his body to rest on his rampant arousal.

His gaze followed hers. "Proof," he repeated softly.

"You look . . . different."

"Different from what?"

"From when I saw you naked before."

"You were only a child." He chuckled. "Besides, you saw me after the fact, not before or during. Proof is not always in evidence." He paused. "Though I've had a damnable time keeping it from becoming so today." He took the candle and started across the room.

She instinctively tensed, her gaze clinging to his.

"Listen very carefully," he said softly. "I do find you desirable, so desirable I ache with it." He stopped before her and set the candle on the bedside table. "Can you doubt it now?"

She couldn't speak.

His hand reached out and touched her hair with exquisite gentleness.

"You're so *tiny*," he whispered. "Last night as I watched you, I kept thinking how tight you'd be around me. Every time I think about you, I grow hard, wondering . . ."

She felt as if she were drowning. He was scarcely touching her, and yet she felt a deep tingling in her palms, in the nipples of her breasts, even in the arches of her feet. She tore her gaze away from his face. "I doubt you'll fit."

"You know better. A female is created to accept a man." His hand moved from her hair to caress her throat. "To want a man. A mare may not appear to enjoy mating, but haven't you seen one back up to a stallion, looking over her shoulder, wriggling her tail at him?" His thumb pressed the hollow of her throat, and she knew he could feel the leap of her pulse beneath the pad of flesh. "Do you know how much I'd like to have you do that for me?"

Shock caused her body to flinch. "I'm not an animal."

"I meant no insult. Sometimes my words have no grace." His hand left her throat and both arms fell to his sides. "I'm not entirely undressed. Help me."

She gazed at him in bewilderment. What was he talking about? He was already naked.

He turned his back to her. "The ribbon tying my queue. Unfasten it for me."

She rose onto her knees and with trembling fingers tried to unfasten the black grosgrain ribbon binding his hair. Her breasts brushed the warm flesh of his back. She felt a shudder go through him. She tried to arch away from him as she worked at the knot, but she brushed him again. This time the shiver that went through him was echoed by hers. Her breasts were aching, the nipples pebble hard, a strange throbbing between her thighs. What was happening to her? "I can't seem to—Perhaps you'd better do it."

"No." His voice was guttural. "In Zalandan it's

traditional for a wife to do this. It symbolizes that only she has the privilege to set her man free."

But the act did not set Tess free. With every passing moment the feeling of being held and possessed by Galen was increasing. She finally managed to untie the ribbon and pull it from his hair. She tossed it on the bedside table and sat back on her heels with a sigh of relief. "It's done."

He shook his head, his back still turned to her. The candlelight caught the thick luster of his black hair as it flowed down to skim his shoulders, the play of muscles in his shoulders. She felt a sudden wild desire to reach out and stroke those muscles, tangle her fingers in his mane and pull him down to—

He turned to face her, huge, primitive, untamed. His eyes were glittering, a dark strand of hair now fell over his forehead, the rest of his loosened hair framed his face. His nostrils flared then, slowly, he slid both palms down his thighs in blatant invitation. Tess gasped, the muscles of her stomach clenching. He had not touched her, but she felt as if he had drawn her against his body with that one sensual gesture.

"Lust can arouse the animal in any of us, *kilen*. As I hope you'll soon discover." He drew a deep, harsh breath and closed his eyes tightly. "Dear Lord, very soon."

His lids flicked open, and he stepped back. He leaned forward and blew out the candle.

Tess supposed she should have felt relieved, but the darkness only made her feel more vulnerable.

She could see Galen's shadowy bulk before her, she could smell his scent.

"Lie down." Galen's low voice vibrated with tension. "I can't take any more. It's over for now."

It had not really begun, Tess thought dazedly. He had only touched her hair and her throat, he had only looked at her body and murmured a few words of need and desire. Why did she feel this sense of bondage?

"*Now.*"

She scrambled under the cover and moved to the far side of the bed.

The next moment she felt the mattress give under Galen's weight.

He lay beside her, not touching her, every muscle hardened with tension.

She lay beside him, her heart pounding, the odd throbbing in her groin.

"I don't understand what this is all about," she said haltingly. "Why?"

His voice was thick, his breathing harsh in the darkness. "I'll have you the way I want you or not at all."

"It's only for the babe. What difference does it make?"

"A great difference." He was silent for a long moment. "We are two civilized people. I will not play stallion to your mare." He was silent, and when he spoke again, his tone was fierce, desperate. "Because, by God, I am *not* a barbarian."

# Chapter 3

Galen was gone when Tess awoke the next morning, and she experienced a rush of relief mixed with disappointment. His presence was exciting; he intrigued her mind while inspiring a curious vitality to possess her body. She wasn't sure she was ready yet to try to understand his effect on her. Last night had been a most unsettling experience. What an unusual and unpredictable man Galen Ben Raschid was proving to be.

She dressed hurriedly in her old dark brown riding habit that she had refused to throw away despite Pauline's pleas, left the chamber, and started downstairs. She had reached the landing when she encountered a young man wearing a

burgundy-and-cream striped robe and flowing white
trousers tucked into brown suede boots. His face
seemed familiar.

"I was just going to your chamber, *Majira*."
He bowed politely. "The *majiron* wishes to depart
within the hour. Is it convenient for me to pack
your valises now?"

"There's not much to pack. I saw no sense in
having my cases unpacked for such a short stay."
She frowned thoughtfully. "You're Said, aren't
you?"

He bowed again. "Said Abdul, *Majira*."

"I didn't recognize you at first." Her eyes twinkled. "You're wearing clothing."

He blinked, appearing slightly taken aback.
"May I pack for you, *Majira*?"

Good Lord, he was as stiff and sober as the
Mother Superior. "By all means," she said solemnly. "Where is the sheikh?"

"In the stable. Shall I tell him you wish to see
him?"

"No, you go about your business." She started
down the steps again. "I'll find him."

"Unescorted?" He looked slightly shocked.
"There are men in the stable, *Majira*."

She glanced impatiently over her shoulder.
"What difference does that make?"

"It is not fitting. You are the *majira*. It would
be unwise for you to—"

"I'll escort her, Said." Sacha was standing at
the bottom of the staircase. "Get to the packing."

Said sighed in apparent relief. "As you wish, my lord."

Tess shook her head as she watched him move quickly away. "He has no humor."

"Said's a good man," Sacha said. "But he does have a highly developed sense of protocol. It's a different world in Sedikhan."

"So I'm beginning to discover." She started down the last few steps. "What's a *majira*?"

He grinned. "That's you. Wife of the *majiron*. The Tamrovian equivalent would be 'Your Majesty.'"

"And Galen is the *majiron*?"

He nodded. "It's one of his titles." His smile disappeared as his gaze searched her face. "Are you . . . well?"

She flushed and avoided his stare. "Probably better than you. You were definitely in your cups last night." She strode past him toward the door. "I'm going to see Selik."

"Not your husband?"

She glanced mischievously over her shoulder. "My husband appeared sound in wind and limb when I last saw him. Selik was not."

"Selik is much better."

Tess swung around to see Galen standing in the doorway. He gazed at her without expression, but his lips twitched betrayingly. "And I'm glad you found me . . . fit."

Tess heard a sound behind her from Sacha that sounded suspiciously like a smothered chuckle.

She flushed as memories surfaced of Galen

standing in naked splendor before her, his dark eyes burning, his hair flowing about his shoulders. Her gaze flew to his hair. It was tied neatly in a queue. He was dressed in a black superfine coat and matching trousers, his cravat wound as intricately as the one gracing Sacha's throat. Somehow that evidence of proper civilized attire restored her composure. "Selik is able to travel?"

He nodded. "But not bear weight. We'll put him on a lead for a few days."

"That's wise," she commented.

"I'm glad you approve." He inclined his head in a slight bow. "I've purchased a mare from the innkeeper for you to ride to Zalandan. She's a little long in the tooth, but adequate for the journey. Now, if you please, we'll break our fast and be on our way. Our escort waits over the border at the Oasis of El Dabal."

A journey to Sedikhan. Who would have believed she would ever go to that barbaric land? She found she was suddenly filled with eagerness to be on her way. "Let's go now. I'm not hungry."

"Nevertheless, you will eat," Galen said. "We won't be stopping until sundown, and you must keep up your strength."

She frowned. "I don't like orders, my lord."

His faint smile faded. "Better mine than your father's."

"True." She gave him a veiled look from beneath her lashes. "But if you recall, I usually found ways to circumvent his orders."

"Those means will not be available to you in

Zalandan." He saw her abrupt stiffening and withdrawal, and his expression softened. "Which doesn't mean I plan to tyrannize you, only to keep you safe."

"My father also took precautions to keep me safe. One of those precautions was to try to kill Apollo, who loved me." She met his gaze directly. "Would you do something like that?"

He gazed at her silently for a moment before he said slowly, "If such a thing became necessary."

She was startled. It was not the answer she expected. He had *saved* Apollo. Yet now he looked at her with implacable resolution shining in his eyes. There was no question he meant what he said. She drew a deep, shaky breath. "Then it's well we come to an understanding." She made an impatient gesture as he started to speak. "I know I have a certain value to you. I will do nothing to endanger it by damaging myself."

"I did not mean—"

"Of course you did. I'm no fool. I know what my worth is to you." She strode toward the common room. "I will eat. Such a small thing does not matter, and I know you must keep me well." She challenged him with a glance. "But you offered me freedom, and I will not let you have it all your own way."

"Freedom comes when you leave me." He smiled. "And I'm very used to my own way in Zalandan."

"I'm ravenous." Sacha moved quickly forward and grasped Tess's elbow, smoothly inserting himself between her and Galen. "If you're both through throwing down gauntlets, may we eat now? Come along, Tess. You know how conflict upsets my delicate nature." He heard a disbelieving snort from Galen and glanced over his shoulder with a hurt expression. "Philistine. You've never appreciated the sensitivity of my feelings." He propelled Tess forward. "Besides, neither of you is giving me enough attention. I'm beginning to become bored."

Judging by the number of tents, Tess would have said a small army occupied the palm-shaded oasis of El Dabal. As she, Galen, Sacha, and Said approached, at least seventy riders, dressed in robes of the same striped burgundy and cream colors worn by Said, thundered toward them.

"Mother of God." Tess reined in her mare to stare at the cavalcade. "Even His Majesty doesn't travel with an entourage this large."

"King Lionel doesn't have to cross a country torn apart by warring tribes," Galen said. "An escort isn't mere panoply in Sedikhan."

"Not when Tamar claims the border country as his," Sacha added with a grimace.

"Tamar?" Tess asked.

"Sheikh Tamar Hassan," Galen said absently as he took off his tailored coat and draped it over the front of his saddle, then removed his cravat, put it carefully on top of the coat, and unfastened the first three buttons of his shirt.

"What are you doing?" Tess asked.

"Getting rid of these foolish trappings. I'm home now."

He smiled recklessly, his white teeth flashing in the bronze darkness of his face. Tess was spellbound. He looked wilder, less controlled than she had ever seen him. The hot breeze lifted his dark hair from his forehead, and barely suppressed excitement glittered in his eyes. She knew he spoke truly when he lovingly called the barren golden sand shimmering under hard blue skies "home." He seemed one with this merciless, exotically beautiful land.

"Bring her, Sacha. I need to go ahead to meet Kalim." Galen spurred ahead into a gallop, with Said pounding at his heels.

Tess sat her horse and watched the uproar of greeting as Galen rode into the troop. At first the men stayed still, merely making shrill, loud noises. Then, suddenly, they surrounded Galen. Even at a distance Tess could see that the faces of the men surrounding Galen showed affection and a respect bordering on worship.

"They do care about him," Tess said thoughtfully.

Sacha nodded. "Of course. He keeps the El Zalan alive and prospering."

"No, it's more than that."

Sacha shot her a thoughtful glance. "Very perceptive, imp. Galen's a chameleon. He's taught himself to become whatever he has to be, to adjust to any situation, to give whatever is demanded. He gives the El Zalan what they need, and in turn they give him unquestioning affection and loyalty. I told you he holds great power."

For the first time since she started the journey, Tess experienced a flutter of uneasiness. If Galen was the chameleon Sacha described, the man she thought she had begun to know might not exist. She suddenly felt very much alone in this wild land.

"It's too late for second thoughts now," Sacha said.

She tossed her head. "I wasn't having second thoughts. Well, only small ones." She spurred her horse into a gallop. "Come on, let's go. I'm hungry."

The tribesmen fell silent as Tess approached; they made her apprehensive, and she was glad Sacha was at her side. Galen was talking with an extraordinarily handsome young man mounted on a superb bay gelding. They were so absorbed in their conversation that Tess again felt estranged . . . and terribly alone.

"What news of Tamar?" Sacha called as they drew within hailing distance of the two men.

"No sign of him," Galen said grimly. "But that doesn't mean he's not here."

The beautiful young man next to Galen flushed and said quickly, "I searched most diligently, *Majiron*."

"That means little. Tamar's a wily wolf." Galen turned his head and said something to the man in a low tone.

Tess was irritated by Galen's ignoring her and

then realized how foolish she was being. Nothing in their bargain demanded Galen must stay by her side every minute, and she must see to her own needs. She boldly rode up to Galen and stopped her mare before him. "I'm tired and wish water and food, my lord."

He looked up absently and gestured casually to the man next to him. "May I present my wife, Kalim? This is my lieutenant, Kalim Ranmir, Tess."

Surprise and then resentment flickered over Kalim's classic features. He bowed his head politely. "*Majira.*"

"My lord Kalim." She nodded and then looked again at Galen. "As I said, my lord, I'm hungry."

He caught the hint of defiance in her tone, and his eyes narrowed on her. He saw the lines of tension around her mouth and the arrow-straight rigidity of the carriage of her slight body. He smiled. "Then of course I must supply food to appease you. We've already discussed my duty in that regard." He turned to Said. "Show my lady to my tent, Said, and fetch her whatever she requires."

"Will you be joining me later?" Tess asked.

He looked a trifle surprised. "Is that your wish?"

"As you like." She shrugged carelessly, she hoped. "I merely want to know if I am to expect you." Before he could reply, she turned and let her mare pick her way through the troop of tribesmen, her back very straight, her head high.

"Who is this Kalim?" Tess asked Said as she rode beside him toward a tent in Galen's striped colors. It was located by a sparkling blue pool that appeared to be directly in the center of the oasis.

"He's the *majiron*'s second in command. Kalim's a very fierce fighter and much respected."

"I thought Sacha was his second in command."

"Oh no!" Said shook his head. "That would not be possible. My lord Sacha is an outsider. He is not of the El Zalan."

Her lips twisted. "Not too much of an outsider to befriend your *majiron* and fight for your cause."

Said nodded. "I meant no insult. He is a true friend to the El Zalan. Everyone likes my lord Sacha."

But they still had clearly not accepted him as one of their own, even after years of service. Her feeling of alienation deepened. "How nice for Sacha."

"He appears to find it pleasant." For an instant the tiniest flicker of smile touched Said's lips. "Our women have a special fondness for him." The smile immediately disappeared, as if he had been startled by his own outspokenness. "Forgive me, I meant no disrespect, *Majira*."

"Of course not." Tess shot him an exasperated glance. "Let's come to an understanding, since we're evidently going to spend a great deal of time together. I'm not like the women of the El Zalan, and I have no intention of behaving like them. I'm more accustomed to the talk in a stable than I am to women's gossip. I will not become offended if you make remarks you deem indiscreet." She paused. "And, in fact, such conversation may make me feel less . . ." She searched for a word that would not reveal her vulnerability and finally ended baldly, "Alone."

Said's expression softened as he dismounted in front of the tent and came around to help her down. "You will not be alone. The women of the court will be honored to become friends of *Majira*. The *majiron* would not permit anything else."

"We shall see." Holding Said's hand, Tess threw her leg over the pommel and slipped from the sidesaddle. "However, I believe I shall fight my own battles and not rely on your master."

She turned and strode into the tent.

Said brought water for washing, and after Tess had refreshed herself, he busied himself preparing to serve her meal. He put out a place setting on the intricate beauty of the Persian rug and served her delicately flavored rabbit stew. It was far better than the food at the café the previous night. "Won't the *majiron* and my cousin be joining me?"

Said shook his head. "They eat with the men by the fire."

"Indeed?" Now that she had rested a bit, her first qualms at the extraordinary situation in which she had been placed were disappearing. "Perhaps I'll join them." She picked up her bowl and started to get to her feet, but Said was frantically shaking his head, his face horror-struck. "No?"

"The *majiron* would be most upset with me if I permitted you to leave the tent. It is not—"

"Fitting," Tess finished for him. "For a barbaric land your customs are annoyingly stringent."

"Barbaric?" The man was obviously insulted. "The El Zalan are not barbaric. Other tribes are barbaric, but we have the *majiron*'s laws." He frowned. "You will not go to the campfire?"

"No." She was too weary tonight to fight the disapproval she would probably meet if she violated the El Zalan's customs. Besides, she was beginning to like Said and had no desire to get him into Galen's bad graces. "But it's too hot to stay in this tent."

He thought for a moment. "I will spread a rug just outside the entrance, and you may catch the night breeze. We will turn out the lantern so that you can see but not be seen by the men."

"Is that nec—" She sighed. "Very well. Anything you say. Please do get the rug."

The breeze was indeed cool on her face as she lounged outside the tent with Said sitting a protective few yards away on his own rug. She didn't really care about the coolness. She could have borne the heat of the tent, but she could not bear being totally isolated from the activity going on around the campfire across the pool from the tent. The air was alive with laughter and casual talk and the camaraderie of men accustomed to living with one another. She wasn't the least bit intimidated any longer, and she yearned to join the men.

She caught sight of Galen on the far side of

the campfire. Her eyes widened in disbelief. He threw back his head and laughed heartily at something Kalim said. She watched Kalim smile and other men sitting in the circle move infinitesimally closer to Galen, as if being drawn by a magnet. She hadn't had so much as a glimpse of this side of Galen. Did he reveal his warmth and openness only to his people? No, Sacha must have seen him thus, for he had followed Galen and fought under his banner for six years.

A bittersweet wail, almost human-sounding, made her turn in surprise. Said was playing a reed flute, and the music was inexpressibly lovely, blending with the night, sand, and fire into a harmony that was completely right for the time and place. When he finally took the instrument from his lips, she said, "That was lovely, Said."

He looked faintly embarrassed as he said gruffly, "The *majiron* does not mind. It passes the time even though for a protector of the *majiron*, it is not—"

"Fitting," Tess finished for him. She was growing weary of that word. "Then it should be fitting. Everything beautiful should be fitting. Play some more."

"You do not wish to go inside now?"

"No, I want to stay here for a while." She added quickly, "You were right, the breeze is cooling." And she wanted to watch Galen's expressions as he talked to the men around the campfire. If she studied him while he had his guard down, might she see into the man?

Said continued to play his flute, and she settled herself more comfortably on the carpet, her gaze fixed in fascination on her husband.

When Galen left the campfire and strolled around the pool toward the tent, it was nearly ten o'clock. Surprised, he stopped in front of Tess. "I thought you would have gone to sleep by now."

She scrambled to her feet. "I was tired, but not sleepy."

"Did Said furnish you with everything you needed?"

"Everything but sociable company." She added tartly, "Which you and Sacha certainly didn't deny yourself."

Galen held the tent flap back, and she preceded him inside. He took off his burnoose and tossed it on the cushions of a low divan. "I've been away for almost two weeks. Kalim had much to tell me."

"You didn't look as if you were conducting state business."

He turned to stare at her with raised brows. "That sounded suspiciously shrewish and wifely."

She flushed. "No such thing. I was curious . . . well, and bored." She frowned. "I would have joined you, but the mere mention of doing such a thing sent Said into a tizzy."

"Quite rightly."

"Why? When members of the Tamrovian court travel, the women aren't stuck away in a hot, stuffy tent."

"You found the tent displeasing?"

"No." She looked around the tent. A thick, beautifully patterned carpet stretched over the ground, and everywhere her gaze wandered were colorful silk cushions, intricately worked brass lanterns, bejeweled silver candlesticks. "I've seen rooms at the palace that weren't as luxuriously furnished as this." She went back to the primary subject. "But I don't like being imprisoned here."

"I'll consider ways to make it more palatable."

"But I don't want to stay here. Can't I join you in the evening around the campfire? If the court does not—"

"The men of your court haven't been without a woman for four weeks," he interrupted bluntly. "And your Tamrovian courtiers are tame as day-old pups compared to my tribesmen."

Her eyes widened. "They would insult me?"

"No. You belong to me. They would offer no insult. But they would look at you and grow hard and know pain."

Her skin burned. "Your words are crude."

"The fact is crude, and you must understand it. I will not make my men suffer needlessly."

"You would rather have me suffer." She scowled. "I would think you'd try to teach your men to control their responses. After all, I'm not that comely."

He smiled faintly. "I thought we'd settled the matter of your comeliness last night."

She had not thought her cheeks could get any hotter, but she found she was wrong. "Not everyone would find me to their taste. I think you must be a little peculiar."

He chuckled, and his face looked as boyish as it had when he'd laughed and joked with his men. "I assure you that my tastes are not at all unusual. You have a quality I've seen in few women."

She gazed at him warily. "What?"

"Life." His eyes held her own, and his expression suddenly sobered. "I've never met a woman so alive as you, *kilen*."

Her stomach fluttered as she looked at him. She tore her gaze away from his face to stare down at the patterns in the carpet. "Your women are without spirit?"

"They have spirit," he said softly. "But they don't light up a tent by merely walking into it."

The flutter came again, and with it a strange breathlessness. "Pretty words. But what you're about to say is that I *must* stay in the tent."

"What I'm saying is that I prefer to save your light for myself."

Joy soared through her with bewildering intensity. She mustn't let him sway her feelings like this, she thought desperately. Sacha had said Galen gave whatever was demanded of him. Perhaps he thought this flattery was what she wanted of him. "As I said, pretty words." She changed the subject as she forced herself to lift her eyes to gaze directly at him. "You look different in your robe."

"More the barbarian?"

"I didn't say that," she said quickly.

"But you thought it." He smiled bitterly. "I've embraced many of your civilized Western ways, but I refuse to give up everything. The material of our robes is thin, comfortable, and the white reflects the sun." He strolled to the small trunk in the corner. "Which reminds me, you look most uncomfortably hot in your velvet riding habit. I think we must do something about it." He rummaged until he found another robe like the one he was wearing. "Here, put this on." He turned and tossed the garment to her. "You'll find it far more satisfactory."

"My habit is comfortable."

"And unattractive enough to satisfy me when you're out of the tent in the presence of my men." He met her gaze. "But not when we're alone. Put on the robe."

She was to dress herself to please him. She knew wives did such things, but the idea was somehow . . . intimate. The air between them changed, thickened. She was suddenly acutely conscious of the soft texture of the cotton robe in her hands, the sound of Said's flute weaving through the darkness, the intensity of Galen's expression as he gazed at her. She swallowed. "Very well." She began to undo the fastening at the throat of her brown habit.

He watched her for a minute before he turned and strode toward the entrance of the tent.

"You're leaving?" she asked, startled. "I thought—" She broke off, her tongue moistening her lower lip.

"You thought I would want to look at you again." He smiled. "I do. But it was easier last night at the inn, with all the trappings of civilization about me. Here, I'm freer and must take care." He lifted the flap of the tent, and the next moment she saw him standing outside, silhouetted by the moonlight against the vast dark sky.

He wasn't going to leave her. The rush of relief surging through her filled her with confusion and fear. Surely, the only reason she didn't want him to leave was because she had felt so alone in such a strange land, she assured herself. She couldn't really care if he went back to the tribesmen by the fire.

"*Dépêches-toi,*" he said softly, not looking at her.

Her hands flew, undoing the fastenings of the habit, and a few minutes later she was slipping naked into the softness of the robe.

It was far too large for her, the hem dragging the floor, the sleeves hanging ridiculously long. On her small frame the robe looked ludicrous and not at all seductive. She strode over to the trunk and rummaged until she found a black silk sash, wound the length three times around her waist, and tied it in a knot in front before rolling up the sleeves to her elbows. The garment was so voluminous she should have felt uncomfortable, but the cotton was light as air compared to her habit. She ruffled her hair before stalking belligerently toward the opening of the tent. "I look foolish. You must promise not to laugh at me."

"Must I?" He continued to look at the campfire across the pond. "But laughter is so rare in this world."

"Well, I have no desire to provide you with more." She stopped beside him and scowled up at him. "I'm sure I don't look in the least what you intended. But it's all your fault. I told you that I wasn't comely."

"So you did." His gaze shifted to her face and then down her draped body. His lips twitched. "You do look a trifle . . . overwhelmed." He sobered. "But you're wrong, it's exactly what I intended."

"Truly?" She frowned doubtfully. How could she be expected to gain understanding of the man when he changed from moment to moment? Last night he had wanted her without clothing, and now it appeared he desired her to be covered from chin to toes. She shrugged. "But you're right, this is much more comfortable than my habit."

"I'm glad you approve." His mouth turned up at the corners. "I should have hated to be proved wrong."

"You would never admit it. Men never do. My father—"

He frowned. "I find I'm weary of being compared to your father."

She could certainly understand his distaste. "I'm sorry," she said earnestly. "I know few men, so perhaps I'm being unfair. I can see how you would object to being tossed in the same stable as my father, for he's not at all pleasant."

He started to smile, and then his lips thinned. "No, not at all pleasant." He reached out and touched her hair with a gentle hand. "But you don't have to worry about him any longer, *kilen*."

"I don't worry about him." She shrugged. "It would be a waste of time to worry about things I can't change. It's much more sensible to accept the bad and enjoy the good in life."

"Much more sensible." His fingers moved from her hair to brush the shadows beneath her eyes. "I drove us at a cruel pace from Dinar. Was the day hard for you?"

Her flesh seemed to tingle beneath his touch, filling her with the same excitement and panic she had known the night before. She had to force herself not to step away from him. "No, I would not admit to being so puny. I did not sleep well last night." She had not meant to blurt that out, she thought vexedly. "I mean—"

"I know what you mean. I did not sleep well either." Galen turned her around and shoved her gently toward the tent. "Which is why I pushed the pace today. I wanted to be weary enough to sleep tonight. Good night, *kilen*."

"Aren't you coming?"

"Presently. Go to bed."

She wanted to argue, but there was something about the tension of the back he turned toward her that gave her pause. Still, for some reason she hesitated, reluctant to leave him. "What time do we leave tomorrow?"

"At dawn."

"And how long will it take to get to Zalandan?"

"Another five days."

"Will we—"

"Go to bed, Tess!"

The suppressed violence in his voice made her jump and start hurriedly toward the entrance of the tent. "Oh, very well." She entered the tent and then slowed her pace to a deliberate stroll as she moved toward the curtained sleeping area. After all, there was nothing to run away from when Galen was not even in pursuit.

She drew back the thin curtain and the next moment sank onto the cushions heaped on the low, wide divan. There was much to say for barbarism, she thought as she burrowed into the silken pillows. This divan was much more comfortable than the bed at the inn. . . .

Tess's curly hair was garnet-dark flame against the beige satin of the pillow under her head. His robe had worked open revealing her delicate shoulder, the skin of which was soft as velvet and even more luminescent than the satin of the pillow below it.

As Galen watched, she stirred, half turned, and a beautifully formed limb emerged from the cotton folds of the robe. Not a voluptuous thigh but a strong, well-muscled one.

Exquisite. He felt a painful thickening in his groin as he stood looking at her. He had deliberately provided her with the oversized garment to avoid seeing her naked as he had last night, but somehow this half nudity was even more arousing.

It was because he was back in Sedikhan, he told himself. It couldn't be this half-woman, half-child who was causing his physical turmoil. He always felt a seething unrest and wildness when he was on home ground. The memories of his past debaucheries were too vivid to be ignored when he was back in the desert. But the wildness had never been this strong, the urge to take a woman so violent. . . .

But he could control it. He had to control it.

Why? She was only a woman, like any other.

No, not like any other. She had a man's sense of honor. She had made a bargain and would keep it. He could have her simply by reaching out a hand. He could put his palm on those soft, springy curls surrounding her womanhood and stroke her as he did Selik. He could pluck at that delicious secret nub until she screamed for satisfaction. He could pull her to her knees and make—

*Make.* The word cooled his fever for her. Only a true barbarian used force on women.

He stripped quickly, blew out the candle in the copper lantern hanging on the tent pole, and settled down on the cushions beside Tess, careful not to touch her. The heaviness in his loins turned painful. He lay with his back to her, his heart pounding against his rib cage.

He could control it. He was no savage to take—

He felt the cushions shift. The scent of lavender and woman drifted over him, and he tried to breathe shallowly to mitigate its effect.

Then he felt her fingers in his hair.

Every muscle in his body went rigid. "Tess?"

She murmured something drowsily, only half-awake, her fingers caressing his nape.

"What"—a shudder racked through him as her fingertips brushed his shoulders—"are you doing?"

She pulled the ribbon from his queue and tossed it aside. "Wife's duty . . ."

She moved away again, and the rhythm of her breathing told him she was sound asleep once more.

Wife's duty? Galen would have laughed if he hadn't been in the grip of hot frustration. He would like to show her a wife's "duty." He would like to move between her thighs and plunge deep. He would like to take her for a ride in the desert *coït de cheval*, cradling her buttocks in his palms, making her feel every inch of him. He would like to— He forced himself to abandon such thoughts and to unclench his fists.

He had put his wild days behind him. He could no longer take with reckless abandon. He must think, consider, wait.

Dear God in heaven, he was hurting.

"Scream and I'll slit your pretty throat from ear to ear."

The voice was guttural, jarring Tess from sleep. Her eyes flew open, but she could see only a shadowy face above her in the darkness of the tent.

And the gleam of the steel of the dagger pressed to her throat!

She was going to die. It wasn't fair. She didn't want to die just as life was beginning to be so interesting.

"Where is he?"

He was talking about Galen, she realized with a wild surge of relief. Which meant he must not have killed Galen yet. The knife bit into her flesh, and she could feel warm liquid flow down her neck.

"Where?"

"Here!" A dark shape appeared suddenly behind her assailant, and she saw the glint of steel as a dagger was held to the man's throat. "Get off her, Tamar."

The man on top of Tess froze. "I can slit her throat before you can draw another breath, Galen."

"Why bother? You wouldn't live to enjoy your victory."

The man hesitated, and then, incredibly, he threw back his head and laughed uproariously. "Ah, Galen, you always did have a persuasive tongue." The dagger moved slowly away from Tess's neck. "Put away your dagger and we'll talk. It's over."

"I think my steel is more persuasive than my tongue," Galen said dryly. "Throw away your knife."

The man carelessly tossed the dagger aside.

"Now, get off her—slowly."

"With great regret. I've always admired your taste in *kadines*." The man swung off her. "Why don't you light the lantern so I can get a better look at her?"

"You light the lamp. I want my hands free."

"Distrustful bastard." The man Galen had called Tamar moved toward the gleaming copper lantern hanging from the tent pole a few yards away. "I told you it was over." A moment after the sound of flint on stone a flame flickered in the copper lantern.

Tess could see Tamar's face now. He was young, no older than Galen, with a black beard, cropped close, flowing black hair, and dark eyes. He stood a little above average height, and his handsome features lit with a flashing smile as he turned to face Galen. "Very good, Galen. When I heard you had a woman with you, I was sure you'd be sleeping the sleep of a dead man tonight."

Galen shrugged into his white robe, covering his nakedness, the dagger still in readiness in his hand. "You made so much noise cutting through the tent wall you'd have wakened the dead, Tamar."

Tamar grimaced. "You were always the panther-footed one, not me." He chuckled. "Do you remember the night you crept into the harem of that old—"

"That was the past."

Tamar shook his head mournfully. "Ah, how I miss those days. What times we had."

"Why are you here?"

Tamar raised his brows. "Why, I came to see my old friend Galen Ben Raschid."

"Why?" Galen repeated.

Tamar shrugged. "I was curious."

"And did you kill any of my men while you were making your way through the camp to satisfy your curiosity?"

Tamar shook his head. "No one got in my way."

"I wonder if you're lying."

"Would I lie to you?"

"If it suited you."

"True, but in this case it's not necessary. I killed no one." His glance turned to Tess. "My sentries told me she had red hair." He studied her critically. "Wonderful skin, but she's not your usual *kadine*, Galen. I think I must examine her more closely to see what drew you to her."

Tess scrambled to a sitting position. "Galen, may I be told who this person is?"

"Her accent is strange," Tamar noticed. "Have you been raiding outside Sedikhan?"

"The woman has just come from France. I found her in a café in Dinar."

Startled, Tess stared at Galen.

"I should have known. You always did like the Frenchies." Tamar strolled toward Tess. "Is she good?"

"Good enough." Galen glanced at Tess and then stiffened as his gaze fell on her neck. "You son of a bitch, you've cut her." He strode across the tent and fell to his knees beside Tess and asked her, "Are you all right?"

Tamar frowned. "What's wrong? It's only a little nick."

Galen didn't look at him. "You've outstayed your welcome, Tamar." He touched the tiny cut on her throat with a gentle finger. "Don't be frightened."

"I'm not frightened." She glared at Tamar. "Why should I be afraid of a man who slithers like a snake in the dark to attack a sleeping woman."

Tàmar flushed, and his lips took on an ugly twist. "Shall I show you, whore?" He gazed at her defiant face for a moment before he said flatly, "She needs teaching. I believe you must give this one to me, Galen."

"When have I ever given you anything belonging to me?"

Tamar looked at him in surprise. "She is only a woman. We have shared women before."

"I've not had her long. She still entertains me."

"I'll make a bargain with you. Give me two nights with her and you're free to travel across my territory with no interference."

"It's not your territory."

"It is if I say it is."

"Not if I say it isn't. Words mean nothing."

"But blood means all," Tamar said softly. "And you know how I love the taste of blood."

"Yes, I know."

"But no more than you," Tamar said. "You go berserk when the battle fever hits you."

"Then you should be cautioned about rousing that fever," Galen said wearily.

Tamar gazed at him, a multitude of emotions flicking across his face. "Are you challenging me, my friend?"

"I'm warning you, Tamar."

Tamar's glance went to his dagger lying on the carpet.

The muscles of Galen's thigh pressed against hers and now Tess felt them tense, as if preparing to spring.

Then Tamar's teeth bared in a grin. "Not tonight, Galen. I have a raid planned against the El Kabbar in two days' time." He bowed mockingly. "So keep your woman. I'll find plenty to amuse me in the El Kabbar camp." He glanced around the tent. "Now, give me a goblet of wine, and I'll leave you."

Galen looked pointedly at the cut on Tess's throat, and his lips tightened. "No wine under my roof, Tamar."

Tamar frowned, then shrugged. "Oh, very well. Then just give me my dagger."

"You'll find it sticking in the big palm by the pool after we leave tomorrow. I'll not risk you slitting one of my sentry's throats simply to ease your frustrations."

"How well you know me." Tamar chuckled.

Then his smile faded. "But you don't know your-self, my old friend. Come back to my encampment with me, and I promise you will learn."

"Good-bye, Tamar."

"Until next time." Tamar tilted his head at Tess. "She is too skinny, but I like them small. It makes a man feel powerful as a bull to gore the little ones." He bowed to her. "At our next meet-ing I'll be delighted to teach your lady to have a more docile tongue." He strode out of the tent.

Tess let out the breath she didn't know she had been holding. "That was . . . interesting."

"Interesting? I've noticed you have a passion-ate fondness for that word." The surprise in Ga-len's expression was wiped away by respect. "But yes, you might call Tamar interesting."

"What else would you call him?"

"Murderer, rapist, bandit. There's no more vi-cious sheikh in Sedikhan than Tamar."

"He spoke as if he knew you well."

"We grew up together in Zalandan. For a time his father's tribe and the El Zalan were joined by a treaty. When Tamar came to power, the treaty was broken, and he returned to the north." He stood up, walked over to the tent pole and blew out the lantern. "You can go back to sleep now. He won't return."

"Why did he come? I could make no sense of him."

Galen shrugged out of his robe and moved back toward the divan. "Who knows why Tamar does anything? Whim directs him." He lay down on the cushions and stretched out his big limbs. "He's a lawless brigand, a total savage."

"But you were once friends."

"Once."

He fell silent, but Tess could still feel the tension emanating from him.

"Why did you lie to him about me?"

"It was best. Tamar has no desire for Sedikhan to be united. He enjoys his life exactly the way it is. He might have been much more determined to have you if he'd known you were part of my plan."

She suddenly remembered the word Tamar had used in referring to her. "What is a *kadine*?"

"A woman of pleasure."

"Couldn't you have named me your wife and still kept my identity a secret?"

"Perhaps, but he would have been suspicious. Tamar knows I have no desire to wed."

A strange pain rippled through her at his words. She swallowed. "Of course, I understand." She lay still, pondering the extraordinary events of the last quarter hour. After a time she spoke again. "You say no one knows why Tamar does anything, but I think you do."

"Yes, I've always been able to gauge what Tamar was going to do next."

"How?"

He was silent so long she thought he wasn't going to answer. "Because he's my mirror."

"What?"

"He's what I was. He's what I could become again."

Startled, she blurted, "But you said he was a vicious bandit."

"Yes."

"A brigand and a rapist."

"Yes."

She became conscious of the waves of emotion radiating from his rigid body. She could sense violence, controlled with difficulty, within, but no trace of the malice that Tamar had exuded. "You're wrong. You could never be like him."

"I'm not wrong," he murmured almost inaudibly. "But it won't happen. Not if I'm strong. Not if I fight it. Not if I'm vigilant . . ."

# Chapter 4

"Galen tells me you had a visitor last night," Sacha said as he lifted Tess into her sidesaddle at dawn the next morning. "You needn't worry that it will happen again. Kalim was mortified that Tamar had managed to slip by his sentries."

"Galen reprimanded him?"

"Galen seldom reprimands. He simply told Kalim he was disappointed in him."

"That seems a strange way to handle the matter."

"It's Galen's way, and it's always proved effective. The *majiron*'s 'disappointment' has more sting than a tongue-lashing from another leader."

She wrinkled her nose. "Kalim probably wishes

that savage Tamar had cut my throat. It's obvious Kalim has no liking for me."

Sacha glanced away from her. "That's only your imagination. How could he dislike you when he doesn't know you?"

Tess recalled the brief look of resentment on Kalim's face when Galen had introduced her and shook her head. "It's not my imagination." She caught sight of Galen. He was riding out of camp at Kalim's side. "What do you know of this Tamar?"

"Not much. There have been a few skirmishes between his tribe and the El Zalan in the past few years, but Galen usually tries to avoid him."

"Why?"

Sacha shrugged. "I have no idea. Galen doesn't talk about him."

"They were children together. Perhaps he still has a lingering fondness for him."

Sacha shook his head. "Galen wouldn't let friendship interfere with the good of the El Zalan. It's probably that the tribes are so widely separated they don't get in each other's way."

And cows could fly. "Yes, that must be it." She gathered the reins. "Let's go. Galen has left the oasis."

"There's no hurry." Sacha swung up into the saddle. "You're to ride in the rear with me until we reach Zalandan."

"I can keep up," she said, hurt. "I ride better than you."

"That's not the point. Galen has to ride up

ahead with Kalim and lead the escort, but he wants to keep you away from the main party."

"Mother of God." Her hands clenched on the reins. "First, I'm penned up in that tent, and now I'm forced to eat the dust. I'm getting very tired of being placed in—"

"I'm hurt," Sacha interrupted, pulling a face. "You've not seen me for years and yet you are already weary of my company."

"You know that's not what—"

"Five more days," he coaxed. "Things will be different in Zalandan."

She scowled. "Freedom?"

"To some extent."

She kicked her horse into a trot. "To a great extent," she said through clenched teeth. "I have no liking for all this smothering. When we get to Zalandan, I will no longer tolerate it."

"*Majira*, wait!"

They both turned to see a young man galloping toward them. As he reined in, he flashed a broad grin and inclined his head in a polite bow. "Greetings, *Majira*. Since you're not to be with the main party, Kalim has sent me to protect and serve you on the journey. My name is Yusef Benardon."

"I believe I can assure my cousin any protection she requires, Yusef," Sacha said dryly.

Yusef stared at him guilelessly, his black eyes like sparkling buttons in his round face. "Very well, then I will protect you, Sacha. It makes no difference to me."

"Protect *me*?" Sacha said blankly.

Yusef lowered his lids to half mask the mischief glittering in his eyes. "You think the honor bestowed on you is too great? I admit having the greatest warrior in Sedikhan put at your disposal is enough to dazzle and humble most men."

Sacha closed his eyes. "I believe I'm beginning to feel ill."

Yusef waved his hand airily. "You see? The *majira* does have need of me, since you're clearly of a delicate nature."

Tess smothered a smile as she saw Sacha's eyes flick open in outrage. It was all very well for her cousin to joke about his delicate sensibilities, but he couldn't tolerate others doing so.

Yusef had caught her glimmer of a smile from the corner of his eye and immediately turned to her with a coaxing grin. "You must not send me back to Kalim. It's very boring and lonely up there for me, as all the other men are jealous of my prowess. We shall get along much better back here together."

"Indeed?"

He smiled solemnly. "I shall immerse myself in the radiant delight of your company, and in return I will tell you many stories that will inform and amuse you. I promise I'll make the hours of the journey fly by."

"A result much to be desired," Tess said.

"Then we're agreed." Yusef gave her another dazzling smile. "I'll go ahead and make sure the road has been made safe for you, but do not fear. I'll not let you linger without me in this abysmal boredom a moment longer than necessary." Yusef galloped out of the oasis after the column of men.

Tess laughed helplessly as she heard Sacha's muttered oath.

"I don't find anything amusing in—" Sacha broke off and smiled reluctantly. "It's no wonder Kalim sent him back here out of harm's way. The scalawag has unerring aim. By the end of five days he probably would have managed to antagonize every one of Galen's men and completely disrupted the escort."

"He's not a great warrior?"

"I didn't say that. He's one of the best fighters Galen has. Unfortunately, he also has a highly developed talent for mischief."

"I think I like him."

"I'm not surprised. Most women have a weakness for Yusef. Which is another reason he's not overpopular with the men."

"He's a womanizer?" The idea surprised her, for Yusef had no claim to the wonderful good looks of Kalim or Sacha, much less the magnetism of Galen. He was only a little above middle height, and appeared wiry and agile rather than powerful. In fact, he reminded her of a rather endearing monkey with his sparkling eyes and round, merry face.

"Let's say he has a weakness where all ladies are concerned. They smile at him, and he forgets trifling realities such as husbands and fathers." He shrugged. "But don't worry—he may be rash, but he's not mad. He won't insult the *majira*, and he may even amuse you." He scowled. "Not that we need the rascal."

Tess's lips twitched. "No, of course not." But she was already feeling her spirits rise as she nudged her mare into a trot. She was sure it had not been Kalim's intention to see to her entertainment when he had sent Yusef to be her escort. But Yusef's mischievous presence just might make the journey bearable.

"There it is!" Yusef gestured jubilantly. "Zalandan." He started at a gallop after the column a quarter of a mile ahead.

"I didn't expect this." Tess paused on the hill beside Sacha and gazed at the great walled city in the valley below. With a gold-dipped brush the late afternoon sunlight gilded the turquoise minarets and the white stone of the houses of Zalandan. The beauty of the city touched her heart and soul. "It's very impressive. Almost as large as Belajo."

"That's where the similarity ends," Sacha said dryly. "Belajo leans toward the West. Zalandan is definitely of the East."

"Yet you preferred to spend the last six years here."

"Because it called to me."

"Called to you?" she asked, puzzled.

"You'll see."

They wound their way down the hill to the city.

"Zalandan has its own allure," Sacha said as they passed through the city gates.

She saw what he meant as they traveled through the crowded streets of Zalandan. Amid the spice shops and silk stalls, vendors carrying huge cages filled with doves and white cockatoos stopped their haggling to watch the troop ride across the huge marketplace.

Yusef rode back to join Tess and Sacha as they reached the market. "Ah, it's good to be home," he said, and sighed contentedly. He added quickly, "Not that I didn't enjoy every moment of your company, *Majira*. The past days will live in my memory through an eternity of—"

"Enough, Yusef." Her tone was abstracted as she eagerly gazed at the shops and stalls on either side of her. She suddenly pointed to a shop where a variety of brilliant-hued pottery containers with strange long handles were displayed. "What kind of place is that? I've never seen vases shaped like those, and they're all exactly the same size."

Yusef glanced casually at the shop she had indicated. "Those aren't vases, they're *carobels*. Camar has the finest *carobel* shop in all of Zalandan." He grinned. "And one of the most beautiful daughters." He glanced wistfully back at the shop. "With a heart as generous as her face is fair. I don't suppose now that you're safely in Zalandan, you would permit—"

Tess shook her head resignedly. She had an idea she would live no longer in Yusef's memory than the moment he saw the shopkeeper's generous and comely daughter, but she would miss the scamp. Thank the saints she'd had Sacha and Yusef's company on the journey, for she had certainly seen little enough of Galen since that first night. Not that it mattered to her, she assured herself quickly. "Go to your shopkeeper's daughter, Yusef."

He smiled. "I look forward to basking in your presence again, *Majira*." He wheeled his horse and rode swiftly back toward the shop.

"At least he made it through the gates before he yielded to temptation," Sacha said. "He's not usually so celibate. I thought perhaps he'd make a side excursion on our journey and visit one of the women of the hill tribes."

Once they left the bazaar, Tess expected to see signs of the poverty she had encountered in Belajo and Paris, but though the houses were small, they seemed spotlessly clean, and the people well-fed and cheerful. Galen's appearance was met by smiles and cheers, but they all drew respectfully aside as the column approached.

"The palace is just ahead," Sacha said as he nodded to the huge courtyard at the end of the street.

She could hardly have missed it, Tess thought dazedly. The palace was only two stories high, but it was a dreamlike turreted structure with arched windows and delicately fretted balconies. It was built of a creamy beige stone that caught the sunlight and glittered like a massive jewel in the center of the courtyard.

"It's . . . bewitching."

Sacha noted her entranced expression and nodded knowingly. "I told you. It calls to you. . . ."

"Welcome to Zalandan." Galen had dismounted and was striding toward them.

She stiffened, jarred out of her bemusement.

He raised his brows as he saw the wariness in her expression. "I hope my home pleases you?"

"Of course it pleases me. Why should it not? It's very beautiful."

"And a surprise." He smiled faintly as he lifted her down from her mare onto the mosaic tiles of the courtyard. "I told you we savages can lay claim to certain comforts. Gold buys nearly anything in this world." Her gaze flew to his face, and he shook his head. "No, I know it didn't buy you. Your price was higher. But gold can make your stay here pleasant." He turned to Said. "Take her to her quarters and be sure Viane makes her comfortable."

"I'll take her," Sacha said quickly. "I have nothing better to do."

Galen turned back to look at him, and for an instant Tess thought she saw a flicker of concern on his face before he shrugged. "As you like." He turned to Tess. "Tell Viane I'll come to your chamber to sup with you at dusk."

"If you're not too busy?"

His brows lifted at the caustic note in her voice. "I won't be too busy." He went toward the stable where Kalim waited.

Excitement mixed generously with resentment rippled through her as she watched Galen join Kalim and enter the stable. He had not supped with her since the night of their wedding. In truth, she had scarcely seen him on the journey to Zalandan. He had stayed at the campfire with the men, coming to their tent only after she had gone to sleep.

"Tess?"

She turned to see Sacha gazing at her with an amused smile.

He gestured with a mocking flourish for her to precede him into the palace.

She quickly climbed the steps, and the doors were immediately thrown open by the two robed guards standing at attention. "Who is Viane?"

"Galen's half-sister."

"I didn't know he had a sister." She shouldn't have been surprised at her ignorance. She was finding she knew very little about her husband.

"Galen's mother died when he was twelve, and soon after his father married again. Viane was the only child of the union." He led her swiftly down the gleaming corridor, his steps springing with a curious eagerness. "You'll grow fond of Viane."

Tess made a face. "I don't seem to make friends with women easily. They find me too bold."

"I can see why." Sacha grinned. "Not many ladies prefer stables to ballrooms, but you'll have no conflict with Viane."

"She likes to ride?"

"No, she's rather timid around horses, but that won't matter."

She looked at him skeptically. She could not imagine a feeling of closeness toward anyone who had no fondness for animals.

He chuckled as he saw her expression. "Truly."

He stopped before a carved teak wood door, threw it open, and then stepped aside for her to precede him into the chamber.

A slight dark-haired woman gowned in flowing light blue draperies came toward them. A deep rose flush colored her olive cheeks as she inclined her head politely to Sacha. "Welcome back, my lord." She turned to Tess and smiled gently. "I have been looking forward to this moment since Galen sent word you were coming. Welcome, *Majira*."

Viane Ben Raschid radiated warmth. Her wide-set dark eyes shone with good humor, and her beautiful features seemed to be lit from within.

"They call me Tess." Tess smiled at her. One could not help but smile at Viane. "And I'm sure I would have looked forward to meeting you also had I known you existed. No one had the civility to tell me."

Viane's smiled widened. "You're very blunt." She smiled. "Frankness is a wonderful virtue. I am too bound by courtesy to speak as honestly as you do."

Tess burst out laughing. "Some people call it rudeness, not honesty."

"Oh no." Viane appeared distressed. "I am the one who was rude. I did not mean to speak without tact. I meant—"

"I know." Tess held up her hand to stop Viane's words. That first strong impression of Viane's gentle dignity had blinded her to the realization that Galen's sister was scarcely older than herself. She doubted if the young girl knew the meaning of the word rudeness. "I was jesting. It's my way." She glanced at Sacha, who was still staring in bemusement at Viane. "Is that not so, Sacha?"

"What?" He tore his gaze from Viane's face. "Yes, you've always been cheeky."

Tess's eyes widened in surprise. She had never seen such an expression on Sacha's face, and Viane's cheeks had gone scarlet again.

"Let me make you comfortable." Viane lowered her lashes, turning quickly away from Sacha. "If my lord Sacha will leave us?"

Sacha frowned and nodded curtly. "I'll see you in the morning, Tess." He turned on his heel and left the chamber.

Viane breathed a sigh of relief as the door closed behind him. "Now, you must bathe while I find you something to wear."

"I have gowns in my valises."

Viane shook her head as she clapped her hands for a servant and moved briskly across the chamber toward an armoire inlaid with mother-of-pearl. "Galen sent word that I should provide you with a few of my garments tonight. Later he wishes to choose things for you himself."

The high-necked gown Viane lent Tess was made of a length of white chiffon shot with silver that draped her small form without clinging and was completely unrevealing.

Galen's gaze ran over her appraisingly when

he entered the chamber that night. "Better than my robe," he commented shortly. "We'll attend to the rest of your wardrobe tomorrow."

"I'm surprised that you're bothering with such a small matter. Ladies' fashions could be of no interest to you."

"I've always found minor details can suddenly become annoyingly abrasive if left untended." He smiled faintly. "And my wife's clothing is of the utmost importance to me."

"Even when you hide her away?" Tess asked flippantly.

"I take care of my own." He moved across the room to the divan. "And circumstances are different now."

"In what way?"

"We're not surrounded by my men." He settled himself on the pillows before the low table that the servants had laid with fine china and jeweled goblets. "There are thick walls around us instead of flimsy cloth." He stared into her eyes. "I'm very selfish," he said softly. "I don't want anyone but me to hear the cries you'll make."

The blood rushed to her cheeks, and she found she couldn't pull her gaze away from his. "I see," she said faintly. She knew the primal cries he meant. From childhood on she had heard Pauline and others scream out in the throes of passion. "You may be disappointed. I've always thought— it lacks dignity."

He burst out laughing. "And you're so very conscious of appearances."

She flushed. "I may be less than womanly at times, but I'm not without dignity."

His laughter faded, but a hint of tenderness lingered. "Yes, you have dignity, the very best kind. Not based on pride, but in confidence of what you are."

Startled, she asked, "I do?"

He nodded. "Even when you were a child, I noticed it. Dignity and honor. I knew you would be a woman to trust."

She felt a warm, sweet melting deep within her. A woman to trust. She felt as if she had been given a gift of great value. "I thought Viane would be supping with us."

He shook his head. "She eats with the women."

Tess frowned. "Why?"

Galen caught the hint of belligerence in her tone and smiled. "Not because I wish it. Viane's mother raised her in the old ways and traditions. She's more comfortable eating in her quarters."

"Then you should have striven to make her comfortable with the new ways."

"It's a battle I fight every day."

"But not in your own palace."

"No, I guess not." His expression was suddenly weary. "I can't fight every minute of every day."

She felt a rush of sympathy that banished her belligerence. She moved toward him across the chamber. "Never mind. I'll attend to it now that I'm here."

He smiled. "I do not doubt it. But please don't pitch Viane into a bog."

"I wouldn't do such a thing. I like her." She sat down on the cushions opposite him. "You have very little European furniture in the palace. I thought since you'd spent so much time in Tamrovia, you would have imported—"

"I spend only as much time as I'm forced to in Tamrovia. This is where I belong." The words were said simply, but with great conviction. "I take what the El Zalan and I need from other countries and no more."

"And you have no need for dining tables?"

He shook his head. "The floor is better."

"Why?"

"Eating is a natural function, and there's an easiness and naturalness about sitting close to the earth. Are you not more comfortable sitting there on your silk pillow than occupying those stiff cushioned chairs used in your country?"

She nodded slowly, as she realized he was right. "You believe life should be simple and natural?"

"As much as possible. We have enough conflict and tragedies without making the everyday functions of living difficult for ourselves." He smiled. "Now, eat. You've probed enough for now."

"You object to questions?"

"No, it is your right to question." He poured wine into a bejeweled goblet and handed it to her. "As it is mine to refuse to answer."

She took the wine, staring down into its red depths. "I have another question."

"Yes?"

"When you saved Apollo and Daphne, I promised you anything you wanted." She lifted her gaze to meet his across the table. "When you made your offer to me at the inn, you made no mention of that promise. Why?"

"For two reasons. First, trust. I wanted you to come to me freely."

"And the second?"

He smiled. "I wanted to save that promise to use at a more propitious time. I wanted to keep you bound to me."

The air between them was suddenly charged with sensual awareness. Tess became acutely conscious of the scent of the gardenias in the giant alabaster vase standing in the corner, the softness of the chiffon pressing against her breasts, his intent gaze on her.

She hurriedly took a sip of wine that flowed warm and heady down her throat. "You're being very honest with me."

"Always." He studied her face. "Would you like to see Apollo?"

"Tonight?"

He shook his head. "Tomorrow. I'll come for you after I've finished with the morning audiences."

Come for her? Then he had no intention of staying the night.

"No." His gaze was reading her expression. "That was just to let you become accustomed to me in your bed. Now, it's time for us to be apart for a while."

"I don't understand." She frowned. "And I'm not sure I like all this dithering about."

His eyes twinkled. "I'm not overfond of it either, I assure you. The 'dithering' will be brought to an end as soon as possible." He smiled slowly. "And then I will spend every night in your bed, and possibly many hours of the day as well."

She again felt the curious tingling and sense of breathlessness. She took another sip of wine and nodded briskly. "To get me with child."

His expression became guarded as he poured wine into his own goblet. "But of course. Isn't that the reason you're here?"

"I thought Apollo would be at the palace stables." Tess frowned as she glanced at the pretty white stone house before which Galen and she had stopped after a long ride through the narrow streets of Zalandan. "Couldn't you have kept him with you?"

"I could have." Galen dismounted from Selik and lifted Tess down from her mare. He tossed the reins to Said and took Tess's arm. "But I decided not to."

"Why not? I know he must have annoyed you on the journey to Sedikhan, but you—"

"He made my life a misery on the journey from Tamrovia," Galen broke in flatly. "But that's not why he's here and not at the palace." He opened the ornamental iron gate and allowed her to precede him into the garden. "Bringing Daphne and Apollo here seemed to solve several problems. I'm forced to travel extensively, and I couldn't provide them with the same attention you gave them, and I didn't wish to cage them in the kennels." He looked down at her. "I didn't think you'd want them to exchange one cage for another."

"No." The frown remained on her face. "But I find this unsettling. Whenever I remembered Apollo, I thought of him with you."

"You gave them into my care. I had to make decisions as to their welfare." He propelled her down the path leading around the house. "When I returned to Zalandan, I found a tribal disturbance had broken out in the hills, and one of my chieftains and his wife had been killed. They left behind a fifteen-year-old son. The boy was alone and grieving, so I brought him here and put him to the task of helping me train Apollo and Daphne."

"Train?" Her gaze flew to his face. "You tried to train Apollo?"

He nodded. "We *succeeded* in training Apollo."

"To hunt?"

"No, that was not his nature. That's where your father erred. Apollo has no killer instincts. However, he did have the potential to be a great tracker." He smiled. "Now, Apollo can track man or beast even through desert country."

She gazed at him in disbelief. "Apollo?"

His smile faded. "He couldn't stay a gamboling pup forever. He wasn't used cruelly, but he had to fulfill his purpose in life."

All these years she had remembered the dog

as her awkward, madcap friend. She tried to smile. "And what of Daphne? Have you solved her problem too?"

He nodded. "She's not as good a tracker as Apollo, but she likes the trail." He paused. "And Apollo is a grandfather many times over."

"Daphne finally accepted him?"

"When it was a matter of choice, not force. I've found opportunity and choice usually win the day."

Opportunity and choice. She suddenly saw the relationship between his behavior with her and his patience with the hounds. "I . . . see."

"No, you don't. You don't understand at all. Besides opportunity and choice, the bitch must also be in heat."

She was startled by the crudity of his words. "I'm surprised you could not control that element as well," she said flippantly.

He smiled. "One must leave something to nature."

The sensuality in his smile caused her to glance hurriedly away. She caught sight of the upper part of a house a few streets away that towered grandly over its neighbors. "That's a fine-looking residence. Who lives there?"

"Yusef Benardon."

"Yusef?" Her gaze flew back to his face. "He has such wealth?"

He nodded. "His father was one of the richest silk merchants in Zalandan."

"Then why was Yusef part of your escort?"

He shrugged. "Town life becomes dull, and young men often prefer battle to bartering." He paused before continuing smoothly, "You appear very interested in our Yusef. You find him appealing?"

"Of course." She spoke absently, her gaze still on the house. "Who would not? He makes me laugh."

"And you find him handsome?"

"I suppose so." She thought about it. "The more one is with him, the more comely he seems."

His lips tightened. "Perhaps it was a mistake to let you become so accustomed to his presence." Before she could answer, he pursed his lips and gave a piercing whistle. The sound was met immediately by an uproar of barking, and two huge white flashes bounded around the house toward them.

Eagerness soared through Tess. Six years . . .

"Apollo!" She fell to her knees on the ground, but the borzois ignored her and dashed past her to Galen to give him a frenzied welcome.

"Down." Galen held out his hand, and the borzois immediately froze, only their tails waving frantically. Galen's gaze narrowed on Tess's disappointed face, and he muttered a low curse. "Don't look like that. They're only dogs."

"I know." She smiled tremulously, blinking back the tears. "I shouldn't have expected them to remember me, but I used to think about them at the convent. . . . They'll have to get to know me again."

"Time goes on, Tess," he said gently. "Nothing stands still."

She got to her feet and busily dusted off her habit. "They appear to have great affection for you. You must have treated them very well."

"For God's sake, I didn't set out to rob you of their affection."

"No, of course not. I knew them both as pups, and missed all the growing years." She smiled brightly. "I understand."

He muttered something beneath his breath. "But you're hurting," he said thickly. "I should have anticipated this."

"You're no seer. You couldn't be expected to know how dumb animals would react." She reached out and touched Daphne's silky coat with a loving hand. "I'm sure I was foolish to—" She broke off as the dogs suddenly tore away from them down the path toward the man approaching them from the house. "Who—?"

It was Kalim . . . but not the fierce, stern Kalim she had come to know. He laughed boyishly as the two dogs launched themselves at him in joyous delirium.

Tess stiffened. "What's he doing here?"

"He lives here. This is the house I gave him six years ago when I brought him down from the hills after his father's death."

"That boy was Kalim?" She was astonished at how affectionately he regarded the dogs. "I would never have guessed."

"He's very conscious of his responsibilities. He

was forced to become a man before he stopped being a boy."

"You like him?"

He nodded. "And understand him. I was only in my seventeenth year when my father died and I became sheikh of the El Zalan." He strode down the path toward Kalim. "Coming here was a mistake. Let's give Kalim our greetings and be gone."

The smile lingered on Kalim's face as he lifted his head to look at Galen. "I thought it must be you. Apollo tore out of the house like a—" He broke off as he caught sight of Tess. His smile vanished, and he bowed formally. "*Majira.*"

She felt a chill go through her. "How do you do, Kalim? I must thank you for being so kind to Apollo and Daphne."

"No kindness was necessary, *Majira*. I am fond of them." He turned back to Galen. "Will you be needing me for the next few days? If not, I thought I'd ride into the hills to visit my great-uncle."

"Go, but be careful. A messenger arrived this morning with news of more raids on the Said Ababa border."

"I'm always careful." A warm smile lit his face as he gave the dogs a final pat. "As you've taught me to be, *Majiron*. I'll bring you back a true report on the raids by the week's end." He bowed to each, then hurried up the path to the house.

Galen watched him with a worried frown. "I don't like him going alone."

"You're truly fond of him," Tess said, amazed.

"I have emotions," he said mockingly as he took her arm and guided her through the garden toward the gate. "I have affection for Viane and Kalim and Sacha and many people of whom you have no knowledge."

"But Kalim seems . . ."—she substituted a word for the rude term she meant—"cold."

"He's not cold. You just don't understand him."

"It's not likely that I will. He resents me."

"Yes."

She had expected him to deny the charge as Sacha had done. "Why? Because you wed me?"

"Partly." He opened the gate. "But principally because you're of the West."

"I don't understand."

"He's been out of Sedikhan on occasion, and he realizes what a pull the West exerts."

She frowned in puzzlement. "On you?"

"No, not on me." He lifted her onto the side-saddle. "Before my stepmother died, she arranged a marriage between Kalim and Viane. Their marriage is to take place next summer."

"With Viane's consent?"

His lips tightened as he mounted Selik. "I would not have sanctioned it otherwise. You persist in thinking me a tyrant. Some of the old ways are best, but I would not cage Viane any more than I would Apollo or Daphne."

"Where are we going now?" she asked, trying to keep up with him.

"Back to the palace," he said curtly. "I made a mistake, but that doesn't mean I can't set it right."

The golden palomino mare in the stall stood fifteen hands high and shone creamy gold in the sunlight.

"Her name is Pavda." Galen patted the mare's nose. "She's been ridden only by the grooms to exercise her. At one time I thought to give her to Viane, but she's afraid of her."

"Afraid of this angel?" Tess moved forward to stand beside Galen. "But why? Look at her eyes. Anyone can see she's gentle as a lamb."

"Tell that to the groom who rides her every morning."

"She doesn't like being cooped up." She shot him a glance. "I can understand that."

"Did I feel a barb hit home?" He made a face. "If you're in such sympathy with her, then you obviously belong together. I take it you'll accept Pavda?"

She gazed wistfully at the mare. "I like Viane. I wouldn't steal this beauty from her."

"You can't steal what has never been given."

"I can't believe it. You're really giving her to me?" Tess's cheeks flushed with excitement as she ran a caressing hand over Pavda's muzzle. "She's going to be mine?"

"Wasn't that part of our bargain?"

"Yes, but my father—" She stopped. "I keep forgetting you don't like being compared to him."

She made an impatient gesture. "You know as well as I that not many men keep honor with women."

"That's because we feel helpless before some of their weapons."

"Nonsense, it's the men who hold all the power in the world." She spoke absently, her gaze on Pavda. "She's mine? You won't take her back?"

"She is yours." He added softly, "And you won't have to fight for her affection. She's had no mistress but you, nor will she ever."

Warmth rippled through her. "Mine," she murmured. "May I ride her now?"

"Not now. Tomorrow is soon enough."

"But I want to—"

"Tomorrow," Galen said firmly. "I have things to do for the next few hours and have no time for lessons."

"Lessons?" she asked indignantly. "I ride very well. Better than most men."

"Sidesaddle." He took her arm and pushed her gently toward the door of the stable. "From now on you ride astride."

She gazed at him, shocked. "Like a man?"

"My mother was killed riding sidesaddle. A horse fell and crushed her," Galen said grimly. "I'll not have you mounted on one of those death traps any longer than I can help it." He chuckled as he saw her expression. "Why do you look at me like that? I would have thought you'd like the freedom."

"I never—I was always told that a woman must ride—" Her eyes began to sparkle as she began to consider the possibilities. "I never thought it possible."

"Many things are possible in Zalandan that aren't possible in the rest of the world." He smiled faintly into her radiant face. "You just have to cast off the old ways of thinking."

"Yet you cling to some of the old ways."

"Choice." He didn't look at her. "Simply because a possibility exists doesn't mean we have to act on it."

"But you gave me no choice in what manner I'm to ride."

"That was different."

"A man's answer. No logic." Tess smiled joyously. "But since you've given me Pavda, I forgive you everything."

"I thank you." He bowed slightly. "Then I hope your indulgence will extend to accepting my guidance in choosing your wardrobe. The fabric vendor and the tailor will be in your chamber at two this afternoon."

"Oh that." She frowned. "I'd much rather go back to the stable and get better acquainted with Pavda."

"Indulge me," he said again.

She shrugged. "Oh, very well. I guess I do need something in which to ride. This habit is suitable only for sidesaddle."

He turned away, but not before she saw the faintest smile touch his lips. "Yes, riding is of the utmost importance."

*     *     *

After she left the stable, Tess immediately went back to the palace to seek out Viane, whose quarters were much like her own. There was one exception. Viane's terrace held a huge aviary with white lattice stone walls and occupied by trees, shrubbery, and a multitude of birds of varying types and hues.

The gate of the aviary was slightly ajar, but Tess stopped just outside. "Viane!"

"Come in, Tess," Viane called from within. "I'm feeding the birds."

"I'll wait." Tess peered warily through the lattice at a huge parrot balanced on Viane's slender arm. "You like birds?"

"Oh yes." Viane lifted her arm and the parrot flew up onto a branch in the tree next to her. "Aren't they beautiful?"

"Very nice."

Viane looked at Tess in surprise as she moved toward the lattice door. "You're afraid?"

"No such thing."

Viane gazed at her in wonder. "Yet you told me you loved horses. How can you be afraid of these gentle creatures when you have no fear of those huge monsters?"

"Horses don't scatter their bounty from above with a singular lack of discrimination."

Viane burst out laughing. "True, but I'd still rather watch one in flight than be on the back of a fierce stallion."

Tess braced herself and said in a rush, "Galen gave me Pavda. I thought you should know."

"Why?" Viane raised her brows. "I have no interest in riding her."

Tess frowned in puzzlement. "That's what Galen said, but I couldn't believe it."

Viane studied Tess's bewildered expression before smiling gently. "You must understand. I'm not like you, either in nature or upbringing. I'm not bold, and I have no desire to go beyond my limits."

"How do you know what your limits are, if you don't try to go beyond them?"

"Why, I don't—" Viane started to laugh. "You see, we're not at all alike." She closed the aviary door and moved gracefully across the terrace. "You left the palace very early. Let me order tea for you."

"How did you know that?"

Viane flushed guiltily. "You must not think I'm spying on you. Since my mother died, the servants have looked to me to oversee the running of the palace, and Galen has made no objection." She continued hurriedly, "But since you are now the *majira*, perhaps you—"

"Me?" Tess looked at her blankly. "You jest. Good heavens no! I intend to spend more time at the stable than the palace while I'm in Zalandan."

"*While* you're in Zalandan?" Viane gazed at her in confusion. "What do you—"

"Are those pigeons?"

Viane nodded.

"The Count owned pigeons. He trained them

to carry messages to his cousin in Paris. It was most interesting."

"Carry messages?"

Tess nodded. "The Count said pigeons have been used to carry messages since the twelfth century before the birth of Christ, sometimes for distances of hundreds, even thousands, of miles." She whirled to face Viane, her face alight with eagerness. "I know, we will train our own pigeons."

Viane frowned. "I do not think—"

"Of course we will," Tess interrupted, her eyes sparkling. "Why not? It's a splendid idea. You'll teach me about birds, and I'll teach you about horses." She linked her hands behind her back as she began to stride back and forth across the terrace. "I learned a little from the Count. It seems the instinct is there in most pigeons, and one must only give them the opportunity. If the Count could manage it, I'm sure we can do even better, for he was not at all clever. By the time I leave Zalandan, I'll know all I need to know about—"

"Leave here? Why should you leave here? This is your husband's home."

Tess hadn't meant to let her enthusiasm run away with her. "That doesn't mean I must stay here forever. It's not that kind of marriage."

"There is only one kind of marriage. You must not think these thoughts." Viane added flatly, "Galen will not let you leave him."

"You will see." Tess paused in midstride and

turned to face her. "I understand you are to marry yourself next summer."

"Yes." A soft flush dyed her cheeks as she glanced back at the pigeons, now on a low branch of a pepper tree. "It was arranged by my mother. Kalim is a good man, and very kind to me."

"And you are content?"

"As much as I can be," Viane said haltingly. "I think some women are not meant for marriage. I feel very shy when I think of Kalim."

"Then don't think of him," Tess said. "Who knows what will come before next summer?" She grinned. "In the meantime we'll have a perfectly wonderful time training your pigeons. Do they have names?"

"Alexander the Great and Roxanne."

Tess laughed. "You see? Alexander the Great was a prodigious traveler. You must have somehow known what his destiny would be."

Viane smiled ruefully. "I assure you that in my wildest moments I had no idea I would ever use my pigeons to carry messages."

"But won't it be exciting?"

Viane's gentle smile widened, her gaze on Tess's luminous face. "Yes, I believe it will prove very exciting, Tess."

# Chapter 5

"You choose. I don't care," Tess said impatiently. She gazed without interest at the bolts of shimmering fabrics spread on every chair, table, and divan in her chamber. "I'm weary of looking at all this."

"You tire easily." Galen leaned back in his chair and stretched his long legs before him, crossing his booted feet at the ankle. "You've scarcely glanced at the fabrics."

"It doesn't matter. This is taking too long." She looked anxiously at the setting sun. "I thought I'd have time to take an apple to Pavda before supper."

"The midnight-blue brocade is exceptional, *Majira*," the bearded fabric merchant said coaxingly.

She cast an indifferent glance at the shimmering fabric unfurled on the floor. "Yes, it's very nice." She turned to Galen. "Did I tell you about the pigeons?"

"Twice," he said solemnly.

"Nice?" the vendor murmured faintly. "The brocade was brought from China, and the pearl embroidery took seven months to complete."

"*Very* nice," Tess said impatiently. "I have no quarrel with your goods."

"She'll take the brocade." Galen stood up. "And the green chiffon and the gold." He strolled around the room, selecting and rejecting fabrics with brisk efficiency. "You have the *majira*'s measurements and my wishes as to the fashioning of the gowns. I'll expect the first to be ready for fittings by next week."

"Certainly, *Majiron*," The little man appeared relieved. He snapped his fingers, and his young assistant began to gather up the bolts. "And the garments for which you previously gave me instructions will be delivered by eight tomorrow morning."

Tess turned to look at Galen. "What garments are those?"

"Your riding habit, among others." Galen waved the merchant and his assistant from the room and sat down again. His lips quirked as he saw Tess's expression of enthusiasm. "Ah, I've fired your interest."

"How is it to be fashioned? Will I wear trousers?"

"Of a sort." He grimaced. "However, I have no desire to see you garbed as a man. The garment resembles a divided gown."

"Velvet?"

"For this climate? I ordered it made of the same material as my robes."

Tess smiled with satisfaction as she remembered its texture. "How pleasant."

"That was my intention." He smiled slowly. "To bring you comfort and pleasure. Of course, you will wear nothing beneath any of the garments."

"No?" She frowned. "I'm not sure I'll like that. Pauline says it's rumored Empress Josephine wears nothing under her gowns, but I always thought it must be rather drafty."

His lips twitched. "Sedikhan's climate is much warmer than France's."

That argument appeared reasonable to Tess. "I suppose we'll have to see."

He looked at her for a moment before he nodded briskly. "Quite right. Why don't we?"

"What?"

"You said we must see." He untied the black sash around his waist and took it off. "Why not do it now, before the garment is finished? Take off your habit."

His sudden change from amusement to sensuality caught her off guard. "Now?"

"Right now." He held the sash loosely, running his left hand slowly down its length. "After all, we have nothing better to do."

She stared in fascination at his hands on the

sash, at his beautiful fingers, strong, graceful, moving with lazy sensuality among the folds of the sable material. Her heartbeat quickened as she watched his index finger lazily delve into a pleat and begin rubbing back and forth.

"And you don't have time to go see Pavda before supper."

She jerked her gaze from his hands, discovering with amazement that she had forgotten all about Pavda.

"You cannot seem to make up your mind whether you wish me clothed or unclothed," she said tartly. "It's most disconcerting."

"Perhaps it's my intention to disconcert you."

She drew a deep shaky breath and slowly began unbuttoning her habit. "I realize what you're doing, you know."

"Indeed?"

She nodded as the habit dropped to the floor. "You're trying to train me as you did Apollo and Daphne." She scowled at him. "And I'm obeying you because I must honor our bargain. But I'm not an animal, and I have no liking for this."

"Yet I believe you'll come to like it." He smiled. "When you realize that no matter how many demands I make, you're in control."

"You said something like that before." She stepped out of her petticoat. "I don't agree."

"And if you search your heart, I think you'll find another reason you're willing to accommodate me."

"What is that?"

"Curiosity. It's entirely in character for a woman who is so vibrantly alive to want to taste every facet of life." His gaze wandered over her. "By the way, you have superb breasts. Small, but quite perfect."

A hot flush seared through her as she saw the blatant sensuality of his expression. She cleared her throat, but the words still came out in a croak. "Are you done with dithering then?"

He smiled. "That's another thing we'll have to see. Anticipation certainly lends the situation a certain 'heat,' doesn't it?"

She caught the slight emphasis on the word as the last of her undergarments dropped to the floor. "I told you I was no bitch like Daphne."

"If you were, you wouldn't be standing there. You'd be on hands and knees, and I'd be moving in and out of you." He smiled crookedly as he saw her shocked expression. "I'm being most restrained . . . for me."

"What do you want from me?"

"Heat," he said thickly. "I want you to come to me because you're hurting too much to do anything else."

She felt the muscles of her stomach clench and a liquid tingling begin between her thighs. "You'd better just do it. It might not ever happen. I'm not like Pauline."

"Nor would I want you to be. Come here."

She hesitated, took a deep breath, and then marched across the floor to his chair and stopped before him. "I'm here."

"Yes." He didn't move; he just sat, his gaze on her breasts as they rose and fell with the increasing tempo of her breathing.

"What next?"

"Why, don't you remember? We're going to see if the material is going to be comfortable for you." He shook out the black sash and draped it around her and across her breasts. The silky fabric was a cool caress on her flesh. "Does this feel pleasant?"

"Yes."

He let the sash fall beneath her bosom, and with the twist of his wrist tightened it, throwing her breasts into prominence. "And this?"

Her breasts were swelling, her nipples hardening to an aching distension. "Not . . . unpleasant."

He kept her lifted, swollen, offering, for another moment before releasing the knot and pulling the silky black sash from her body with an excruciatingly slow movement.

It made no difference. Her breasts remained enlarged, taut, and aching.

"Is . . . that all?" she asked unsteadily.

"Not quite." His eyes were glittering, his cheeks flushed as he slowly rose to his feet. "There's another place that must be tested." She inhaled sharply as his fingers brushed her inner thigh. "You'll be riding astride. . . ."

His arm went around her waist, catching the other end of the sash as he thrust it between her thighs.

She gasped, her gaze flying to his face. "What—"

"Sometimes the rhythm will be soft and smooth."
He moved the black sash gently and slowly back
and forth, letting her feel the soft folds of the fabric like a sensual whisper against that most sensitive part of her. "But since your nature is not of
the tamest, more often it will be hard and fast."
He lifted the material, jerking the sash in a
stronger, firmer seesaw movement.

She cried out, her spine arching as waves of
sensation spiraled through her. She could tell he
was being careful not to hurt her, but the silky
friction caused an erotic shock. She reached out
blindly to clutch Galen's shoulders as the sash
moved back and forth, tingling, teasing her softness. It was like nothing she had ever felt before.
She was dying, in a fever, swelling, starving. . . .

"Galen!" Her teeth sank into her lower lip as
the force of the movement between her thighs
strengthened, accelerated. "It's too—"

The sash was gone, whipped away, and instead
his hard hand was cupping her, petting her, stroking her. "It's all right." He pushed her gently
down on the cushions of the divan. "You had to
know."

What had she to know? she wondered dazedly
as she looked up at him. That sensation could send
you mad, enslave you, make you want to hold,
buck, devour? She gasped. "Why?"

He dropped the black sash beside her on the
silk cushion. "Because I want you to remember
me every time a fold of material touches your

body. I wanted you to remember *this*." He smiled grimly. "One of my more possessive and less civilized impulses." He smiled sensually. "But you will remember, won't you, Tess?"

How could she help it? She was still throbbing, tingling, her breath coming in gasps. "Yes," she whispered.

"And when we're riding and I look at you, you'll know I'm thinking about what I just did to you." His breath was coming fast, harsh in the silence of the chamber. "And you'll remember what it felt like to be in heat." Color mantled the bronze of his cheeks, and his dark eyes glittered with excitement as he looked down at her. He said hoarsely, "I think we'll not sup together tonight. I need time to—" He moved toward the door. "I'll meet you in the courtyard at nine tomorrow morning."

The door closed behind him.

Tess braced herself as she straightened her shoulders and marched down the steps toward Galen. "Good morning." She kept her tone carefully casual as she moved across the courtyard toward the fountain where Said was holding the reins of the horses. "How is Pavda this morning?"

"Pavda is very well." Galen's brows lifted. "And so is Selik. I believe Apollo and Daphne are similarly disposed." He paused. "I'm in fairly good health myself."

"I was getting to that." Tess stopped before

the mare and reached up to stroke her muzzle. "Though I had no concern on that score. You seem well able to care for yourself."

"You're annoyed with me." He took a step nearer and murmured in a low tone. "I made you feel helpless last night, and you resent it."

"Yes."

"It wasn't me who made you feel that way. It was your own nature. You could have fought me. All you had to do was say no, and I would have stopped."

She flushed. "You caught me by surprise. I wasn't expecting you—"

"You were expecting me to take but not to indulge in play?" He shook his head. "That's not my way." He took a step back, and his gaze went lingeringly over her from booted feet to the hood that loosely covered her hair. "Your new riding clothes are quite lovely on you."

She avoided his stare. "The fabric glitters too much. I thought it would be simpler."

"It is simple." He studied her expression. "And I think you like it very much."

She did like it, but she was making no admissions to him when she was still feeling so vulnerable. The white divided skirt of the gown flowed when she walked, and yet gave her a sense of freedom she had never known. The loose hip-length hooded cape that completed the outfit was trimmed in rich gold embroidery and billowed gracefully with her every movement. "It will do." She reached up and touched the barbaric golden pendant that hung from a rope necklace encircling her throat. "Viane gave me a great casket of jewels, and this was in it. She said you insisted I wear it whenever I go out." Her lips tightened. "I have no liking for trinkets."

"Still, you'll wear it."

"I will not be—"

"It's not an ornament. Only the members of my house are permitted to wear that pendant."

She felt suddenly branded, possessed as she had when she lay naked before him on the cushions last night. "Let Viane wear it then."

"She has one she wears when she goes abroad in the city." His gaze raked her mutinous face. "Why do you argue? It will protect you."

"I'll think about it." She moved around to Pavda's left side, passing Said, who was looking desperately into space, trying to appear invisible.

"You'll wear it or you won't leave your chamber."

She glanced defiantly back at his grim expression. "I said I'd consider it."

He jerked his head toward the palace. "Leave us, Said."

The young man gave a relieved murmur and thrust the reins into Galen's hand. "Yes, *Majiron*." The next moment he was taking the steps of the palace two at a time.

"There's no question about this, Tess," Galen said softly. "I know you're looking for a battle to win from me, but it isn't going to be this one. The pendant will keep you safe, and you *will* wear it."

"What?" Tess asked absently, her gaze on

Said's back as he entered the palace. She looked back at Galen. "Why did you send him away?"

He blinked at the sudden change of subject. "I told you I meant to win this battle."

"And you didn't want him to see my defeat?" She looked at him in surprise. "How very odd. My father never cared if servants saw my mother's humiliations." She held up her hand as he opened his lips to speak. "I know. I did it again. I'll try to keep a more cautious tongue. Now, help me get on Pavda. I'm not at all sure I can swing my limb over her back. Do you suppose there's a physical reason women ride sidesaddle?"

He frowned. "We've not finished our discussion."

"But of course we've finished." She scowled at him. "Am I not still wearing this gaudy necklace?"

"But you will continue to wear it?"

Her scowl vanished. "Help me onto Pavda." He took a step nearer, lifted her, and she awkwardly threw her leg over. "I feel most . . . peculiar."

"That will pass." He stood looking up at her with narrowed gaze. "Why aren't you angry any longer?"

"I wasn't ang—" She broke off as she met his gaze and then said simply, "You're right, I don't like to be made to feel helpless, but I can bear it as long as you allow me to keep my pride."

He looked away from her toward the stable. "A man also feels helpless when the rutting need seizes him. He aches and cannot sleep and wants only to thrust deep into a woman. I wanted to go to another woman, any woman, last night after I left you."

She stiffened. "And did you?"

"No."

"Why not?"

"We've just been wed."

"I don't understand."

"My movements are watched. I would not have anyone think I didn't find you pleasing."

She blushed. "I'm no fool. I know all men are unfaithful. I wouldn't care."

"I would care for you."

"You would?" She frowned. "You're a very strange man, my lord."

"Admitted." He smiled crookedly. "And since I met you, I've taken note that my actions are becoming even stranger."

"I would like our relationship to be . . . more clear. I do not like to play cat to your mouse."

"Not even a little? Tell me, Tess, don't you find the situation 'interesting'? Isn't your heart beating a little faster because you don't know what to expect of me?"

"Perhaps, but that doesn't mean I'm at all comfortable with the feeling."

He burst out laughing. "It will become easier. Lust cannot be maintained twenty-four hours a day. It must ebb and flow."

"It sounds a tedious process, and you don't appear to me to be a patient man."

"Only when the prize is worth it." His hand suddenly reached out and touched her thigh.

She gasped, and her gaze flew to his face. She felt the warm heaviness of his palm through the thin material, and the memory of the intimacy of his touch last night flooded back to her. She moistened her lips with her tongue. "The guards—"

"They can't see." His body was blocking the view of the guards by the palace door as he slowly rubbed back and forth, his gaze never leaving hers. He said thickly, "I can be a patient man, but I'm not a monk. That's why there will be moments like this when I have to touch you."

His hand seemed to scorch through the material, and she found her breasts swelling, pushing against her bodice as she looked down at him.

Then his hand fell away from her, and he stepped back. "But I've taught myself to wait." He swung onto Selik's saddle. "I've even learned to enjoy the anticipation, if it doesn't go on too long."

She asked shakily, "And if it does?"

For an instant she glimpsed a flicker of recklessness beneath the control of his expression. "Then nature would probably triumph over will. Let us hope that doesn't happen." He turned Selik and grabbed Pavda's reins. "Grip Pavda with your knees, and keep your back straight. I'll keep you on a lead until you become accustomed to the new rhythm."

"Hold, dammit." Selik pounded behind, rapidly overtaking Pavda. "Rein her in, Tess."

Galen's tone was sharp, and she supposed she

should obey him. But, dear heaven, she didn't want to stop. This morning the sky was blue and the sun hot and the wind tore at her hair, taking her breath and stinging her cheeks. The blood pounded through her body, and Pavda's gait lengthened into a gallop that was like gliding on silk. She nudged Pavda to go faster.

Then Selik was drawing alongside her, and Galen was grabbing the reins.

"No!" she protested. "Not yet!"

She heard his low chuckle as he pulled Pavda to a trot. "Another two miles and you'd have been halfway to Said Ababa." His smile faded. "And you disobeyed me."

She laughed joyously. "Pavda wanted to run this morning." She patted the mare's neck. "And Selik was too slow."

"How odd that he still managed to catch you." Galen's lips tightened. "Never disobey me again, Tess. Particularly not when we're outside the city walls."

"There was no danger. We've ridden this road every day for the last week and never chanced on anyone." Tess gazed around the barren landscape to the green hills in the distance. "You see, there's no one in sight for miles. I told—" She broke off as she pointed to a tall round structure on the second hill she had never noticed before. "What's that?"

He glanced at the gray stone tower she had indicated, and his expression immediately became guarded. "It's a watchtower. It was built by my grandfather in order that the sentries could watch over the passage of the wagons carrying gold from the mines in the hills to Zalandan and prevent bandit raids. It's not been used for some time."

"Why not? Are there no longer bandits?"

"Yes, bandits aplenty. Some things never change."

"Then why isn't it—"

"It's time to go back." Galen turned Selik with an abruptness that startled her. "I've wasted enough time this morning."

Yet he had not considered it a waste until she had caught sight of the tower. "It looks . . . lonely. Pauline once told me a tale of a witch who imprisoned the daughter she loved in a tower to protect her from the harshness of the world and keep anyone from stealing her."

"An unlikely story to have attracted our lusty Pauline's interest."

Tess chuckled. "Not so strange. The daughter grew her hair very long, and let her lover climb it to reach her. Every night he would call, 'Rapunzel, let down your hair.' Then she would loose her hair, and her lover would climb to the tower and spend the night with her. It's just the kind of intrigue that would appeal to Pauline."

"How did it end?"

"I don't know. Pauline was only interested in the part of the tale she told." She glanced curiously over her shoulder at the tower. "May we go see inside it tomorrow?"

"No!"

The harshness of his tone surprised her, and she looked at his face. She inhaled sharply, her hand instinctively tightening on Pavda's reins as she saw his expression.

"Stay away from the tower, Tess."

"Why?"

"*Merde*, isn't it enough that I tell you to do it?" he asked fiercely. "Must you question every order? Stay away from the tower."

"It's unreasonable of you not to tell me why," she said, stung. "If there is danger, tell me."

"There is danger." He enunciated precisely.

"Bandits?"

"No."

"Is the tower in disrepair?"

"I don't know. I haven't been there for years."

"Then I can see no reason—"

"You don't have to know the reasons." His eyes glittered in his taut face. "It's enough for you to know there's danger for you there."

"But if there are no bandits, I cannot—"

"From me." Threat vibrated in Galen's low voice. "From *me*, dammit."

He whipped Selik into a run and galloped away from Tess toward the gates of Zalandan.

"I saw a watchtower in the hills yesterday, Sacha. A great gloomy place." Tess kept her tone carefully casual as she glanced down at the chessboard. "Galen said his grandfather built it."

"Did he?" Sacha moved his knight.

Tess studied the board. "Why isn't it used anymore?"

"Didn't you ask Galen?"

"Yes."

"If Galen had wanted you to know, he would have told you."

"You're being most exasperating." She looked up and scowled at him. "Why shouldn't I know?"

"You don't have to know everything, imp." Sacha leaned back in his chair. "For the past week you've dragged me all over the city, gobbling sights and information like a greedy little girl."

"Zalandan interests me." She fingered the ivory queen in front of her. "I don't see why Galen must be so secretive about the tower."

Sacha's smile faded. "Stay away from the tower, Tess. You wouldn't like what you'd find there."

"Cobwebs and mice."

"And memories."

"Memories?" She looked into his eyes. "You do know something about it. Tell me."

He shook his head.

She muttered an oath beneath her breath. "Memories are no threat."

"Galen's memories could be."

"Why?"

"Because Galen's memories are bitterer and more savage than most."

"What memories?"

Sacha slowly shook his head. "Stop probing, imp." He paused before adding, "Galen has always been two men, and there's a struggle between them even now. As long as he keeps the memories at bay, he's no danger to you."

She made a face. "You exaggerate. Galen is always in control of his emotions."

Sacha smiled curiously. "And you want to prod the tiger."

"Certainly not. I'm just curious."

"And impatient," Sacha said softly.

She hadn't realized how transparent she had been. Dear heaven, she hoped Galen had not noticed. For the past week she had been aware that Galen had deliberately struck a balance between teasing affection and raw sensuality that continually kept her off guard. In the midst of a joke or discussion he would suddenly insinuate a glance, a touch, a word, between them that would send her flailing in the darkness of yearning. Tension was building in her; she waited breathlessly for his sweet, torturing words and looks. You would think she was eager for him to reach out a hand and take—

She flushed and quickly stood up. "I don't know what you mean. And I'm tired of this silly game. I think I'll find Viane and go to the aviary. Are you coming?"

He glanced down at the chessboard. "I think not. I'm leaving for Tamrovia this afternoon."

She whirled back to face him. "Why?"

"Galen wants to know the moment your father learns you've left France. I seem to be the logical one to be on hand when it happens."

"It's only been three weeks. He couldn't know yet, could he?"

"It's not likely." He pushed back his chair and stood up. "But Galen doesn't wish to be caught by surprise."

She moved restlessly across the terrace to look out at the hills in the distance. "Belajo seems like another world. I like it better here, Sacha."

"So do I."

"At first I didn't think I would. Most of the people here seem so stern, but I'm very fond of Viane, and I like Yusef and Said and—"

"Kalim?"

"How can I like Kalim? He freezes me to stone when he looks at me." She grimaced. "I can't believe Viane is going to wed him."

"Neither can I."

The underlying bitterness in Sacha's voice made her turn and look at him. The expression on his face caused her eyes to widen. "Sacha?"

The vulnerability vanished from her cousin's expression as he made a rueful face. "Don't worry about it, Tess. I'll get over it."

"Viane?" She shook her head in bewilderment. "I don't understand. You're not at all alike."

"Perhaps that's why she touches me. It seems similarity is not a requisite for grand passions." He shrugged. "All I know is that I took one look at her and felt calmer and more serene than I ever had before in my life."

"Serene? You?"

"Perhaps that's what I've always been searching for."

She gazed doubtfully at him. Serenity and Sacha did not ride tandem, but who was she to know what would please her mercurial cousin. "Then you must have her," Tess said. "There should be no problem. You're far more charming than that scowling Kalim."

He chuckled. "You make it sound so easy."

"It is easy. We only have to think of a way to accomplish it. Galen would have no objection?"

"No, but Viane would."

She gestured impatiently. "We'll change her mind."

"You can't alter nature to suit yourself, imp."

"We can try. Viane is kind and clever." She frowned. "She lacks an independent spirit. I must try to instill that quality in her while you're in Tamrovia."

He shook his head. "Worry about yourself, Tess."

"But I want to help." She could feel the tears sting her eyes as she looked at him. "I have great affection for you, Sacha."

"So you want to set the world right to suit me?" Sacha reached out a hand to gently touch a bright curl tumbling over her temple. "Viane belongs in this world, Tess. Her roots are here."

"And you do not?"

He wearily shook his head. "I'm not of the El Zalan, and they don't accept strangers readily. I don't belong anywhere."

And neither did she. Tess felt a curious pang. "You're a prince of Tamrovia."

"Which means nothing to the El Zalan. Kalim has more stature than I do here." He leaned forward and brushed a kiss on the tip of her nose. "I'm leaving within the hour. I'll send you a message when I reach Belajo. Keep well, Tess."

"I'll come to the courtyard to bid you farewell. God go with you."

At the doorway Sacha glanced over his shoulder. "Stay away from the tower, Tess."

He left and she shivered. She had no intention of pursuing her fascination with that dark, forbidding tower. Let Galen keep his secrets and his memories. She would only be here for a short time, and had no desire to knock down the barriers he erected against her.

Still, it would do no harm to make Viane see what a splendid husband Sacha could be.

Sacha. Husband. She grinned as she realized how foreign the two images were to each other.

However, if Viane was the woman her wild cousin wanted, then Tess had to help him win her.

# Chapter 6

An hour later Tess heard the sound of horses' hooves on flagstone and men's voices even before she reached the front door, and Sacha was riding out of the stable as Tess reached the courtyard where thirty or so robed, mounted men were milling about. Galen, mounted on Selik, walked the horse over to her.

"You're leaving too?" she asked, trying to keep the shock and disappointment from her voice. "Why didn't you tell me?"

"I don't like farewells. I'm taking Said with me, but I asked Kalim to deliver a note to you later."

"How kind."

Galen muttered a curse. "I'm only traveling as far as the border. I didn't like the report Kalim brought back from the hill tribes. Sacha's going back to Tamrovia on my behalf, and I must assure him safe conduct through Tamar's territory."

"You have no need to make explanations. I'm not arguing with you. I shall be glad to be on my own again." She lifted her chin. "I simply think it would have been courteous of you to tell me in person."

"I said I have no use for farewells."

"Nor for courtesy either." Her voice was faintly tremulous, and she steadied it before she continued. "We all must do things we don't like. Why else am I in Zalandan?"

"To plague and torment me? Very well, I was discourteous, but I had no wish to hurt you. Will you wish me good journey?"

"Certainly. Good and speedy journey, my lord."

He hunched his shoulders as if buffeted by a cold wind. "It's as well I'll be traveling in desert country." When she didn't answer, he went on, "If you have need of anything, go to Kalim. He'll be in charge during my absence."

"I'm sure he'll do very well. His arrogance almost equals your own."

"Tess, dammit, this is for the best." His dark eyes glittered in his taut face. "My patience is nearly gone. I need to be away from you for a time."

"And, naturally, the decision is always yours. You make me feel like a chess piece moved across the board according to your own rules." She gazed at him directly. "I think it's time we started a new game, my lord."

"Indeed?" He went still, and then recklessness suddenly flickered in his expression. "We'll discuss it when I return in a week."

She shook her head. "Impossible from Tamrovia. Why, it took us five days from the border to reach here."

"But I had no strong incentive then." His gaze narrowed on her face. "Now, I have every reason to hurry back."

Heat tingled through her, and her lungs seemed to constrict. "You do?" she whispered.

"Oh yes." His gaze held hers. "And do you know what that reason is?"

She was beginning to have an excellent idea. The tension with which she had become so familiar had returned, settling upon both of them like a sensual cloak. She realized with surprise that this was precisely the reaction she had wanted to stir in him. Perhaps Sacha was right, and she had wanted to prod the tiger. She swallowed, feeling the dark excitement envelop her as she looked at him. "I'm sure you're going to tell me."

"You're damn right I am. Shall I put it in your own words?" He smiled. "I'm done with dithering."

He and Sacha rode out of the courtyard then,

the men following in loose formation. Her heart pounded, the exhilaration of the adventure to come making her almost dizzy with excitement.

She impulsively took a half-step forward and then stopped. She couldn't go after him. He would only send her back. She had to wait for his return.

Dear Lord, how she hated to wait for anything!

Well, she must resign herself to it and find some occupation to make the time pass quickly.

She turned and ran up the steps into the palace and then through the corridors until she reached Viane's chamber.

Viane was on the terrace, and looked up in surprise when Tess blew into her presence like a storm-driven leaf, cheeks ablaze, eyes sparkling.

"I've decided that we've been entirely too lax in our efforts with Alexander and Roxanne," Tess announced as she marched toward the aviary. "It's time we set our minds to teaching them their duties."

"Why can't you understand? I tell you I wish to speak to your—" Tess looked beyond the woman servant who had opened the door to see Yusef coming down the steps to the foyer. "Never mind. There he is." She brushed by the protesting woman and rushed over to Yusef, who appeared to be frozen on the third step. "I'm glad you're here. I couldn't seem to make her understand that I had to come in and speak to you. I was sure I'd have to—"

"*Majira!*" His open mouth shut with a snap. "I cannot blame her. Virtuous women do not pay visits to men in Zalandan."

"Not only in Zalandan. Women are surrounded by iron bars and silly rules wherever they live." She waved a dismissing hand. "No matter, I've learned to escape most of them. One absolutely must be determined and persevere."

"I . . . see." Yusef waved the servant away and descended the last three steps. His alarmed gaze searched the hall behind her. "Dear God, where is your escort?"

"Don't be ridiculous. I had no need of guards to come to visit you."

"No?" Yusef asked weakly. "I may have need of guards if the *majiron* hears you've paid me a visit without them. It's not fitting for—"

"You sound just like Said." Tess made a face. "Sweet Mary, I'm beginning to detest that word. I refuse to encumber myself with a covey of roosters clucking around me."

The suspicion of a smile broke through the shock and disapproval on Yusef's face. "I believe roosters crow, not cluck."

"The distinction is of no importance. You haven't asked me why I'm here."

"Terror struck me dumb."

She chuckled.

Yusef merely shook his head.

"You seem somewhat perturbed, so I'll get straight to my reason for visiting you," Tess said. "I wish to use your roof."

"What?"

"I noticed when Galen and I visited Kalim that this house is very tall. Its roof is higher than any in town. I need it to launch Alexander."

"Alexander?"

"My homing pigeon. Well, he's not that yet, but he will be when I've finished training him properly. Viane and I actually have two, but it seems Roxanne is regrettably lacking in natural instinct, so we've had to concentrate on Alex—"

He said quickly, "You cannot come here. It would not be fitting."

"You mean I must find another house? Oh dear, I'm sure I won't be able to find another roof this suitable, and it will be most awkward going from house to house asking strangers if—"

"No!" Yusef interrupted. "You cannot do—" He stopped as he saw her determined expression and gave a deep sigh. "How long would you need to use the roof?"

She brightened. "Oh, not long, I'm sure. Perhaps only a few days, if I came every afternoon."

"And when the *majiron* returns to the city, you must immediately cease your visits."

She nodded. "I'm sure Alexander will be clever enough to learn the trick of it long before the week is out."

"I hope so," Yusef sighed again. "I can send the servants away to avoid gossip and only hope no one else notices you." He glanced at her red hair blazing in the sunlight streaming into the foyer. "Though that's probably too much to ask."

"I'm sure everything will go splendidly." She smiled at him. "I do thank you, Yusef. I knew I could count on your help." She moved briskly toward the door. "I'll see you tomorrow just after noon."

Yusef nodded gloomily. "I'm afraid you will. I'll be waiting, *Majira*."

The sand in the dunes shifted, lifted, then swirled in the moonlight with eerie grace.

The desert seemed empty, but that impression might be wrong. Galen gazed out into the darkness.

"Do you think Tamar's out there?"

Galen turned to see Sacha strolling toward him from the encampment. "Probably, we're on his territory."

"Will he pose a problem?"

"Not unless the whim takes him." He shrugged. "I've posted many sentries tonight. After we cross the border into Tamrovia tomorrow, there won't be any danger."

"Except total exhaustion." Sacha's brows were lifted as he looked at Galen. "I've never seen you push the men so hard as on this journey."

"I wanted to get you safely to the border. News travels fast among the tribes, and there was a chance Tamar might have guessed the reason for my marriage and decided to cause trouble."

Sacha continued to look at him skeptically.

Galen shrugged. "Very well. So I'm restless and want to get back to Zalandan." He turned and strode back toward his blanket by the fire. "I've been away too much these past months."

A smile tugged at Sacha's lips. "Ah, how fraught with responsibilities and the burden of state affairs is the life of a ruler." Sacha dropped down on his blanket and curled up with his backside to the fire. "What a relief it is to me that I'm just a dissolute popinjay who does only what he wishes to do."

Galen realized ruefully that Sacha knew why he wanted to return quickly. They had been too closely associated for too long. Sacha had to see that lust was driving him back to Tess. He wondered why he hadn't answered him with the earthy bluntness that was common between them. Sacha knew Galen needed a woman frequently, and was probably aware that since he had reached Zalandan he hadn't visited any of the *kadines* who usually serviced him.

It wasn't only because of his desire not to heap shame upon Tess that he had not indulged, he told himself. He had also been busy. There had been no time to—

How long did it take a man to wrest his satisfaction from a willing woman? *Merde,* he was lying to himself as he had to both Tess and Sacha. He didn't want a *kadine*. He only wanted Tess.

He had wanted her since that first night in the stable, and the fever had grown until he couldn't look at her without his loins readying.

As he was readying now just thinking about her.

He muttered a curse and turned to face the fire.

The flames shone as brightly as Tess's auburn locks. No, Tess's hair shone with a deeper, softer fire.

He closed his eyes tightly, trying to push the thought of her from his mind. It would be different once he had bedded her. The hold she had on him would lessen, the lust fade, the tenderness—

He would *not* think about the tenderness she stirred, or the amusement she prompted. It was perfectly reasonable for him to be eager to be with her after only a few hours apart. She glowed with the joy of life, and naturally such joie de vivre would draw him to her. Still, it was best not to dwell on anything but his physical response. Lust could be satisfied. Lust could not hurt him.

The hell it couldn't. Right now it was damnably uncomfortable, he thought grimly. However, the wait was almost over. When he returned to Zalandan, he would be able to satisfy the hunger he had kept at bay for almost a month.

He firmly locked away thoughts of Tess. Tomorrow he would start back to Zalandan, but it would be so long before he reached there . . . before he could be with Tess. . . .

Someone was following her!

Tess hastened her pace as she turned the corner. It was the time of the evening meal, and the streets of Zalandan were deserted. The entrances to the shops were dusky caverns on either side of the street. She shivered with apprehension.

She could have been wrong about the footsteps that slowed and quickened in tempo with her own. Why should anyone be following her? Her hand instinctively went to the golden pendant around her neck. She had discovered in the last few days that although Zalandan might have its share of scalawags, she could move about without anyone bothering her. The pendant. She was sure it was responsible for her freedom. It was invisible armor enveloping her. Galen's armor.

But Galen had been gone for three days. Perhaps the man following her was more interested in the gold of the necklace than the warning it sent out to—

"Stop!" The voice behind her was harsh, male, commanding.

Her heart leaped, and she broke into a run.

*"Majira!"*

The voice was familiar, she realized with relief. She turned to see a tall, robed figure stalking toward her. Kalim.

"Kalim, you frightened me. I didn't expect—" She drew a trembling breath and drew herself up proudly as she saw his forbidding expression.

"You should not be wandering in the streets."

"No harm has come to me."

"I'm responsible for your safety—and your behavior—while the *majiron* is gone." His lips tightened. "From now on you will not leave the palace."

A flare of anger seared through her. "I will go where I wish."

He smiled mirthlessly. "And you wish to g.
the house of Yusef Benardon."

Her eyes widened in shock. "*Merde*, have you
been spying on me, Kalim?"

"I have only been doing my duty to the *majiron*." He paused. "It aroused my curiosity when
the grooms at the stable said you hadn't taken
Pavda out since the *majiron* left the city."

"So you followed me today."

"For your own protection." He inclined his
head. "Naturally, I assumed you were on your
way to a special shop or to the bazaar to buy
trinkets."

"Why would you assume that?"

"I should not, I realize, considering who you
are. Western women seldom have innocent pleasures in mind when they leave the safety of their
husband's chamber."

Her gaze narrowed on his face. "What do you
mean?"

"I think you know."

"Say it."

He smiled crookedly. "Yusef is young and
strong, a bull of a man. The ladies have always
liked him."

"Go on."

"The *Majiron* is away, and Western women do
not like to wait for their pleasures."

"I believe you know very little about Western
women," she said hotly.

His smile faded. "Enough to know that I will
not permit my friend to be dishonored in the eyes

of the El Zalan. You will not go again to Yusef's house."

"I will go where I please."

"Go again and you will find him dead."

Her eyes widened in shock. "What?"

"I cannot touch you without the *majiron*'s permission, but otherwise my authority is absolute. I can dispose of Yusef." He paused. "As I would any threat to the *majiron*."

She shook her head dazedly. "Just because I visited him?"

"Because you've spent the past three afternoons alone with him. I admit you have been discreet, but if it continues, it will become known, and the *majiron* will suffer shame."

"And a man dies to prevent that from happening?"

"Casual infidelity is not sanctioned here as it is in your own country." His eyes glittered in his stern face. "And Galen will not tolerate it in you. He allows you much freedom, but he won't allow you to take another man."

She drew a trembling breath, trying to smother her fury. "You insult me."

He gazed at her impassively.

"Would you believe me if I told you that I have not been unfaithful?"

"Lies come easily to Western women."

"*Impossible*." She threw up her hands. "I refuse to waste breath denying your foul accusations." She turned on her heel and strode quickly up the street.

"You will not go back to Yusef's house," he called after her.

"I'll do exactly as I choose." She glared back at him over her shoulder. "I won't allow you to interfere in my life, Kalim."

"Visit him again and I'll deliver his head to you in a basket."

Stunned, she gazed at him, a shiver running down her spine. For the first time she believed he actually would carry out his threat. "You're a savage without conscience."

"At times." He smiled. "But be warned that Galen taught me from boyhood. Compared to him when he is enraged, I'm quite tame."

"Is he here?" Tess burst onto the terrace, her gaze searching the shadows beneath the pepper tree. "Did he come back?"

"An hour ago." Viane's delighted smile lit her face as she hurried out of the aviary. "It's the third time, Tess."

"And you fed him the grain?"

Viane nodded. "As soon as he perched beside Roxanne."

"Only an hour?" Tess frowned. "He didn't make very good time. I released him from Yusef's roof over two hours ago. He must have been meandering."

Viane laughed. "What difference does it make? I think it's magical that he found his way home at all."

"It's instinct, not magic." Tess shrugged. "But perhaps feeding the grain will help make him more eager. The Count said that was the secret of training them." Another frown wrinkled her brow. "But I'm beginning to believe pigeons are very stupid. Yusef's house is only an hour's walk away. I almost made it on foot before he got here."

"On foot?" Viane's eyes widened. "You walked through the town? You know that is not fitting. I would never have—"

"I was quite safe." Tess mentally cursed her unruly tongue. She hadn't meant to let Viane know that she hadn't ridden Pavda through the town. Viane was anxious enough that Tess moved about without Galen's permission, and now she would fret. "The first time I rode Pavda to Yusef's house, the jouncing seemed to upset Alexander. It took a terribly long time to quiet him before I felt I could release him."

Viane shook her head. "Well, as long as you took the groom—"

"I think Alexander's ready for a longer test," Tess broke in quickly.

"What did you have in mind?" Viane asked warily. "Yusef's house is almost at the city gates."

"Then it's clear we must go beyond the city gates," Tess said lightly.

"No! It's forbidden for the women of the household to go beyond the gates."

"Galen often took me for rides outside the city."

Viane frowned. "You know he wouldn't permit

you to go without him, even accompanied by a groom. We must be satisfied with Yusef's house until Galen returns. Then perhaps we can persuade him—"

"Persuade?" Tess made a face. "It's another word for plead, and leaves a bitter taste in my mouth."

"Galen has been very lenient with you. No other woman is permitted such freedom," Viane said soberly. "You must understand it's not usual for women to ride abroad with their men, much less alone. I'm sure Galen has been criticized for indulging you so."

"He doesn't appear to mind."

"He's accustomed to fighting battles," Viane said. "Since my father died, he has tried to bring to Zalandan all that is good of the West. Many do not like to be driven from the old ways."

"Like Kalim."

"And me."

"You?"

Viane nodded. "In that way Kalim and I are alike. I find the old ways have grace *and* reason."

"It's reasonable to be imprisoned in this chamber as you've penned in your birds?"

"Their pen is beautiful, and they will never know hunger."

"Or freedom."

Viane's eyes were suddenly twinkling. "Alexander knows freedom whenever you loose him on the wind."

"But even then we tie him to us with bribes

of food so that he'll return to his cage." Tess shook
her head. "If he wasn't so stupid, he'd fly free and
fend for himself."

"But then you would have no messenger bird."

"True." Tess suddenly scowled as she remembered her last meeting with Kalim. "You're not at
all like Kalim. He's an uncivilized beast."

Viane arched a delicate brow. "You seem upset
with him. Has he done something to disturb you?"

Tess didn't dare tell about her confrontation
with Kalim. "I just don't like him," she said
weakly.

"He appears surly at times, but he has his reasons. He grew up in one of the wild border tribes,
and has known nothing all his life but warfare and
bloodshed. . . . He can be very kind when he
wishes."

"But not the least amusing. He's all frowns and
boring lectures and duty." Tess gave her a side-
long glance. "Sacha would not bore you."

Viane flushed and glanced away. "No, I doubt
if he would bore anyone."

"And he can be kind." Tess added in all fair-
ness, "When it occurs to him."

"You know him better than I."

"And he's handsome. All the ladies think Sacha
is wondrously handsome."

"Very handsome." Viane moved across the terrace to the balustrade and looked out over the city
to the hills beyond. "Why are we speaking of
Sacha, Tess?"

"Because he is fond of you."

"I know."

"And you are fond of him."

"He stirs me." Viane's hands tightened on the stone balustrade. "It is most unsettling."

"You would be so much happier with Sacha than Kalim. He would give you freedom."

"I have told you that freedom has little value for me."

"But it should," Tess said earnestly. "If you knew how wonderful it is to be—"

"I don't wish to speak of this any longer. It disturbs me."

Tess was sure she had made progress and was tempted to continue, but decided she had pushed enough for the time being. "Oh, very well. I only wish the best for you."

Viane's huge eyes glistened like polished onyx as she turned to look at Tess. "And I hope I have not hurt you by avoiding the conversation. I have come to care very much for you."

"You have?" Tess asked, surprised. "I thought I might be too abrasive for you. I know I sometimes nudge you."

"Nudge?" Viane chuckled as she shook her head. "Your 'nudges' resemble being pulled behind Selik at a full gallop." She added quickly, "But I don't mind. I've found life much more exciting since you've come to Zalandan."

Tess couldn't resist the opportunity to insinuate just one more idea. "Sacha is much more exciting than I've ever managed to be. Let me tell you—" She broke off and smiled sheepishly as she met Viane's reproving stare. "Well, it's true. I haven't lived long enough to compete with Sacha, yet I do look forward to overtaking him shortly." Her smile faded as she continued haltingly, "I haven't had a woman for a friend before, but I consider you my—" She stopped and then went on with a rush. "That is . . . if you would like . . . if you wouldn't mind being—"

"But of course we're friends." Viane smiled radiantly. "Friends and sisters. I knew as soon as I met you that it would be so."

"How . . . clever of you." Tess turned and stared out at the sun going down beyond the hills. Her throat ached, and she knew her voice sounded gruff. "I'm never certain about anyone or anything. I only hope. . . ." She cleared her throat and said briskly, "Now, about Alexander's next journey."

Viane frowned. "I thought we'd agreed it would be from Yusef's house."

"No, I believe we've imposed enough on Yusef." She carefully avoided Viane's gaze. "I've decided it might become awkward for him if we continue to use his house."

"Awkward?"

Tess had a sudden gory vision of Yusef's head in a wicker basket. "Extremely awkward . . . perhaps. I'll send him a message tomorrow that we won't be using his roof again." She would also include a postscript that it might be wise for him to leave Zalandan until Galen returned. She glanced at Alexander on his perch in the aviary. "We'll let him rest for a few days and then set him a harder task."

"What task?" Viane asked warily. "And what place will we use if not Yusef's house?"

"I'll have to think about it," Tess hedged. She had no intention of divulging her new plan at the moment. Viane could be very obstinate when her sense of propriety was offended. Tess intended to use the next two days to drop hints and information and bring Viane around. She looked to the horizon. From this distance she could not see the watchtower, but she had no need to see it. She could visualize it standing tall, strong, mysterious, beckoning to her as it had the first time she had seen it. "I'm sure something interesting will occur to me."

Kalim met Galen just after he'd galloped through the city gates. "You made good time, *Majiron*."

"Good enough." Galen looked at the palace and felt a predictable quickening in his loins, quickly accompanied by a bewildering flicker of joy. Not yet. Control. Soon. "We rode hard. Is all well?"

Kalim didn't answer as he nudged his horse into a walk beside Selik.

Galen stiffened and shot him a keen glance. "I take it all is not well?"

Kalim didn't look at him. "Nothing of importance has occurred to the El Zalan."

Galen's gaze flew to the palace.

"Viane is also well." Kalim added haltingly, "It is the *majira*."

Galen's heart lurched, and he muttered a curse. "Damn you. I told you to care for her. Is she ill?"

"Her health is excellent." Kalim's cheeks flushed as he gazed uneasily at the men surrounding them. "This is not the place."

Galen kicked Selik into a trot that sent them ahead of the escort. He didn't stop until he reached the courtyard of the palace. He reined in before the steps, slid from the saddle, and whirled to face Kalim. "Why must you have privacy for what you have to tell me?"

Kalim swallowed and said hoarsely, "I would not have you dishonored before them."

Galen went still. "Dishonored?"

"The *majira* visited the house of Yusef Benardon three times this week and stayed a number of hours." Kalim paused. "Alone."

Galen felt as if he had been kicked in the stomach. "You're certain?"

Kalim nodded. "She went on foot and took no groom. I spoke to Yusef's neighbors, and they say he sent his servants away while she spent the afternoons with him." Kalim continued quickly, "They will not gossip. I told them I would put anyone to the sword who spoke of this shame."

Shame. Galen felt a burst of primitive rage. Tess in Yusef's bed, writhing on the cushions, Yusef above her. . . . The blood pounded in his veins. A red haze formed before his eyes. He valiantly tried to think clearly. "Sometimes things are not as they seem."

"I confronted her, and she did not deny it. She was . . . bold."

Yes, Tess would be bold. He could almost see her standing before Kalim, eyes flashing. "You confronted her?"

"I told her if she continued, her lover would have no head," Kalim said fiercely. "It would have given me great pleasure to have destroyed him for you, *Majiron*."

Galen carefully kept his voice level. "And did she continue to see him?"

Kalim shook his head. "His servant said Yusef received a message the next day and left the city immediately."

"Bound for where?"

"To visit one of the hill tribes." Kalim took a deep breath. "I thought it was over."

Galen turned his face so that Kalim would not see his expression. "And it's not?"

Kalim miserably shook his head. "The *majira* left the city shortly after noon today. I felt it was my duty to follow her." He paused. "She went to the tower."

Galen whirled to face him. "The tower?"

"I don't think she could have known that a tryst there would add to your shame," Kalim whispered. "She might not have been told."

"If she didn't know, Yusef certainly did." Galen's lips twisted. "Just as he knew how convenient the tower would be to reach from the hill encampment."

Kalim's eyes were bright with moisture. "Believe me, I did not want to tell you. I wanted to take care of it myself before you returned."

"I know, Kalim." On one level Galen was aware of how upset Kalim was, but he could not extend comfort now. His entire being was consumed with the effort to subdue the untamed anger writhing through him. He must think, reason, he couldn't let himself uncage the wildness.

"What shall I do? Shall I go and bring her back?"

"No." He turned and mounted Selik. "It's no longer your concern, Kalim."

"Let me go with you. Suppose Yusef is—"

"I hope he is." Galen smiled chillingly. "Then I won't have to seek him out."

Kalim's hands clenched into fists. "I knew the Western woman would bring trouble down on you."

"I brought it on myself. I know how bored women can get. They must be kept under control." Dear God, he sounded like his father. Well, why not? He felt like his father. Betrayed, angry, the blood lust rising within him. "I should have taken her with me." He turned his horse. "Tell Viane I won't return tonight."

He galloped out of the courtyard and through the town toward the city gates.

He was not his father.

*Yet the blood was there, the savagery was there.*

Tess was not without honor.

*She had found Yusef comely. She had laughed and joked with him.*

She was still a child in many ways.

*Yet in those days before he left, he had purposely teased her, primed her to take him into her bed. In the courtyard that last day she had challenged him. She had been ready for a man.*

Any man?

Galen found his teeth clenching, his hands tightening on the reins.

He must maintain his composure. He would be calm and reasonable. He would give her the opportunity to explain.

*Mother of God, he hoped he could keep himself from hurting her.*

He rode through the gates and turned Selik toward the hills.

Tess lifted Alexander carefully from his cage. "All right, lad, we've done this before. Just set your mind to it." She straightened, leaned far out the window, and tossed the pigeon into the air.

Alexander's gray wings flapped wildly, the tiny bells affixed to his leg jingling merrily as he rose into the sky, wheeled gracefully in a circle . . . and headed west.

"Not that direction, you idiot," Tess grumbled as she watched the bird fly away from the tower.

"You're flying toward Said Ababa. Who'll feed you grain there?"

The pigeon soared blissfully away from both the tower . . . and Zalandan.

Tess leaned her elbow on the windowsill, chin in hand, and made a face at the swiftly retreating bird, quite definitely headed toward the border. "Very well, you'll find out." But Sweet Mary, there was no telling how long it would take the stupid bird to discover his error. In the meantime she'd have to stay at the tower in case he returned instead of winging his way home. Who could know? The dratted bird might become addled and never make it back to the palace.

She cast a speculative eye at the sunlight filtering into the room. She judged it would be at least another two hours before the sun set and Viane started to worry.

She would give the pesky bird until sundown to return. If he didn't, she would set out then for the palace to see if he had come to his addled senses and flown back like a proper homing pigeon.

In the meantime this chamber in the tower was not a bad place to wait. The guardroom downstairs had been in total chaos, tables and chairs broken and overturned and every nook and cranny wreathed in cobwebs, but here in the tower room there were even touches of luxury. Evidently, the officers who had commanded this outpost liked their comfort. The wide bed across the room was encased in heavy blue velvet curtains to keep out the chill of the desert night; the blue-and-cream patterned carpet stretching over the stone floor was as thick and fine as the one in her chamber in the palace. No matter the luxurious quality of the furnishings, there was no denying the coat of dust and mildew layering everything, and if her judgment of Alexander's intellect was correct, she might have a long wait. She had no intention of lying on that filthy bed or sitting on the stone floor until he came back.

Tess moved the large thronelike chair before the huge fireplace. She snatched up the mildewed cushions on the dusty chair and threw them carelessly on the hearth before taking off her cloak and draping it on the chair. She settled herself gingerly on the hard seat, leaned back, and sighed.

On the whole the tower had been a disappointment. She had found nothing mysterious or intriguing about the place, and certainly no reason why Galen had forbidden it to her. The only inhabitants were mice and spiders.

She was lying to herself, she realized impatiently. She knew very well why she had wanted to come here. The attraction had been not the tower itself but Galen's reaction to it. She had hoped she would find some clue to a new aspect of Galen's character. He was so guarded, he would yield little to her voluntarily. She knew when he returned, their relationship must change, and she had thought she would feel safer if she—

Safer? How odd that word had occurred to her. She had never been afraid of Galen. She had always been aware he could be a danger to those around him, but his control was so absolute, she was sure it could never falter.

Well, she had learned nothing about Galen from this tower. She would have to wait until he returned and probe the man himself. He should be back in Zalandan in two days' time, three at the most, and the new game would begin. She stifled the tiny flutter of excitement that rippled through her. It was too unsettling to think of coupling with Galen. Instead, she would fasten her thoughts on that idiotic bird winging his way toward Said Ababa.

Dust motes danced on the narrow path of sunlight streaming through the long, narrow window into the chamber. The ride to the tower had been long and hot, but now the heat was abating. In truth, it was quite pleasant in this circular room, the sun bathing her face . . .

In the distance Galen could see the watchtower silhouetted against the blood-red setting sun. Pavda was tied to the tree that grew beside the brass-bracketed door.

One horse. She was alone in the tower.

It could be a mistake. Kalim could be wrong.

But Kalim would not lie to him.

She could have a purpose for being here.

Of course she had a purpose. Her lover had told her to meet him.

*Rapunzel, let down your hair . . .*

The narrow tower window was dark. Was she

waiting for her lover to arrive before she lit the candle?

He could feel the shadows of the tower reach out with iron claws, dragging him into darkness.

He was a civilized man. He should think, he should try to search out reasons, delve into his soul for understanding.

Yet the closer he came to the tower, the more his thoughts became blurred. Time seemed to shift. The man he had become was lost. The wild, primitive boy he had been when he had last ridden this serpentine road toward the tower was found.

The flamelike rage licked at him, surrounded him, devoured him, became one with him . . .

# Chapter 7

She should be afraid, Tess realized drowsily, as she opened her eyes and first saw the huge dark silhouette framed against the blood-red sky beyond the slit of window. In his billowing cloak he reminded her of a fierce hawk limned in fire. Galen.

She wasn't afraid. There was something supremely natural in waking and seeing Galen watching her. She was glad the waiting was over. The years had passed so slowly, the loneliness had gone on too long. "Galen . . ."

"Yes, I regret to disappoint you." The harshness in his voice jarred her into full wakefulness. "But life is full of disappointments, isn't it?"

She shook her head to clear it as she struggled

upright in the chair. "You're not supposed to be here. I didn't expect you for another two days."

"What bridegroom could resist rushing back to his beloved?" The heavy irony in his voice made her flinch. He moved across the room to the fireplace and knelt on the hearth. "Imagine my disappointment to find you had fled my eager arms."

"You know I'm not your beloved." She watched him strike flint to the wood in the grate, wishing desperately the room was not dark so she could see his expression. She was aware of something different in his demeanor, in the inflection of his voice. "You're angry with me?"

"I was, but I'm not any longer."

She was not reassured and blurted out quickly, "I know you told me I wasn't to come here, but it was necessary." She frowned as a thought occurred to her. "How did you know I was here?"

"Kalim followed you."

"Kalim . . ." She leaned forward in her chair, peering at the shadowy contours of his face. Now, she was beginning to suspect the reason for his anger. "I suppose he told you about that foolishness he—"

"I don't want to discuss Kalim." The spark caught, and suddenly the wood burst into flame. "His role in this is done."

"I have to discuss Kalim, if I'm to—" She inhaled sharply as he turned his face toward her. The features were the same, but his expression made them alien to her. He looked younger, harder, his dark eyes glittering in the firelight, his lips curving in a reckless smile that held an element of cruelty. "I think it would be best if we talk," she murmured.

"I'm done with talk." He shrugged off his cloak and dropped it on the carpet in front of the hearth. "And I'm done with waiting."

Waiting. The word stirred something in her memory, a realization that had come to her in that half-waking state only a moment ago. "You're not yourself. Let's go back to the palace and we'll—"

"On the contrary, you've never seen me more myself than I am at this moment." He unbuttoned his shirt, took it off, and dropped it carelessly on the floor. His tone was soft, easy, almost carefree, and yet Tess found herself tensing as if confronted by a wild animal. The comparison was apt because in this moment Galen seemed a magnificent cat-like creature, lithe, silken, completely sensual.

He crossed to the windowsill and half sat, half leaned against it as he pulled off his boots, then his trousers. "Remove your clothing." The words were spoken casually. "I wish you to be ready for me." He glanced up at her and smiled faintly as he saw the way she stiffened. "As you must always be ready for me from this time on. At any hour and in any way I want you. I may not be sure your babe is mine, but I will not be cheated. There *will* be a child for the El Zalan."

"Not yours?" She should be arguing with him, perhaps even be growing fearful, but she found she was only curious, fascinated by this new side to him.

"My pleasure will be in the result, if not the

creation." He was naked now and moving toward her across the chamber. She was again aware of his vibrant animal grace, the rippling muscles of his thighs that flexed as he walked, his arousal.

"Stand up," he commanded.

She jerked her gaze from his lower body and slowly got to her feet. She could feel excitement pounding through her as she stared at him. "You really should listen to me."

"That's what I told myself." He smiled. "But then I realized a man can blind himself with logic. Why try to find excuses for what is a woman's nature? You were brought up by a strumpet, and it was unreasonable for me to expect you not to have the same morals." He began to unfasten her gown. "You lusted, and I was not here to satisfy." His smile widened as he saw the shiver run through her when his knuckles brushed against her breasts. "I won't make that mistake again. You'll travel wherever I go from now on." He parted the bodice of her gown and looked down at her breasts. A dark flush mantled his cheeks, and his voice became thick. "But you'll learn to please only me with your body." He reached out and cupped her left breast in his hand.

She bit her lower lip to smother a cry. His palm was hard, callused against her softness, and sent a strange heat through her body.

His thumbnail flicked back and forth across the nipple, watching it grow hard and distended. "You like this, don't you? Tell me, was Yusef a good lover?"

"Yusef wasn't—" She broke off as his thumb and finger closed on her nipple, not roughly, but with just enough pressure to send hot flame tingling through her. Her spine arched helplessly toward him. She had not dreamed her flesh could be this sensitive to mere touch. She couldn't breathe. Her breasts were lifting and falling as she tried to force air into her lungs.

"I believe we won't talk of Yusef."

"I wasn't the one who brought him up," she said indignantly.

"I was wrong. I didn't know how angry I'd feel hearing his name on your lips." He drew a deep breath, his hand opening and closing on her breast. "And I didn't think I'd care if I hurt you, but I find the idea oddly distasteful."

He was only squeezing her breast, yet the caress was generating a mysterious aching emptiness between her thighs. She moistened her lips with her tongue. "I wouldn't let you hurt me."

"A woman is helpless in certain positions. . . . And I intend you to know every one of them." His hand dropped away, and he turned his back on her. "I'm growing impatient. Strip off your other garments if you don't wish me to tear them from you. You must have clothing to wear back to the palace."

She hesitated, trying to decide what to do. Instinct urged her to continue to try to explain, but he clearly didn't want to listen. Besides, wasn't this what she, too, wanted? The anticipation he had fostered in her for this new experience was approaching fever pitch. She wanted to *know*. Why should she deny what she wanted because his words annoyed her?

She slipped the divided gown off her shoulders and let it fall into a pool at her feet.

"Why did no one feel compassion for the witch?" Galen asked in a low voice.

She blinked. "What?"

"The witch must have felt affection for Rapunzel to have wanted to keep her safe from the sorrows of the world. Yet the sympathy is for those who betrayed her."

"I don't know what to—"

"Never mind. The thought just occurred to me."

She stepped over her gown, sat on the chair, and took off her stockings and suede boots. Then she stood. What did she do now? What did he want of her? She stepped closer and began to loosen the ribbon tying his queue.

The muscles of his back rippled as her breasts brushed his flesh. "What are you doing?"

"Isn't this why you turned your back on me?"

"No." His voice was hoarse. "I turned my back so that I could keep myself from lifting you and thrusting in you as you stood there."

She was immediately interested. "Is that possible?"

"Yes." His breathing was uneven. "More. Probable."

"I don't believe I ever saw Pauline do—" She stopped as he turned to her. "Will it hurt?"

"Not if you're ready for me."

"How do I know if I'm ready?"

"How? Yusef must have proved very inadequate if you don't know—" He broke off with a sardonic smile. "Good, I dislike the thought of him teaching you everything." His lips tightened. "Anything." He stepped closer, his hand cupping her womanhood, rubbing, caressing. Two fingers probed, explored. "Lord, you're tight."

She gasped as she felt the intimate intrusion. "Perhaps we'd better not—"

"The hell we won't," he muttered. "But not this way." He pulled her down on his cloak and knelt, facing her. "You're too little."

She dimly remembered what he had told her on their wedding night. "You said a woman was meant to take a man."

"I obviously shouldn't have been so general. You were meant to take *me*." His tone was almost a growl as he pushed her onto her back and parted her thighs. "Be quite still, and let me look at you."

But looking wasn't the only thing he was doing. His fingers were parting, probing, his gaze fastened on that most private part of her. Sudden shyness overwhelmed her, and she quickly shut her eyes. She felt as if she were melting into the cloak beneath her. Her breasts lifted and fell with every breath as she lay exposed and vulnerable before him while shiver after hot shiver stabbed through her.

His palms moved upward, sliding over her hips to fasten on either side of her slim waist.

"*Merde*, you're tiny. My hands almost reach around you." His grip tightened, letting her feel the hard power of his hands. "I could break you, if I wished." He released her waist, and his palms glided slowly over her flesh down her belly to the curls surrounding her womanhood. "But I'd have to be mad to destroy this." His fingers tangled, combed, petted the soft curls. "Look at me."

Her eyes opened. He was bending over her. His dark eyes glittered wildly in his flushed face as his hand searched. "I want to see you enjoy me. Do you know how many times I've thought about doing this?" He found what he had been searching for, and his thumb and forefinger closed upon her.

Her eyes widened in shock as a hot wave of convulsive pleasure tore through her.

He plucked and squeezed gently, skillfully, his gaze narrowed on her face, absorbing every nuance of expression. "Heat, Tess?"

"Yes . . ." She could barely force the word through the haze of pleasure he was bringing her. The tempo of the plucking accelerated, and she bit down on her lower lip to keep from crying out. She could feel the muscles of her stomach clenching, her spine arched helplessly up from the floor toward him. "Dear heaven, what—what are you doing to me?"

"I don't want to hurt you," he muttered as he widened her thighs and moved between them, nudging at the heart of her womanhood. "You had to be ready for me."

She tensed and immediately felt his hands on her belly, stroking, smoothing, soothing her. "Easy . . ." he murmured.

She doubted if he was even aware of that last action, for his expression reflected only a heavy dazed sensuality, and the words were spoken abstractedly. A flutter of warmth surged through her as she realized that no matter how deep his anger, he was instinctively trying to make the experience more palatable for her. She mustn't be such a coward about an act that happened to all women, she thought impatiently. This was what she had wanted him to do to her. "Go ahead," she whispered. "Now. I'm ready."

A harsh sound burst from him as he plunged forward.

She cried out as he broke through the barrier and buried himself deep within her.

She heard his shocked oath as he froze above her, but she was too busy trying to adjust to the intruder in her body. Pain was fading, and she was beginning to feel a delicious fullness.

"The hell you were ready," he said hoarsely. "Why didn't—"

"Hush." She was savoring their joining, but rapidly discovering it wasn't enough. The aching emptiness was still not satisfied. "Don't talk. Move. I want to feel you."

He was still a moment, and then a crooked smile crossed his face. "Oh, you will. You're right, it's too late for talk." He withdrew, then began to thrust, slow, fast, shallow, deep. "Like this?"

She nodded frantically, her head moving back and forth on the cloak as a hot tension began to build within her.

He stopped for a moment, his hands reaching blindly out to cup her breasts. "*Merde,* you're holding me too tight—you're *killing* me."

Did that mean she was doing something wrong? Yet he didn't look in pain. He hunched over her, driving in and out, his dark hair streaming about his shoulders, his eyes shut, and an expression of agonized pleasure on his face.

She tried to move, to help him, but he was losing control, bucking, lifting her from the floor with each thrust. She could only hold on to him, lost in a delirium of sensation.

He rolled over, muttering wild words beneath his breath as he pulled her on top of him and bucked upward, again and again and again. Then, still not satisfied, he rolled over again and sat up, lifting her legs to curve around his hips. "You're not taking enough." His flesh was pulled tight over his high cheekbones, his lips heavy with sensuality as his hips jerked feverishly back and forth. "I need you close, part of me . . ."

"I'm trying. . . ." She didn't know if he heard her. There was no trace of the controlled Galen she had come to know in this untamed sensualist leading her through an erotic haze. He shifted again, changed positions, and fresh waves of sensation jolted through her.

Her nails bit into his shoulders as the pace quickened. She couldn't take any more. The heat was too intense, yet it continued to rise feverishly within her.

Beauty. Hunger. Searching.

He plunged deeper, stronger. She could hear the harsh rasp of his breath above her. "Close." His teeth were clenched. "So close. I can't—"

From somewhere far away she heard the low animal cries she was making deep in her throat. Mating. Splendor.

Completion.

She heard Galen's low groan above her as he threw back his head, a massive shudder racking his big body.

Beautiful, she thought dazedly as she looked up at his face above her. Galen's expression in this moment was almost as beautiful as the release climaxing through her. She had given him that look of supreme pleasure, she realized with fierce satisfaction.

He fell forward, his elbows braced on either side of her to spare her his weight. His chest moved in and out as he tried desperately to catch his breath. He didn't move for a moment, flexing within her. She could feel his heartbeat heavy, fast against her breast.

Then, slowly, jerkily, he sat up, his chest still heaving painfully with every breath. He muttered an oath as he got off her and stood up. He padded barefoot to the hearth, snatched up her cloak from the chair, and came back to where she lay on the carpet. "Sit up."

"Not yet." She didn't want to move. She

wasn't sure she would ever want to move again. What a delicious languor, she thought dazedly. It was almost more delightful than the sensations that had gone before. "Later . . ."

He frowned down at her. "Did I hurt you?"

She tried to remember through the after-haze of the emotional storm through which she had just plummeted during the last moments. "I think so. A little. At first . . ."

"It was entirely your fault. *Merde*, what stupidity. Don't you know what I could have done to you?" The roughness of his voice was belied by the gentleness of his hands as he knelt and tucked the cloak about her. "You should have told me Yusef hadn't touched you."

"You didn't want to listen."

"You should have made me listen." He sat down on the carpet beside her and linked his arms over his knees, the muscles of his shoulders and arms ridged with tension. "It was a matter of the utmost importance."

"Would you have believed me?"

He was silent a moment. "Probably not. I—I was not myself."

Yet she believed the passionate recklessness she had discovered in Galen tonight was as much a part of him as the disciplined man she had learned to know. "Then why are you angry?"

"I believe the question should be why you aren't angry with me for forcing you."

"Because you didn't force me." She sat up and drew his cloak around her. "You should know that.

*Merde*, you took long enough arousing my curiosity about the act."

His gaze narrowed on her face. "I hope more than your curiosity was satisfied."

She nodded briskly. "Oh yes, I enjoyed it very much. No wonder Pauline is so fond of the sport."

The faintest smile touched his lips. "Then you've decided she doesn't indulge herself merely because she has nothing better to do?"

She frowned thoughtfully. "It's very . . ."—she searched for a word—"strong, isn't it? I never realized . . ."

"It has to be experienced." He was silent a moment. "Do you still hurt?"

"I'm a trifle sore." She wrinkled her nose. "But no more than I was after that first day I rode astride. Actually, your pounding was far gentler than Pavda's gait."

Surprise crossed his face, and he threw back his head and laughed. "Dear God in heaven, if you're not comparing me to your father, you're likening me to your horse."

She grinned. "You shouldn't object. I've heard gentlemen delight in calling themselves stallions."

His smile faded. "With strumpets a man can be a stallion. A virgin deserves gentleness."

"I didn't mind. I found it all very interesting. I believe I must not have been a proper virgin."

His eyes twinkled. "A virgin cannot be anything but proper, else she wouldn't be a virgin."

"You know what I mean." She glanced away

from him. "As usual, I was too bold. I liked it too much."

"To my infinite delight."

Her gaze shifted back to him. "Truly?"

"Truly," he answered solemnly. "I should have expected nothing else from you." He gently touched her hair with his fingertips. "Life, *kilen*."

Joy surged through her with a heady force that dispersed the languor. She smiled radiantly. "I'm glad you don't mind my lack of meekness. I should hate to have to—" She broke off as she heard a familiar tinkle of bells, a dry rustling. "Alexander!"

"What?"

She threw the cloak aside, scrambled to her feet, and ran across the chamber. "It's Alexander. He's back."

"Who in hades is Alexander?"

She ignored the question as she reached the window. "Come in, you idiot. It's a wonder you didn't get lost in the dark."

Alexander flew through the window and landed on the mantel above the fireplace.

Galen stared in astonishment as the pigeon waddled along the wide stone mantel. "A bird?"

"Not just any bird. He's my homing pigeon. I told you about him the second day I arrived in Zalandan."

"Ah, yes. How could such an important tidbit of information have escaped my memory?" He watched her pick up the bird and carry it toward the wicker cage under the window. "I confess my mind was occupied by a few trifling matters. Bandits, tribal wars, unity . . . I take it this Alexander has something to do with why you're here?"

"Of course." She glanced at him in surprise. "Kalim was going to cut off Yusef's head. Besides, the flight from Yusef's roof was no longer a challenge for Alexander." She frowned down at the bird. "No, I'm not going to give you any grain. You don't deserve it. You were supposed to go back to Zalandan." She closed the cage. "I get very impatient with him. The silly bird probably flew all the way to Said Ababa and back."

"You used Yusef's house to train your pigeon?"

"It has the highest roof in Zalandan. Alexander's not at all clever, and I thought he'd have a better chance of finding the palace if he could see it." She scowled down at the warbling bird. "Listen to him coo at me. He probably doesn't even realize he did anything wrong." She took three grains from the leather pouch beside the cage and slipped them through the wicker bars and told the bird sternly, "This isn't a reward, you understand. I just don't want you to starve to death."

"Why didn't you tell Kalim?"

She didn't look at him. "He wouldn't have believed it. He has no liking for me." She turned and lifted her chin defiantly. "Besides, why should I explain myself to him? Why should I let him tell me what I must do or what I must not do?"

"Because in this instance it might have saved you a modicum of unpleasantness."

"I experienced no unpleasantness." Her brow

wrinkled. "But for a moment or two you made me uneasy when I first woke up. You behaved most peculiarly."

He turned to look down at the fire. "As I said, I was not myself. I do not like this place."

"Why not?"

"It reminds me of what I was." His lips twisted. "I think for a while tonight I became what I was then."

"And you believe that is wicked?"

"Don't you?"

For a moment she could sense an uncertainty and loneliness beneath the guard he usually kept around himself. She wanted to help him, comfort him in some way, but she knew he wouldn't let her. Yet she had discovered one comfort they both enjoyed he would accept from her. "No." She met his gaze fearlessly as she moved across the room to stand before him. "Not wicked. Different and . . . interesting."

He shook his head. "But then you find the entire world interesting."

She nodded. "But I know the difference between wicked-interesting and intriguing-interesting."

"And what is that?"

"Tamar is wicked-interesting. I would not like him to touch me." She reached out and put her hand on the triangle of dark hair thatching his chest. "But I like you to touch me."

He went still. "How fortunate for me."

"I would like to do it again, please."

"Now?"

"If it's not too much trouble." She found it difficult to meet his eyes, so she flowed into his arms and laid her cheek on his chest. "I find looking at you is causing me to feel . . . I would like to do it again."

"You're not too sore?"

"No." She lifted her head and whispered, "And I would like you to kiss me. You haven't done that yet."

"Oh yes." His lips brushed hers as he gently pushed her back on the carpet. "There are many kinds of kisses, and we enjoyed one of the most pleasant ones. But I shall be delighted to show you many more." He parted her thighs and moved between them. "By all means, we must keep life interesting for you."

Tess cradled her head on her arm and gazed contentedly across the chamber at Alexander in his cage. His beady eyes stared back at her as he gave a soft warble. She felt an odd kinship for Alexander at the moment. She had soared herself this night. She had never dreamed when she had come to the tower this afternoon that she would be lying here replete and wondering at the pleasure touch could bring. She had only wished to know more about the puzzle that Galen posed. For that matter she still wished to know, and this might be a very good moment to broach the subject.

"What happened in this place?" Tess turned over on her other side to look at Galen. "Why didn't you want me to come to the tower?"

Galen was silent for a long time, and she wasn't sure he was going to answer. "My mother died here."

"Here in the tower? You said she died in a fall from her horse."

"She died running away from the tower." He looked at the leaping flames curling around the wood in the fireplace. "My father killed her lover in the guardroom downstairs. She ran out the door, jumped on her horse, and tried to get away from him." He paused. "Fifteen minutes later we found her crushed beneath her horse on the road to Said Ababa."

"We?" She stiffened with shock. Galen had told her he was only a boy of twelve when his mother died. "You were there?"

He nodded jerkily. "When my father learned that she was meeting her lover in this tower, he sent for me. He told me my mother was a whore who had betrayed us both and must be punished. He said she had never had any affection for either of us and was planning to flee with her lover to Said Ababa."

"Harsh words."

"True words. I knew she had never loved me." He paused. "But I didn't want her to die. I thought if I went with my father to the tower, I might find a way to save her."

"Perhaps you were mistaken. Most mothers have some affection for their children."

"Not mine. When I was old enough to leave the nursery, she immediately abandoned me to my father."

"That could have been by his will."

He shook his head. "She hated me. She told me so." He shrugged. "Perhaps she had reason. My father saw her for thirty minutes on the streets of Diran and kidnapped her and brought her to Zalandan to be his concubine."

"That was your father's sin, not yours."

"She saw only my father in me. She once told me that I would grow up to be a barbarian like him, and she wished I had died in her womb."

Tess shivered with distaste. "She sounds a very unpleasant woman. You were probably better off with your father."

"Better a barbarian than a whore?"

"Was he a barbarian?"

"Yes, he was far worse than Tamar. And he taught me well. By the time I passed my thirteenth year, I was the savage my mother had called me." His glance shifted from the fire to her face. "I remember on my sixteenth natal day I got drunk and brought several whores and a few friends here for a feast to celebrate." He saw her eyes widen. "Ugly? Oh yes, but that was what I was. Tamar and I drank and feasted and orgied for three days. Something about the place drove me into a frenzy."

Despair. Desperation. Tess didn't voice the words, but she moved closer to him.

"Tamar killed one of the whores in a drunken rage." Galen looked back at the fire. "He strangled her."

"You couldn't stop him?"

"I was drunk too. I woke the next morning and found her lying dead on the bed between us. For a moment I thought I had done it myself. I was sick and cold with disgust. Then I looked at Tamar and realized what I was becoming, what I already was." His voice turned fierce. "What we all were. There had to be another path, the blood lust and lawlessness couldn't go on." He got to his knees and stoked the fire. "That was the last time I came to the tower."

She shivered as she looked around the chamber. Now that she realized the debauchery and violence that had taken place here, the very walls seemed to exude a sinister air. In this tower Galen had known enough pain and disillusionment to have destroyed a weaker man. Instead, he had been hammered, honed to greater strength. Yet this place must abrade his spirit.

She sat up and threw off the cloak covering her. "I've had enough of this place." She stood up and grabbed her gown from the floor and stepped into the divided skirt. "It no longer interests me. I wish to go back to the palace."

"Now?" Galen turned to look at her. "I thought we'd wait until first light."

She shook her head. "I wouldn't sleep." She dropped down on the huge chair and pulled on her boots. "This is not a good place."

He sat back on his haunches and smiled faintly. "I believe I could pique your interest, if you cared to stay until dawn."

She smiled cheerfully. "I'm sure you could. I

find I like bed play very much, and you are most skillful at it, aren't you?"

"I endeavor to please." His voice lowered as his gaze fastened on her breasts. "While pleasing myself."

"Well, we can do that back at the palace." She stood up, located his clothes, and tossed them to him. "I'm sure we'll be more comfortable, and Alexander will be happier home in his aviary.

"Ah, yes, the well-traveled Alexander." He smiled. "We mustn't forget him."

"Not *well*-traveled." Tess grimaced. "He does everything badly." She shrugged. "But he'll learn in time. I have three years before he has to be proficient."

He stopped in midmotion of pulling on his boot. "You've set yourself a time limit?"

"Of course. I've grown very fond of Viane, and if I can train Alexander, I see no reason why we can't exchange messages after I leave Sedikhan."

"Indeed?" He jerked on his boot with sudden force and stood up. "You're already planning your departure? I might remind you that there are certain goals to be reached before you'll be permitted to leave Zalandan."

"The babe?" She crossed to the window and stooped down to pick up the wicker cage. "That shouldn't take long now that we've made such a good start. I'm young and healthy, and if God wills, I should be heavy with child by autumn." She looked at him. "If I cannot use the tower, we must find another place to free Alexander. Do you know of such a place?"

"Possibly," he muttered as he stood up and moved toward the door. "I'll think on it."

He was angry, she realized with surprise. She could feel the tension and displeasure emanating from him even at the distance separating them. "You need not trouble yourself to accompany me. Just tell me where—"

He turned to her. "Listen well," he said deliberately. "From this moment on I will be behind you, beside you, or within you. When you return to the palace, it will be to my chamber and my bed. You will *not* travel over the countryside alone or under the protection of any other man. I may have only three years, but they are going to be *my* years."

Before she could answer, he had flung open the door, and the next moment she heard the sound of his boots on the stone steps.

Tess hesitated, gazing after him in confusion. Alexander gave a low call, and she glanced down at him absently. "Be quiet. We're going."

She shrugged as she began to negotiate the spiral stone staircase. Galen's attitude might be bewildering, but many good things had come out of this night in addition to the pleasure he had taught her. She had begun to understand the experiences that had created him and the battles he constantly fought.

No, she was not at all sorry she had come to the tower.

# Chapter 8

A murmur of voices, the sudden absence of warmth.

Tess murmured protestingly as she felt Galen sit up on the divan. "It's all right. Go back to sleep."

Tess opened one eye to see Said standing by the divan, striving valiantly not to look at her. "What is it?"

"Said says Kalim wishes to see me." Galen swung his feet to the floor.

Tess glanced at the lattice window. Only the first pink streaks of dawn showed through. They had not arrived back at the palace from the tower until after midnight, and could not have been asleep for more than a few hours. "Now?"

"Kalim says it's important."

She raised herself on one elbow. "Where is he?"

"In the anteroom." He paused. "Don't worry, I won't permit him to be brought into your presence. I'll go to him."

She gazed at him in surprise. "Why? I may not like the man, but I'm not so missish that I must hide my face when he appears before me."

His gaze shifted to the outline of her naked breasts beneath the silk sheet. "It wasn't your face I was trying to hide. I thought you might be feeling . . . vulnerable."

"You mean defeated." She shook her head. "You're not being sensible. No one has defeated me. Not you, and certainly not Kalim. I've only kept my bargain, and there's no dishonor in that." She airily waved her hand. "Tell him to come in, Said."

"I'm glad you've shown me the error of my thinking," Galen said gravely. He nodded to Said as he lay back down and draped the sheet over himself. He tucked her bare arm beneath the sheet and drew the silken coverlet up to her chin. "I hope you won't mind if I object to your appearing in *déshabille* in front of another man. I find I'm experiencing a certain primitive possessiveness."

Her brow wrinkled in puzzlement. "I don't mind, but I don't understand. It doesn't seem reasonable for you to feel—"

"I'm sorry to disturb you, *Majiron*." Kalim

strode across the chamber toward them. "There's been a raid in the hills. A messenger arrived from the encampment of El Sabir."

"El Sabir!" Galen sat straight up in bed. "What raider?"

"They're not sure." Kalim hesitated. "It could have been Tamar."

"This far south?" Galen shook his head. "He's never raided the El Zalan before."

Kalim shrugged. "The leader matched his description, and he took women and horses as well as gold and seemed very selective about choosing the horses. You know what a passion Tamar has for fine horses."

"Who brought the message?"

"Yusef." Kalim carefully avoided looking at Tess. "He wasn't at the encampment at the time of the raid, but rode in directly afterward. It was he who said descriptions of the leader pointed to Tamar."

Galen smiled crookedly. "You needn't be so discreet, Kalim. I assure you that Yusef wasn't with the *majira* yesterday."

Kalim nodded without expression. "I didn't think he would have remained in such splendid health if that had been the case."

"Quite right." Galen stood up and reached for the robe Said hastily held out to him. "And it appears my wife was not enamored of Yusef, but of his house. She needed a high roof from which to launch her pigeon."

Kalim blinked. "Pigeon?"

"It's actually Viane's pigeon. We're teaching him to—" Tess broke off. Why was she making explanations to Kalim? She turned to Galen. "Where is this El Sabir?"

"It's one of the encampments that guards the gold mines in the hills. The El Sabir is one of the vassal tribes of the El Zalan." Galen took the goblet of wine Said held out to him. "It's about a four-hour ride from here." He took a sip of wine and turned back to Kalim. "What damage?"

"Not good. He set the encampment to the torch, and there were six deaths." Kalim paused. "One child. The young son of Hanal."

Galen swore. "Mother of God, when will it end?" He thrust the goblet at Said, turned, and strode toward the dressing room. "We'll leave within a half hour. Rouse the men." He disappeared into the dressing room, followed closely by Said.

Kalim started for the door, then stopped and slowly turned to face Tess again. "I was mistaken?" he asked haltingly.

Tess gazed at him without answering.

"You should have defended yourself. You should have told me—"

"That I'm not a strumpet? Why should I defend myself to you? Why should I care what you thought?" She raised her chin. "I knew you were not my friend."

He flushed. "Perhaps not your friend, but I would not wish harm to an innocent woman." He inclined his head in a formal bow. "You have my regrets if my action caused you undue pain. I owe you reparation."

Tess stared at him in surprise. He was a proud man, and she had not expected an apology. He was undoubtedly more complex and perhaps less arrogant than she had thought. She tilted her head to gaze at him curiously. "It isn't only that I'm a woman of the West, is it? You dislike me."

"I have no right to dislike you. You are the *majira*. I should—"

"Sweet Mary, cease." She scowled at him. "Tell me the truth."

He opened and closed his mouth without speaking. Finally, he said jerkily, "I do not dislike you. I fear you."

Before she could recover from the shock of his words, he turned on his heel and strode from the chamber.

Tess gazed blankly at the door. His words had astonished her not only because of their content, but because of the admission itself. Kalim represented all that was alien and forbidding in Zalandan for her, and yet, for an instant, she had detected something vulnerable and sensitive beyond his proud, cold facade.

Perhaps she had also been arrogant in expecting these people to welcome her warmly when she had done nothing to earn such a welcome. Since she had come to Zalandan, she had not really tried to get to know the El Zalan. Like a child, she had played with the pigeons, ridden Pavda, and sought only to amuse herself.

"I'll be back tomorrow evening, if all goes well. Lord knows, I can't be certain." Galen, fully dressed, strode out of the dressing room. "I'll probably have to spend hours in the council tent trying to talk them out of starting a tribal war. Stay inside the city gates. Though I doubt if Tamar will be anywhere nearby. He usually strikes and then carries his booty back to his own encampment, but there's no sense taking risks." He started toward the door.

"Wait." She blurted out, "I want to go with you."

Galen shook his head. "This won't be a pleasant journey. No tents or satin cushions. We'll travel fast and sleep on the ground."

"I know that. I still want to go."

His gaze narrowed on her face. "Why?"

"I'm not sure." She moistened her lips with her tongue. "I think perhaps I might learn . . ." She shook her head and repeated helplessly, "I don't know."

"You'll see things you won't like."

She nodded. Her hand clutched the sheet covering her body; the texture was soft and silky, as her entire life had been since she arrived in Sedikhan. But there were other, rougher textures and patterns to this country, and people she had not experienced yet. "May I go with you?"

He nodded curtly. "You have a right to see why I brought you to Sedikhan. Dress. I'll meet you in the courtyard within the half hour."

\*     \*     \*

The fires were out in the encampment of the El Sabir, but the flames had left devastation in their wake.

Tess had begun to smell the smoke from over two miles away. Her eyes smarted as she rode beside Galen through the encampment, but she didn't know whether the stinging was from smoke or tears. Over half the tents had gone up in flames, and it was heart-wrenching to see entire families searching among the blackened rubble of their possessions, trying to salvage a cooking pot, a bit of bedding, a straw doll.

"Did he have to burn the tents?" she asked huskily.

"No." Galen's expression was grim. "But he probably enjoyed it." He reined up before a scorched, ragged tent. "This is the tent of Dala, the mother of the child who was killed. You don't have to come in with me."

"I'll come."

Galen dismounted, came around, and helped her down from Pavda. "You may be sorry."

Tess *was* sorry. The moment she entered the small tent, she saw the child.

The little boy lying on the pallet couldn't have been over three years old, and his long lashes curled peacefully on tan cheeks that still held the silky bloom of babyhood. He could have been asleep, but slumber did not have this quality of tragic stillness.

The thin young woman who knelt beside the child was not long out of childhood herself, but the eyes she lifted as they came into the tent were old with pain.

"I sorrow with you, Dala," Galen said gently. "Is there anything I can do to ease you?"

The woman shook her head. "They broke him, *Majiron*," she whispered. "They rode him down as if he were a mongrel dog that got in their way."

Galen's hand clasped the woman's shoulder.

"They saw him." The woman dazedly shook her head. "They saw him and still did not swerve aside. He was barely three, *Majiron*."

"Where is your husband?"

"With the other men at the council tent." Her eyes were brimming with tears. "He cannot bear to look at him." Her hand reached out and caressed the little boy's unruly curls. "And I cannot bear to let him go."

Tess's throat ached as she looked at the woman. She wanted to run far away from this place of sorrow and death. Dear heaven, she was full of pain.

"I'll send him to you," Galen said.

The woman shook her head. "I must prepare my son for burial. My husband feels my pain as well as his own. He cannot bear the burden of both right now."

"The village women?"

"They have their own families to care for. It is a bad time."

"I'll stay." Tess didn't realize she had spoken until the words were out. She took a step forward and fell to her knees beside the woman. "If you

will permit me?" Dear God, why had she made
the offer? She had no wish to be here.

"I don't care," the woman said dully, still looking at the child. "Whatever the *majiron* wishes."

"You wish to stay?" Galen asked Tess in a low
voice.

"No." Her voice was trembling. "But I've got
to stay."

Galen's gaze searched her face before he nodded slowly. "I'll station Said outside the tent. If
you have need of anything, send him to the council tent to get me."

She could not stop looking at the face of the
child. Sweet Jesu, he was almost a baby. How
would she have felt if this babe had been her own?

Galen hesitated, and she could feel his stare
on her face.

"Go on," she whispered. "You can do no more
here."

She heard him move and then felt a current of
air as the tent flap was opened. After the flap fell,
she was silent a moment. What did she do now?
Dala seemed to be in a stupor of grief, and Tess
had never been good with people. Yet she had to
do something.

Very well. She wasn't good with people, but
she knew horses. She would apply what she knew
of animals to Dala. Dala was beaten and wanted
only to lie down and wallow in grief. But if a sick
horse was allowed to lie down, that was often the
end for him. So, Tess reasoned, she must keep
the woman moving.

She reached over and shook Dala's thin shoulder. "I know it's not fair, but you must guide me."

Dala lifted dull eyes. "What?"

"I want to help you with him, but I don't know how to go about it. What's the first thing we must do?"

The woman stirred, temporarily brought out of her numbness by the necessity of responding to Tess's ignorance and need. She rubbed her temple and then said haltingly, "First, we should bathe him."

Tess nodded briskly. "Then that's what we'll do. I'll go ask Said to fetch water." She stood up and moved toward the flap of the tent. "Yes, that sounds sensible."

But what was sensible in a world where innocent babies were murdered?

She didn't leave Dala's tent until the sun was setting.

Said immediately rose to his feet as she stepped out of the tent. "You have not eaten. We've set up our own camp near the stream at the edge of the El Sabir encampment and found enough game for a stew. May I get you something, *Majira?*"

"Not now." She was too weary and heartsick to think of food. "Where is my husband?"

He nodded at a large tent several hundred yards away from where they stood. "Still at the council tent."

"Take me to him."

"It's not fitting for a woman to disturb—"

She wheeled on him, her hands clenched into
fists. "*Merde,* I have no intention of intruding on
the men's precious council. Though only the sweet
Virgin knows why a woman should have no say in
these matters when their children are butchered
like—" She turned away. It wasn't Said's fault
that life was unfair to women. Or perhaps it was
his fault, and Galen's fault, and her father's, and
all the men who dictated that women should bear
children and then fail to give them a safe world
in which to raise them. She strode past Said
toward the council tent. "I'll wait until the meeting is done, but I must speak to the *majiron* as
soon as possible."

To her surprise Kalim wasn't inside the council
tent but sitting cross-legged on the ground outside, waiting. "Why aren't you attending the council? I would have thought Galen would need your
support."

Kalim shook his head. "I was born in these
hills and raised with these people. He knows I
wouldn't be able to keep a cool head."

Tess gazed bleakly at the destruction around
them. "Can he?"

"It's not easy for him." Kalim's expression became shadowed. "But he's stronger than the rest
of us."

"That poor baby." Rage flared again in her
eyes. "*Canaille.* I'm not sure I won't go after
Tamar myself."

"Such ferocity." The faintest hint of a smile

touched Kalim's lips. Then it faded, and she could feel him withdrawing from her again. "Why are you here? How may I help you?"

"You can get Dala's husband out of that meeting and send him back to her." Tess wearily ran her fingers through her hair. "I've done all I can. She needs him."

"Hanal doesn't wish to—"

"Dear God in heaven," Tess exploded. "I don't care what he wishes! She is going to bury her son tomorrow, and she needs him. Do I have to go in and get him myself?"

He stared at her impassively for a moment before turning and moving toward the closed flap of the tent. "No, that's not necessary. I will go in and find him and make sure he goes to her."

"You will?"

"Why do you look so surprised? How could a savage like me withstand the wisdom of a woman of the West?"

She ignored his mocking words. "Why are you doing this?"

Kalim glanced over his shoulder. "Because you're right," he said simply. "Hanal has no right to indulge his own grief and rage for vengeance and give no comfort to his loved ones."

Kalim was clearly very effective when he chose to act. A few moments later she watched a grim Kalim hustle a surly-faced young man from the council tent and half-push, half-lead him down the street toward Dala's tent.

"What's amiss?"

She turned to see Galen.

"Why did Kalim come for Hanal?"

"Because I told him I'd go in and get him if he didn't," Tess said. "Dala needed him."

He frowned. "How is she?"

"A little better, I think. I treated her like a horse, and it seemed to work, but—"

He blinked. "A horse?"

"You know, I kept her walking."

For an instant the tension and weariness in his expression lightened as a smile tugged at his lips. "Very wise."

"I don't know about the wisdom of it. But it was all I could think to do."

"Instincts are usually correct in situations like this."

"Are they?" She shook her head. "I wouldn't know. I've never been in a situation like this." She added quickly, "But I'm doing very well, you understand. I just realized Hanal could help Dala more than I could now. You didn't have to leave the council."

"You're doing splendidly," he said gently. "As for the council, I left them to their quarreling." His voice was heavy with weariness. "I'll go back later." He took her elbow and propelled her toward the camp the El Zalan had set up at the far end of the El Sabir encampment. "It's much worse than I thought here. I'll order food to be prepared and then send you back to Zalandan with Kalim."

"Said's already prepared a meal." She shook

her head. "And I'm not going back. I promised
Dala I'd be here to bid farewell to her son." Her
glance traveled around the burned tents of the
encampment. "And God knows there's work enough
to be done."

"Your work?"

"I'm here. Why should I not make myself useful? We'll have to send back to Zalandan for food
and supplies, and I'll have to visit each family and
determine what and how much is needed." She
shrugged. "Besides, I believe it would be benefi-
cial for Dala to keep stirring after the funeral tomorrow, and I cannot count on her husband to
keep her too busy. I believe if I show her I de-
pend on her to help me, she'll heal faster."

"You have it all planned." Galen's gaze was on
her face. "This isn't your problem. You needn't
involve yourself in it."

"They need me."

Galen nodded. "Yes, they need all the help
you can give them."

"Then let us speak no more about it. I'll stay
until you return to Zalandan. Do you think you'll
be able to persuade them not to go after Tamar?"

"If I have the eloquence of Lucifer and the
patience of Job."

"They've lost a great deal."

"And will lose more if they start after Tamar.
He's a raider, skilled in the battle and the chase."

She offered tentatively, "You could help them."

"Yes." He paused. "But I won't. The bloodlet-
ting has to stop." He released her arm as they

reached the camp. "There has to be another way."
His lips tightened. "*Damn* Tamar!"

She had been a witness to this pain and violence for only a single day, and yet she felt
wounded and scarred. How much worse it must
have been for Galen, who had grown up in the
midst of this slaughter and bloodshed. "What will
you do now?"

He shook his head. "I don't know. Go back
and argue with them, I suppose." He reached out
and traced the dark imprints beneath her eyes.
"It's not been an easy day for you."

"Easier for me than for the El Sabir." And she
was not sorry she had come. These sad hours had
enriched and deepened her in some mysterious
fashion. She felt as if she had started down a path
that never could be retraced. "Easier for me than
for you."

That truth was also clear to her. The tragic
sights with which she had been assaulted had temporarily blinded her to Galen's agony of spirit, but
now she became acutely conscious of it.

*"He's stronger than the rest of us."*

But what price did he pay for disciplined
strength?

"Don't go back tonight," she urged impulsively. "You're too weary. Wait until tomorrow."

"I'm touched by your concern."

She grimaced. "But you won't change your
mind."

His expression softened miraculously, but he
shook his head. "Tempers are too hot. I have to

calm them." He glanced back at the council tent.
"I should be there right now."

"Nonsense. You can wait at least until you eat.
Sit down." She pushed him down on a log near
the campfire and moved toward the large pot simmering over the blaze. "I'll get you a bowl of stew
and a cup of tea."

"I have no time to—"

"Of course you do." She frowned sternly at
him over her shoulder. "Rest."

A flicker of amusement that held an element
of tenderness crossed his face. "As you command,
*Majira*."

It was nearly dawn when Tess roused to find
Galen slipping under the blanket beside her,
drawing her back against him spoon fashion.

"Did all go well?" she asked drowsily.

"No." He stretched out his long legs and buried his face in her hair. "Go back to sleep."

"Don't be absurd." She yawned and turned on
her side to face him. "If you wanted me to sleep,
you should have lied to me. They're going after
Tamar?"

"They've agreed to wait for three months. If I
haven't brought Tamar before a tribunal in that
time, they'll launch a foray against his encampment."

"What kind of tribunal?"

He paused. "A tribunal of the United Tribes
of Sedikhan."

Her eyes widened. "In three months? You said
it might take years."

Galen's lips twisted sardonically. "That's why they felt it safe to compromise. They'll appease me and still have their bloodbath."

"What are you going to do?"

"What can I do?" His face lit with a sudden reckless smile. "I'm going to unite the whole damn country in three months."

She stared at him in fascination, held captive by the forceful magnetism he was emitting. "You're not discouraged?"

"How could I be discouraged? The situation is beyond ridiculous; it's completely impossible."

And he was responding to a challenge with an excitement and exhilaration she had never seen in him. It was because his waiting had at last ended, she suddenly realized. No matter how slim the chances of success, he was now free to act. "You're going to tilt at windmills?"

He shook his head. "I'm going to talk them into stopping their whirling."

He was striking a spark within her. She leaned forward, her face alight. "How?"

"First, I'm going to visit the sheikhs of the nine principal tribes of Sedikhan and try to persuade them to come to a meeting to discuss unity."

"Will they come?"

"Oh, they'll come all right. I'll call a *carobel*."

The word was vaguely familiar, but she couldn't place it. "What's that?"

"A festival. Food, music, dancing, and the *carobel* race. Some of the sheikhs may not want to talk unity, but they'll come anyway if a festival is in the offing. Once I have them together, I'll have the chance of molding them to my will."

"Where will this festival take place?"

"In the foothills near Zalandan. It's as close as I can manage to neutral ground." His brow creased with absorption. "If I can make some progress with the visits to the individual tribes, I'll have a chance. There's a possibility I may be able to use Tamar's raids to advantage. He's been growing too strong for the liking of most of the sheikhs, and his raids have caused a good deal of bitterness. With the threat Tamar's posing and the added prestige of my marriage to a Tamrovian princess, I may be able to manipulate them into the fold."

"Then why not take the Tamrovian princess with you and display her properly?"

He looked taken aback. "What?"

She raised herself on her elbow. "Isn't that why I'm here?" Her face flushed with eagerness. "Take me with you."

"You wish to go?"

She nodded briskly. "We'll need to spend a few more days here helping these poor people, but then I'll be free to go." She frowned. "Of course, I'll have to send a message to Viane, asking her to continue Alexander's training. He mustn't get out of practice."

"By all means, we must make arrangements for Alexander." His gaze narrowed on her face. "You're very enthusiastic. Why?"

She wasn't sure. Perhaps she was moved to share his weariness and loneliness, or perhaps she simply wanted to be a part of his great adventure. Either explanation would reveal a vulnerability she wasn't ready to display, and she quickly lowered her gaze to the pulse beating in the hollow of his throat. "We struck a bargain. It's only honorable for me to fulfill my part as soon as possible."

He stiffened. "And you'll be free to leave Sedikhan sooner."

Leave? The thought was the farthest thing from her mind. She felt hurt, but rallied to say coolly, "That's true."

"Then there's no question I should let you accompany me." He drew her close, cradling her cheek in the hollow of his shoulder. "I must take full advantage of your presence while I have it."

# Chapter 9

Tess smiled politely at the old sheikh, but received a haughty glare in return.

After only two minutes in his presence she knew that their visit to Sheikh Sarum Hakim of the El Kabbar tribe was not going to be particularly pleasant. She kept her smile firmly in place while she wondered what the old dragon would do if she stepped forward and tugged on his long white beard.

A flash of amusement lightened her fatigue and discouragement until the sheikh rudely turned his back on her and spoke to Galen. "We sup with the elders in an hour, but I wish to have conversation with you before." He snapped his fingers,

and a veiled woman in dark robes came scurrying
forward. "Take the *majira* to the visitors' tent."

"We've brought a small tent of our own,"
Galen said. "We need not trouble you."

"You refuse my hospitality?"

Galen shrugged. "That was not my intention. I
merely sought to save you the bother." He smiled.
"Naturally, we shall be glad to accept whatever
arrangements you've decreed for us." Galen nodded to Said, hovering a few steps behind them.
"Make sure the *majira* has whatever she needs."

The old sheikh smiled unpleasantly. "You pamper her? The El Zalan has grown soft since you
built your fine city and no longer roam the countryside. The women of El Kabbar know their place
and display proper respect for their husbands. We
teach them meekness with a whip." He flung out
his hand toward Tess. "Look at her. She wears no
veil."

"She comes from Tamrovia, a country that
doesn't require their women to cover their faces."

"I've heard you do not demand it in Zalandan
from your own women. Pah, weakness!"

"You're entitled to your own view." Galen's
expression was bland. "However, you lost five of
your women and six of your best horses to Tamar
two months ago. Your strength didn't prevent that
from happening."

Hakim stared at him without answering.

"Perhaps other measures are needed to prevent such a thing from happening again," Galen
said softly.

"Your mouthing unity again?" The sheikh hesitated before turning abruptly away, the carriage of his tall, thin body rod straight. "It will do no harm to talk. Come."

Galen fell into step with the old sheikh, and they moved toward the large tent a few yards away.

"Come, *Majira*." Said's tone was gentle. "It may be hours before—"

"I know that." Tess gestured impatiently. "I doubt if I'll see Galen before morning." She turned and followed the veiled woman through the encampment, acutely conscious of the heat of the sun's rays on her own naked face. The women they passed were all gowned in black, their kohl-outlined eyes staring fearfully at Tess and Said above their heavy black veils. She had never felt more alien than she did at that moment. Zalandan was a liberated paradise compared to this tribal encampment. She should be accustomed to it, she thought wearily. The El Kabbar was the seventh encampment they had visited, and her reception had been the same at each. Well, not precisely the same. She was usually met with reserve and curiosity, not this hostility. Yet it didn't ease the feeling of loneliness to know the women were downtrodden rather than resentful.

Said's gaze was fastened sympathetically on her face. "The *majiron* says we stay only one night here. The attack by Tamar has made the sheikh amenable to argument. They are not so strict with their women in the next tribe we visit."

"You mean they permit them to go unveiled and not to bow and kneel before their masters? How generous." Tess's gaze went to the woman hurrying ahead of them. "Dear Lord, I feel sorry for them. I want to strike out. Or shake them or—"

"No!" Said's expression was alarmed. "You must not do that. It would make the *majiron*'s task more difficult."

"Don't worry." She raked her fingers through her tousled hair. "It would do no good. They would just stare at me with those big eyes and . . ." She shook her head. "My own mother is the same. If my father lived in Sedikhan, I've no doubt he would force her to wear a veil."

The woman had stopped and was drawing back the flap of a small tent. She held it back for them to enter.

"Thank you," Tess said.

The woman merely nodded, then swiftly lowered her lashes.

Sweet Mary, the woman was even afraid of *her*. Tess felt the frustration welling up within her as she strode into the tent. She stopped short just inside, her senses assaulted.

Heat, dimness, incense.

She was vaguely able to discern various cluttered objects, a scattering of pillows, but they were all strange, alien. It was a cage. . . .

She couldn't *breathe*.

The panic was rising within her, her heart pounding painfully.

The impression of closeness was overpowering.

"No!" She turned on her heel and bolted out of the tent, almost colliding with Said. The air outside was hot, too, but not smotheringly oppressive. She gasped frantically.

"You're pale." Said was beside her. "Are you ill?"

Tess shook her head, trying to stop the shudders racking her. "I can't stay in the tent. Where did they put Pavda?"

Said nodded to an enclosure a few yards distant. "Shall I get the *majiron*?"

"No, of course not." She moved away from the tent, trying to ignore the eyes of the women staring at her. "I'll be all right soon. I just need to get away from here. I'll go for a ride and—"

"I'll get the horses."

"No argument, Said? Aren't you going to say such an action wouldn't be fitting?"

He shook his head. "Sometimes it is necessary to break with custom. I know these past days have not been easy for you."

She gazed at him in surprise.

"I know of a small oasis within two miles of here. You can sit and become serene, and I will play my flute." He paused. "If you will permit?"

A sudden surge of affection coursed through her as she looked at his concerned expression. Said still didn't approve of many of her actions, but over the last weeks they had begun to understand and accept each other. "I'll be happy to have your company, Said."

\*    \*    \*

The moon had risen when Tess saw a lone rider approaching the oasis. Galen.

She glanced at Said, who was sitting on a folded blanket under a palm tree a few yards away from the one against which she was leaning. "I suppose you sent someone to tell him where we were going?"

"It was only courtesy, *Majira*." He began playing his flute again.

She should have thought to do that herself, but she had been desperate to get away from that tent . . . from all the pitifully staring eyes of the women. Besides, she had been sure Galen's discussions with the sheikh would last well into the night as they usually did.

Galen reined up beside Pavda and slid from Selik's back. Was he angry? She couldn't tell; his expression was hidden in the shadows of the palm trees.

She straightened. "Did the talks go well?"

"Well enough." He strode over and knelt beside her. "How are you?"

"There's nothing wrong with me. I just wanted to get away from—" She broke off. "I'm better now. We can go back to the encampment."

"Presently." He sat down beside her and called to Said, "Go back and present my apologies to the sheikh. Tell him the *majira* is ill, and I won't be able to meet with him until morning."

"No! I told you I wasn't ill. I'll be—"

But Said was ignoring her protest and already

striding toward his horse. Tess turned quickly to Galen. "Don't be foolish. The sheikh already thinks you're weak to pamper me. This isn't a wise move."

"I don't give a damn what the sheikh thinks of me. I don't stand or fall by any man's opinion."

"But the unity of Sedikhan might. I have no intention of having you fail to reach your goal after all I've gone through these last two months." She got to her knees on the blanket. "Now, call Said back and tell him—"

"Why? I don't want his company." Galen stretched out on the blanket and put his arms beneath his head. "I think we'll stay here awhile. This is the first time I've felt free and relaxed since we started this journey."

"But the sheikh—"

"The sheikh will think I'm weak where women are concerned." He smiled lazily. "But I'll have no trouble convincing him that I'm not vulnerable in other areas, and it will probably make him feel safer to consider himself superior to me."

She shook her head. "This isn't necessary."

"It wasn't necessary for you to bear loneliness and weariness for my sake," he said quietly. "It wasn't necessary for you to stand and let yourself be insulted and then watch me walk away from you without offering defense."

She gazed at him, startled. "I knew you couldn't defend me without weakening your position."

"I wasn't sure you understood." He reached

out and pulled her down in his arms, cradling her head in the hollow of his shoulder. "I can only fight one battle at a time. Once I've assured the unity, I can turn my thoughts to other problems."

She found herself relaxing against him, the weariness and discouragement miraculously easing. She found herself drawing nearer, taking strength from him. She suddenly blurted, "It was the women."

He was silent, waiting.

"They were like slaves, caged and beaten into submission. Then I went into that tent, and it was like another cage." She laughed shakily. "I think it frightened me."

"Frightened?"

"That it could happen to me. All my life I've wanted to be free, but I knew that women couldn't—one slip of fate and I could be caged like them and . . ." She trailed off and then said with sudden fierceness, "It isn't right. Women shouldn't be treated as chattels. Those poor women creeping around afraid to lift their eyes, and Dala losing her son but not allowed to have any say in deciding the fate of his murderer. It's not *fair*, Galen."

"No."

"I always knew it wasn't fair, but I accepted it as the way of the world. Dear heaven, even the priests tell us we must be meek and dutiful." She gazed straight ahead into the darkness. "But I've been sitting here thinking, and I've decided you're not entirely to blame. It's our own fault for letting you do it. We haven't had the courage to fight, to prove our worth. It has to change, Galen."

"I'll shoulder my own sins, but I refuse to bear the rest of mankind's."

"Actually, you're better than the rest."

A smile tugged at his lips as he inclined his head. "I'm most grateful for such extravagant praise." His smile faded. "I told you I cannot—"

"You're not listening to me. I'm asking nothing of you. It's because we've relied on men to fight our battles that we didn't deserve to win them."

"And you intend to fight this battle yourself?" He gently brushed the hair from her face. "God help us all."

"God has already helped the men of the world. It's time we had our turn."

"And when do you intend to launch this offensive?"

"I haven't decided." She grimaced. "It's a difficult task."

"And it may take more time than you've allotted yourself." His hand continued to stroke her temple, but he looked away from her. "Providing it's the women of Sedikhan you've decided to save."

His words brought pain. She knew Galen found intense pleasure in her body, but he knew her well enough to realize she would probably be a great deal of trouble to him. She was a stranger in his land, and in these last weeks she had found just how suspiciously a stranger was regarded by his people.

"They certainly appear to need saving." She deliberately made her tone noncommittal and changed the subject. "Will Hakim attend the *carobel* in two weeks?"

Galen nodded. "And probably vote for union. He's suffered too much not to grasp any remedy for his troubles."

"We only have two more sheikhs to visit." She paused. "Unless you intend to invite Tamar."

"I'm not mad. We'd have war before we reached the council tent."

"Won't he be angry not to be invited and disrupt it anyway?"

"I won't let him."

"How will you—"

"I'm tired of talk." He began to unbutton her riding habit. "Lord knows, I'll have enough of that when I get back to Hakim." His head lowered, and his lips brushed her nipple as he whispered, "Hakim offered to give me a *kadine* to pleasure me tonight."

She stiffened. "What did you tell him?"

"What could I say? I told him you were a goddess of love and that the reason I indulged you so extravagantly was because you sent me to paradise every time I moved between your thighs."

She could feel the familiar ache igniting in her womanhood as his teeth pulled gently on her nipple. She swallowed. "You didn't have to lie to him."

He moved over her, drawing down the gown

and parting her thighs. He muttered, "I didn't. It was no lie. . . ."

"It's like a small village," Tess murmured to Galen as they paused on the rise to look down at the festival site below.

Over a hundred tents dotted the landscape in the valley, and the encampment was bustling with activity. Women tended huge kettles before their tents; men wandered about, laughing and talking; fine horses, their coats gleaming in the sunlight, moved restlessly in the enclosure at the far end of the encampment.

"No children," Tess noticed. "If this is a festival, where are the children?"

"No one who has not passed their thirteenth natal day is permitted at the *carobel*." Galen nudged his horse forward. "The children are left behind to be tended by the elders."

"Why?"

"Both the race and the prizes are for grown-ups, and are taken very seriously." Galen pointed at a small clearing at the western end of the encampment. "There's Viane."

"Where?" Then Tess caught sight of Viane's small figure moving gracefully and serenely through the crowds in the clearing. "Never mind, I see her!" She kicked Pavda into a gallop that sent the mare hurtling down the road ahead of Galen toward the encampment. "Viane!"

Viane looked around, and a smile lit her face.

She stood waiting until Tess reined in Pavda and slipped down from the saddle. "It's good to see you. You look well."

Tess gave her an affectionate hug. "Did you bring Alexander?"

Viane chuckled. "Why did I know that would be your first question? Of course I brought him. Didn't you ask me in three separate dispatches to do so? He's in my tent, and we can release him whenever you wish. I've told my maid to feed him his grain when he comes back to the palace." She held up her hand as Tess started to speak. "And yes, I've been keeping him in practice. Kalim has been helping me."

Tess frowned. "Kalim?"

Viane nodded. "Each evening he took him to Yusef's house and released him." She paused. "And for the last week he's traveled about the city letting him go from different points. Alexander is getting quite proficient at finding his way home."

"Kalim didn't mention helping you in any of the dispatches he sent to Galen."

"I'm sure he wouldn't. It's hardly a matter of state affairs."

"True." It was surprisingly considerate of Kalim to give his time and effort to their project, but Tess wasn't sure she approved. "If Sacha had been there, I'm sure he would have done the same thing."

Viane smothered a smile. "Possibly."

"Of course he would," she said staunchly. "Is Kalim here?"

"Of course, everyone comes to the *carobel*. It's

tradition for all men of stature to participate in the games."

"Even Galen?"

Viane nodded. "He says it's very important to observe the small traditions when you seek to break the big ones. He's won the last four *carobels*." Her smile faded. "I must not stand here talking. There is much to be done before the festival begins day after tomorrow. Food must be prepared." She gestured toward a large tent. "And special quarters readied for the *kadines*."

"*Kadines*? Here?"

"But of course. Did you not know it's the custom to provide the winner of each event with a night with the woman of his choice? In the beginning there was much bloodshed when a winner chose the wife or daughter of other competitors, so it was decided to bring the most beautiful *kadines* to the *carobels* to avoid such a choice." She shrugged. "Though the women service most of the men in the encampment before the festival is through. It's not only the feast and games that bring the chiefs and their followers here. It's tradition for each man to take his pleasure at least once with a *kadine* while at the festival."

"I . . . see." She should have not been surprised. She had discovered that *kadines* were completely accepted even by wives and concubines. "Have they arrived from Zalandan yet?"

Viane shook her head. "Tomorrow. But I must make sure their tent is comfortable and suitably furnished. They receive many visitors."

"I imagine that's true enough."

"I brought a trunk containing suitable clothing for you and also your jewel box." Viane said briskly, "Naturally, you'll want to add to Galen's consequence by appearing in proper attire." She cast a disapproving glance at Tess's habit. "I suggest you change at once. Half the sheikhs have already arrived."

"There's still time." Tess glanced thoughtfully at the *kadine*'s tent. "Are they very beautiful?"

"Of course, I selected them myself," said Viane, surprised. "Why else would they be considered as prizes?"

"I don't know. It seems—"

"Greetings, Viane." Galen reined up beside them, his glance taking in the order and cleanliness of the encampment. "You've done well."

Viane flushed with pleasure, "There's still much to do—I was explaining to Tess—but all will be ready by tomorrow." She frowned sternly at Tess. "Change your clothing."

"Oh, very well." Tess made a face. "But I refuse to smother my face in a veil, regardless of Galen's consequence."

"A pity." Galen's eyes twinkled. "I'm sure old Hakim would regard such a concession as a major victory for me."

"No veil." Tess's tone was firm. Her glance fell on the *kadine*'s tent again, and she added carelessly, "However, I see no reason why I shouldn't change into a gown."

"I'm grateful," Galen said gravely.

"After all, I'm quite weary of these habits after wearing nothing else for the past two months. And I'm not unreasonable."

Pearls framed the low square neckline of the gold brocade gown, the only ornamentation disturbing the graceful simplicity of the high-waisted garment.

Not that she had overmuch to fill the bodice, Tess thought ruefully as she gazed into the polished bronze mirror. Still, the gold did seem to make her hair shimmer in contrast.

Galen shifted his position on the divan, leaning his chin on his palm as he watched. "Quite splendid."

"It has a matching fringed shawl and even a foolish gold parasol to carry with it." She touched her bare throat. "It's not at all modest. Perhaps I should wear the shawl. Hakim will glare at me again."

He lifted his brows. "Do you care?"

"Well, Viane said I mustn't damage your consequence." She looked straight ahead at her reflection and said casually, "She seemed to think you would follow the traditions of the *carobel*."

"Whenever possible."

"She said most of the men visit the *kadine* tent."

"True."

"Will you?" She still avoided his glance as she rushed on, "Not that it matters. I only wanted to know."

"If it doesn't matter, why are you interested?"

She scowled at him. "I don't like . . . it bothers me."

"Why?"

"How should I know?" she asked in exasperation. "I just don't like to think of you with—" She broke off. "Are you going to them?"

"It would break tradition not to visit them." He stood up and started toward her. "The other men might doubt my virility."

"Nonsense."

"Hakim would think me crazed."

"Stop toying with me. Are you going to visit them?"

His index finger traced the pearls on the bodice of the gown. "Did you wear this to persuade me not to visit them?"

"Certainly not."

"That's good. Because it would have been a mistake."

She frowned uncertainly. "It would?"

He nodded. "If you wished to persuade me, you should have worn nothing at all. I much prefer you without clothes." He smiled. "But it pleases me that you don't wish me to fornicate with another woman. You do realize that if I make this supreme sacrifice, it's only fair that you make a special effort to please me? The *kadines* have been taught many delightfully wicked ways to pleasure a man." He slipped a finger into the bodice and rubbed it back and forth across her nipple. "Would you like to learn them?"

She could feel her body flowing helplessly toward him. "Would I find them interesting?"

"I guarantee it."

She moistened her lips with her tongue. "Then I see no reason why I shouldn't—"

"Galen, Tamar is here!"

Kalim burst into the tent.

"Tamar?" Galen's hand fell away from Tess, his muscles tensing. "Are you sure?"

Kalim nodded. "I saw him riding into the encampment myself."

"How many?"

"Alone."

A little of the tension ebbed from Galen's stance. "Good. Then there's no immediate threat. Bring him here."

Kalim nodded and strode out of the tent.

"Tamar," Tess whispered. "Dear God, and the festival hasn't even started."

"I expected him to appear sometime. Now is better than later." Galen turned to face her. "Go to Viane's tent. I don't want him to see—"

"Galen, how could you be so unkind?" Tamar walked into the tent. "Would I have had a *carobel* and not have invited you?"

Galen's face became expressionless. "Your raids have made you less than popular to the majority of my guests. I doubt if you expected to be welcomed."

"Not by those swine." Tamar shrugged as he strolled over and selected a plump fig from a large wooden fruit bowl. "But you're always glad to see me, aren't you?" His strong white teeth sank into the fig as his gaze wandered to Tess. "How grand you look. Like the princess you are." His voice was low and silky. "It was truly wicked of Galen not to tell me of his plans for you. I hear you've been traveling the countryside with my old friend. Have you properly impressed these fools with your splendor?"

"I believe we've had a certain amount of success," Tess said coolly. "And possibly my presence contributed to it."

Tamar took another bite of the juicy fruit. "So haughty." His white teeth flashed in his bearded face. "I believe I like the princess better than the strumpet, Galen. Shall I tell you why?"

"No, but you can tell me why you're here."

Tamar's gaze shifted back to Galen. "Why, to give you one more chance to turn your back on this foolishness. Send these sheep back to their own encampments and forget trying to persuade them to a unity nobody wants but you."

"One you certainly don't want."

"I admit it wouldn't suit me. My nature wouldn't tolerate the chains of union." His smile widened. "And neither would yours. I'd wager you'd break your own fine laws within six months after a union was formed."

"You're wrong, Tamar."

Tamar shook his head. "Oh no, I know you very well, my friend. Your silly ideals will stand only as long as the provocation is not too great."

His smile faded. "And I assure you I'd provide that provocation. Send them away, Galen."

Galen squarely met his gaze. "By the time they leave, there will be a united Sedikhan."

Tamar muttered a curse. "And it will declare me an outlaw?"

Galen nodded.

Tamar glared at him. "This is ceasing to amuse me. You're going too far. I warn you—" He struggled with his rage. Finally, a tight smile curled on his lips. "Unfortunate choice, Galen." He turned and moved toward the opening of the tent. He stopped in the entrance to look back at Tess. "You didn't want to know, but I think I'll tell you anyway. The reason I like the princess better than the strumpet is that I've never rutted with a princess." He paused. "Yet."

The next instant he was gone.

Tess tried to suppress the shiver that rippled through her. No knife had been drawn, but this meeting had been inexpressibly more menacing than her last with Tamar.

"I'm sending you back to Zalandan," Galen said flatly.

She whirled to face him. "Because of Tamar's ugliness?" She shook her head. "I won't go. I have a purpose here. No matter whether they disapprove of me or not, whenever those sheikhs look at me, it reminds them of your connection with Tamrovia."

"You leave in the morning. I'll tell Kalim to escort you."

"And when he leaves me in Zalandan, I'll be
ten minutes behind him riding back here. Would
you rather have me traveling alone and unescorted
than under your protection?"

His hands clenched into fists. "You don't know
Tamar. I won't have—" He broke off as he saw
her set lips and squared jaw and muttered a low
oath. "Lord, you're obstinate. Don't you understand? Tamar doesn't make idle threats, and he
*threatened* you."

"And you also."

"It's my battle, not yours."

She didn't answer.

He threw up his hands and uttered another
curse before turning on his heel and striding from
the tent.

He was wrong, she thought. Didn't he realize
that his battles would be hers always? As long as
she lived she would be—

As long as she lived.

Shock made her go rigid as she stared blindly
at the tent opening through which he had disappeared. *Merde,* what was she thinking? She
wanted to be bound to no man.

Yet she was bound to Galen Ben Raschid, not
only by vows and the pleasure of the flesh, but by
a deeper bond.

"No!" She wanted no bonds that would hold
her to either Galen or Sedikhan. She wanted to
be free. It was not love. What she felt was only
lust and respect for a man possessing unusual
qualities. Their companionship and joint purpose

had brought them closer than was common, but it couldn't be—

And he did not love her.

Pain swept through her, catching her off guard. If she didn't love him, then why did that realization hurt her?

She glanced down at the brocade gown she had donned to keep him from going to another woman. She should have realized how dangerous a reaction that had been.

She was only dazzled by the pleasure he gave her. Pauline had been similarly besotted with one of her swains for a full two weeks before she came to her senses.

But Tess was not Pauline, and she did not forget easily.

She would not think about it. She would keep herself so busy that she would not have time to think about Galen or this mysterious link they had forged. She would distance herself from him.

Yes, that was the thing to do. As she had kept Dala active in her time of trial, so she would treat her own affliction.

It was after midnight when Tess heard Galen enter the tent and begin disrobing. She breathed shallowly, hoping he would believe she was asleep.

Soon he slipped onto the divan beside her and lay there without speaking for a few moments.

"You're not sleeping." Galen turned over to look at her in the darkness.

"No."

"I would have returned earlier, but Hakim wished to discuss the laws of justice of—"

"It didn't matter."

He was silent a moment before he said haltingly, "I didn't mean to swear at you. I was . . . concerned."

"My feelings aren't so tender as to be damaged by harsh words."

"Aren't they?" He reached over and gently touched the plane of her cheek. "I believe they are, *kilen.*"

She shut her eyes tightly to keep back the tears. Foolishness. This wave of emotion sweeping through her was madness. Just because he touched her with tenderness was no reason to weep like an infant not yet out of swaddling clothes. Yes, the decision to distance herself from him had been even wiser than she had thought. "You're mistaken. I'm only awake because it's too hot to sleep."

"Odd. I thought the night cool." His hand reached out and cupped her breast. "Your flesh isn't warm." He chuckled as he felt her nipple hardening beneath his palm. "But I do detect a certain heat."

"You've trained me well, haven't you? You should be very proud." She removed his hand and edged away from him. "I doubt that even Daphne learned her duty so quickly."

"Duty?"

"To pleasure you, to bear your child. Isn't that my duty?" Her voice was uneven, and she quickly steadied it. "Well, I've been thinking, and I believe I've done enough for the time being to demonstrate my compliance."

He stiffened. "And?"

"I do not wish you to touch me."

He muttered an oath. "Dammit, Tess, I told you I regretted—"

"Your words had nothing to do with my decision. Bed play was amusing, but I've grown weary of all this fondling."

He gave a disbelieving laugh. "You weren't weary early this morning when you rode me like a wind demon on a—"

"I do not wish to speak of it." And she did not want to think of that joining. The memory was already starting a tingling through her body. "However, I'll tell you if my feelings change."

"Thank you." The irony in his voice verged on sarcasm. "I'll be grateful for any small crumb you deign to toss me. I believe we'd best come to an understanding. I have no intention of—" He abruptly fell silent. When he spoke again, his tone was coaxing. "Talk to me, Tess. Tell me what's wrong."

"Nothing." She closed her eyes and edged a little farther away from him. "I'm weary. I wish to sleep now."

"*Now*, you wish to sleep?" Exasperation and frustration had banished gentleness. "You throw me into this turmoil and then you decide you'll just go to sleep?"

"Yes."

"Well, that's not going to be—"

She sensed he was subduing emotion, gathering control about him again.

"Very well, sleep." He turned over and presented his back to her. "I can wait."

He had been waiting all his life. Waiting for affection that never came, waiting for the wars to end, waiting for his task to be done. Dear Lord, she wanted to touch him in comfort. She wanted to hold him close and rock him and tell him . . .

Her nails bit into her palms to keep herself from reaching out to him. She must not touch him. If she could endure this night, tomorrow would be better.

She just must not touch him. . . .

# Chapter 10

She hadn't stopped since dawn.

Galen paused in the entrance of Hakim's tent and watched moodily as Tess moved swiftly across the clearing with Viane, talking brightly, gesturing almost feverishly. She had been gone when he awakened, and he had only caught glimpses of her for the greater part of the morning. She had been a whirlwind of energy, trailing behind Viane, helping to supervise the erecting and furnishing of the tents, and the setting up of the refreshment tables. He had even seen her frowning seriously as she tasted stew from one of the kettles simmering over the wood fires.

Cooking, for Lord's sake. Tess hated the hum-

drum details of even supervising the kitchens at
the palace. He knew very well that something was
amiss when she lingered over a cooking pot. But
what was wrong, dammit?

She had changed, grown evasive and cool. Yet
coolness was foreign to her nature, and no one
was more blunt than Tess. Last night when she
had turned away from him, he had felt angered
and betrayed, as if her withdrawal had robbed him
of something precious.

Pleasure. She had robbed him of the pleasure
of her body. She had made a bargain, and had no
right to cheat him. This rawness he felt was not
hurt but frustration, because he had become accustomed to her body and no one else could satisfy
him. He should have told her that he would not
tolerate her spurning him as she had done last
night. He should have forced her to give him
what—

"Is something wrong?"

He had been so deep in thought that he hadn't
heard Kalim's approach. "What could be wrong?
Every sheikh of the nine tribes has arrived, and
they're even listening to me."

"You were frowning." Kalim shrugged. "I came to
tell you that we've received a message from one
of the hill tribes."

Galen stiffened. "Tamar?"

Kalim shook his head. "Tamar seems to have
vanished into the air since he rode out. No, the
word was about Sacha Rubinoff. He was sighted a
half day's journey from here."

"Sacha." This news was probably not good if Sacha had chosen to leave the court and come back to Sedikhan, but still feelings of warmth surged through him. He had missed the dry humor of his old friend. "Send an escort to meet him. I doubt if Tamar has truly vanished."

"I've already dispatched an escort." Kalim smiled. "I'm not a fool, Galen."

"No." His gaze went back to Tess. He was the fool, watching his wife like a lovesick swain when his mind should be on important matters. "I'll be with Lomed and Hakim for the rest of the afternoon. Let me know when Sacha arrives."

"Shall I bring him to you?"

"No." He glanced back at Tess. "Send him to the *majira*." Perhaps Tess would confide to Sacha how he had offended her. Lord knew, he couldn't take much more of this without exploding.

The irony of the thought made him smile sardonically. He had waited patiently for almost twenty years for his dream of a united Sedikhan to come into flower, but one night of rejection from a small red-haired woman had him clenching his teeth and ready to rape her. "Tell him to come to my tent this evening for supper, and we'll talk."

"Sacha!"

Tess rushed across Viane's tent and hurled herself into Sacha's arms, then hastily backed away, wrinkling her nose. "Sweet heaven, but you stink of sweat and horse."

"Insults!" He drew back in mock hurt. "I rush

to your side because Kalim told me you'd be devastated if I failed to let you greet me, and you offer me only insults."

"I could have waited until you had bathed. Never mind, I'll hold my breath." She went back into his arms and hugged him affectionately. "What news?"

"Not good." Sacha's smile faded. "The Mother Superior wrote your father a letter inquiring if your journey had gone well and if Captain Braxgan had proved trustworthy."

Tess's eyes widened. "Not good indeed."

"It may not be so bad, imp." Sacha touched her nose with his index finger. "Your father was going to set off the day after I left to find the captain and question him. Perhaps the good captain may have set sail from Diran."

"Or he may not." She nibbled at her lower lip. "My father doesn't know you're involved?"

"Not yet."

"He suspected nothing when you left hurriedly?"

"My august father and brother were about to go on a fishing expedition on the Zandar River, and I told your father I was joining them." He pulled a face. "The excuse was a trifle flimsy considering my feelings for their royal absurdities, but it served."

"Not for long. Diran has few inns, and you would be easily remembered." She frowned. "And Galen is even more memorable."

"Denigration again," Sacha said mournfully. "Only to you, brat."

"Sorry." Her tone was abstracted. "My father's not stupid. He'll ask questions in Diran and find out about the marriage and be on his way to Zalan-dan in—" She stopped, trying to estimate. "How long do we have?"

Sacha ceased trying to comfort and told her the truth. "A week. Perhaps less."

She breathed a sigh of relief. "I was afraid he was on your heels. It may be enough. The *carobel* race is run tomorrow morning, and the final coun-cil meeting follows. Galen could have his union of the tribes before my father arrives."

"Events have progressed amazingly since I left Sedikhan. What was the impetus?"

"Tamar."

Sacha nodded. "Every tribe we passed had news of his raids." He turned and moved toward the entrance of the tent. "Well, as you so rudely suggested, I must bathe and change before I sup with Galen. You'll be there?"

"No."

He turned to look at her in surprise.

She smiled with an effort. "I still have much to do. I'll sup with Viane and perhaps join you later."

He studied her thoughtfully for a minute be-fore he shrugged. "As you like." He paused. "How is Viane?"

"Well." She frowned. "But it's just as well you've returned. Kalim has proved much too obliging with the pigeons."

"I suppose that remark has deep significance,

but I don't think I'll take the trouble to fathom it."
He opened the flap of the tent. "Kalim is riding in
the *carobel*?"

"Yes." Tess frowned. "Are you?"

"Probably, it usually proves amusing."

"Amusing? Just exactly what is this *carobel*
race?"

He raised his brows. "You don't know?"

"I've been more concerned with the festival
itself. Galen said only it was a race of some sort."

"A very special race. The course is laid out
over six miles of desert and rough hill country."

"Jumps?"

He nodded. "Five. That's where most of the
*carobels* are shattered."

"What?"

"A *carobel* is a two-foot pottery jar that's
filled with heavily perfumed water, corked, and
strapped on each rider's back. The pottery is
paper thin, and only the best riders have a good
enough seat to return to the encampment without
breaking their jars and drenching themselves with
the perfume."

"What a challenge." Tess's face was suddenly
alight with eagerness. "It must be very interesting."

Sacha's smile faded. "It's not for you, Tess."

"I didn't say I wished to race. I only said it
was interesting."

Sacha gazed at her skeptically. "The other riders would be outraged if a woman rode in the
race."

She lifted her chin. "But I wager I could best

them. Perhaps it wouldn't be so bad for them to know a woman could ride as well as they."

"You're the *majira* of El Zalan. It would throw the shiekhs into a turmoil and possibly disrupt the council."

Her eagerness was submerged in disappointment. "True." She shrugged. "I was only thinking anyway. I suppose it doesn't matter."

Sacha breathed a sigh of relief as he turned to leave. "Second thoughts are always best."

Tess asked dryly, "How would you know?"

His eyes twinkled as he glanced over his shoulder. "Not from experience. I stumbled across that truth in one of the boring tomes my tutor once made me read."

Sacha was gone when Tess returned to the tent late that night, but the lantern was still lit. Fully dressed, Galen sat on the divan.

Tess braced herself when he glanced up from a stack of papers on the low table before him. His face was expressionless. "I was wondering if you intended to come back at all tonight."

"I would not cause you such embarrassment." Tess moved across the tent toward him. "Sacha told you about my father?"

Galen nodded. "It doesn't matter. By the time he arrives, I'll either have a united Sedikhan with which to intimidate him, or—"

"Or?"

"Or we'll have disintegrated into a pack of ravening wolves." He smiled grimly. "Either way, he'll not find the prospect pleasant for him here in Sedikhan."

She glanced away from him. "You won't give me up to him?"

"I promised you that you'd not have to go back to him. How many times do I have to tell you that I'm not like your father?"

"I thought . . . if Sedikhan is united, isn't my part over?"

"It's over when I say it's over."

"You think you'll still have need of me?"

He looked down at the papers before him. "We have a bargain. You promised me a child, and I won't be cheated."

She didn't have to leave him yet. The relief she felt was frightening in its intensity. She turned hurriedly away and moved toward the curtained alcove. "You won't need a child now."

"I'll decide what I need." A hint of ferocity tinged Galen's voice. "And what I'll take."

Raw anger and frustration vibrated in the tent, and for the first time Tess became conscious of the air of suppressed violence surrounding Galen. "You won't take anything that—"

A scream tore through the night!

Tess went rigid.

Another scream. A woman's scream of agony.

"Stay here." Galen was on his feet, running toward the entrance of the tent.

She was supposed to stay and listen to that poor woman screaming?

Dear God, what if it was Viane?

Galen was already several yards away when Tess reached the entrance of the tent.

Another scream.

Half-dressed men streamed out of the tents, lanterns were being lit.

Tess darted across the clearing toward Viane's tent.

"Tess, what is it?" Viane, her maid at her elbow, held back the tent flap. "That scream . . ."

"I don't know."

However, Galen seemed to know. He was striding through the tents toward the north end of the encampment.

Tess hurried after him. They were now passing through the area of the El Kabbar, but no one was coming out of these tents.

Another scream . . . closer.

She rounded the corner and almost ran into Galen, who had stopped and was standing watching something occurring before Hakim's tent. "What's happening?"

Galen didn't look at her. "I told you not to come."

A slight black-gowned figure was kneeling in the clearing. The woman was still fully veiled, but her back was bare, the flesh striped with livid weals and bleeding cuts. Hakim stood over her, a bloodstained whip in his hand. As Tess watched, he lifted the whip to strike again.

"No!" Tess started toward them.

Galen grabbed Tess's wrist and jerked her to a stop. "Don't interfere."

"Don't you see? She can't—"

"Galen." Hakim looked up and scowled. "I suppose my wife's screams woke you. I apologize for disturbing you, but the girl's not only clumsy, she has no courage." He shrugged. "She's only thirteen. I suppose she has time to learn."

Galen didn't look at the kneeling girl. "We all need our rest if we're to perform well in the *carobel*. Perhaps her punishment could be postponed until after the race?"

Hakim shook his shaggy white head. "She shattered my favorite *carobel*, and has three more lashes to bear. Women must be punished at the time of the offense if it is to be effective. They're like hounds or horses, too stupid to remember for long." His gaze moved to Tess. "Pay heed to my words and actions, and you may yet make a true woman of that one."

Fury soared through Tess, and she took a half-step forward. "If you didn't beat them, perhaps fear wouldn't make them so clumsy that—"

"Silence." Galen's hand clamped over Tess's mouth.

She started to struggle, but he lifted her and slung her over his shoulder and started back through the encampment.

"That's right!" Hakim called after them. "Well done, Galen. Never let them speak without your permission."

Tess pounded on Galen's back. "Let me down!"

She heard Hakim's voice fading away as they neared the El Zalan section of the encampment.

"Don't worry, there will be no more disturbance, Galen. I will gag her."

Galen didn't let Tess down until he had entered their tent. He dumped her on the divan and then strode back across the tent and tied the flaps closed.

Tess jumped to her feet and ran toward the entrance.

"No!" Galen turned to face her. "Try to leave and I'll tie you up until morning." He grabbed her shoulders and shook her. "Listen to me, if you interfere, I'll be forced to punish you as Hakim's punishing that poor child. He would consider it an insult, and retribution would be the only action he'd understand."

"With a whip?"

"Better at my hands than Hakim's. I can't afford a disruption now."

"He's a beast, an animal." Her voice was shaking with anger. "Dear Lord, over a *pottery* jar!"

"Hakim's very proud of his horsemanship and performance in the *carobels*."

"You defend him?"

"No, I'm merely explaining that a *carobel* is more than a pottery jar."

"You could have stopped him."

"If I'd wanted to destroy my hopes for unity. I need Hakim to influence the desert tribes."

"You told me once your people didn't beat their women."

"I was speaking of the El Zalan. Hakim's tribe has other customs, other laws."

"And you can do nothing?"

"Not without unity, not until we have common laws."

"So women will be beaten and stepped on like animals until then?"

"Do you think I enjoyed seeing that girl hurt?" Galen asked fiercely. "Do you know how many times I've seen it and been able to do nothing?" He paused, struggling for control. "And I won't lie to you. Even after union it may take years to change the laws regarding the treatment of women. I can't change in a day what's been going on for centuries."

"We aren't animals." Tess's hands clenched into fists. "Someone should punish him. Someone should make him see."

"Yes." He turned wearily away. "For God's sake, cease. I told you I can do nothing about it. Not yet. Perhaps not for a long time." He began to gather up his papers that had fallen on the floor when he had run out of the tent. "Go to bed."

"Oh yes, I should be able to go right to sleep. After all, he's gagged her, and we can't hear her screams."

He muttered a curse and wheeled to face her. "Why does it so disturb you? Your own father beat you until you bled, and you've told me you accepted the beatings without protest."

"Because I was a child, afraid and believing I had no choice but to accept. I've changed."

"But you cannot change the world."

"Why not? Isn't that what you're trying to do?"

"That's different. I'm—"

"A man? And I'm only a woman, to be beaten and caged like an animal." She threw up her hands. "Sweet Mary, you're as much a barbarian as Hakim." Suddenly, her anger lessened, faded as she saw the expression that flitted across his face. She had hurt him. She had used the one word that could wound him.

The vulnerability vanished, and his expression hardened. "If I were a barbarian, you wouldn't have heard that woman scream." He smiled recklessly as he moved forward to stand before her. "You would have been screaming yourself as I drove in and out of you." His fingers tangled in her hair. "I should have thrown you down when you walked into the tent tonight and kept you too busy to think of anything but pleasure."

"I would have fought you."

"But would a barbarian care?" He jerked her head back and smiled down into her eyes. "Wouldn't a barbarian merely enjoy the battle?" He reached out and began stroking her arched throat. "There were moments when I would have enjoyed having you on your knees. Perhaps Hakim's right, and I should—" He drew a deep, shaky breath. He slowly released her and stepped back. "No." He turned and moved across the tent. He undid the flap closure with shaking hands and threw it open.

"Where are you going?" she whispered.

"Why should you care?" He smiled bitterly as he glanced back at her. "Perhaps to the *kadine* tent. Would you like to come along? Do you wish to observe the barbarian at his pleasure?"

"My words were hasty," she said haltingly. "I didn't mean it."

"I think you did. It explains much. I'm letting you go tonight because I'm sickened of violence." He paused. "But that doesn't mean I'll feel the same tomorrow."

Before she could answer, he strode out of the tent.

Tess gazed after him. Was he going to the *kadine* tent, or had he said that to hurt her?

What did she care if he did go?

She did care.

She was filled with a wild mixture of anger, rebellion, pain . . . and regret.

She had hurt him. She had flung the one charge his mother had hurled at him. All his life he had fought to overcome the savagery within— and she had told him he had failed.

It had been the fault of that old demon Hakim. If she had not been so upset, she would never have thrown that word at Galen. Now, she had a double score to settle with Hakim.

She moved to the entrance of the tent and gazed out into the darkness. Hakim should be punished, not only for beating that poor half-grown girl but for Galen's hurt as well. Yet Galen had said that he could do nothing.

Which didn't necessarily mean Tess was equally bound. Punishing Hakim might be a trifle difficult considering the delicacy of the situation, but she wasn't stupid. If she thought carefully and weighed all aspects of the problem, there should be a way . . .

Galen tightened the leather straps of the burgundy-colored *carobel* about his waist before swinging carefully into the saddle. Twenty-six riders were already at the rope barricade at the other end of the encampment. The men had stripped down to only trousers and flowing shirts, the *carobel* jars bright, multihued patches of color on their backs. An elder of the El Zalan who had won many races in his youth had been given the honor of dropping the yellow silk *camosa* to start the race and was pacing solemnly back and forth before the rope barricade.

Hakim nodded unsmilingly to Galen as he rode past him to the barricade. Evidently, the bastard had found another *carobel* adequate to his needs, Galen thought bitterly as he noticed the sky-blue jar fastened on the old man's back.

"Good fortune, Galen."

Galen looked away from Hakim to see Sacha strolling toward him. "You're not riding? I thought you told me last night you were going to participate."

Sacha didn't meet his gaze as he reached out and patted Selik's neck. "I feel too lazy this morning. I'm travel-weary." He made a face. "Besides, I never make it past the fourth jump before my *carobel* breaks and I'm drenched with perfume. I have no desire to spend the rest of the day in the bath trying to get rid of the odor." He stepped back and gestured to the crowd gathered behind ropes where the riders had assembled. "I'll stay here and wait and watch with the rest."

But Tess was neither watching nor waiting. Galen's gaze went to their tent, and his hand tightened on the reins. After their argument last night, he had not expected her to bid him good fortune, but still a frisson of anger went through him.

"Are the jumps bad?" asked Sacha, still looking at the crowd.

"No worse than at any other *carobel.*"

"Which is bad enough," Sacha muttered.

Galen raised his brows quizzically. "I'm touched by your concern."

Sacha smiled with an effort. "He's ready to drop the *camosa.* You'd better join the others."

Galen nodded jerkily as he nudged Selik forward. He must rid himself of emotion and concentrate only on the race. It was not necessary that he win, but it was important he present a powerful and dignified figure to the other sheikhs, and that meant keeping his *carobel* intact for the entire race. He kept his face turned away from his tent as he joined the other riders at the rope barricade.

A hush fell over the crowd behind the confining ropes.

The yellow *camosa* fell to the ground.

The second jump was a fallen tree with great gnarled branches that had been dragged across the trail.

Selik jumped, faltered as he landed, and then was up and running again. Kalim followed, but Galen could hear him cursing as his *carobel* shifted on his back. He carefully adjusted the leather straps and rode on. Not so with many of the riders behind him. One horse was already down, flailing desperately to gain its feet. The horse of Ladar, the young sheikh of the El Zabor, shied, sending him crashing into a tree on the side of the trail, shattering his *carobel*. The sickening sweet stench rose to mingle with the dust-clogged air.

"You smell like a strumpet I wouldn't bother to bed, Ladar," Hakim called jubilantly as his horse made it across the fallen tree with *carobel* intact. "See how a real warrior does it."

Galen bent down in the saddle, murmuring to Selik.

"What is this?" Hakim's roar was so outraged that Galen glanced again over his shoulder.

He was just in time to see another rider lift effortlessly over the barricade and race past Hakim down the trail.

Tess, a bright red *carobel* fastened on her back, was leaning forward, urging Pavda on. She passed Hakim, then Kalim, gaining on Selik.

"What in hades do you think you're doing?" Galen shouted as she came within hearing distance.

Her laugh answered him as she bent low, her red hair gleaming in the sunlight.

He heard Hakim's muttered curses as Pavda sprayed dust in his face.

Tess took the next jump across the stream only

yards behind him. Two riders fell, their *carobels* shattering and spilling the heavy, perfumed liquid into the waters of the brook. Kalim had lost speed and was falling behind. Hakim made the jump and pounded after them.

A four-foot brush barricade barred the path a mile farther along. Selik was still in the lead, but Pavda was on his heels as they drew close to the barrier. "It's too high for Pavda. Go around it, dammit," Galen called over his shoulder.

She shook her head, the color in her cheeks as brilliant as her glittering eyes.

Galen muttered a curse and then turned back as the jump was upon him. Selik made the jump, not without difficulty, and Galen wheeled to watch Pavda sail over the brush pile with only inches to spare.

He breathed a sigh of relief, feeling a flicker of possessive pride mix with his anger as he watched Tess straighten, her carriage and balance perfect, her *carobel* intact.

Dear God, if he didn't pay more attention to the race, the little minx would be making *him* eat her dust as she had Hakim!

He turned Selik and touched his whip to the stallion's withers. The horse responded instantly with more power, more strength. Selik and Pavda made the last jump across a nettle-strewn barricade almost together, but Selik drew ahead again on the straightaway leading back to the encampment.

Galen glanced over his shoulder. Hakim, Kalim, and several others were still in the field. He

crossed the finish line ahead of Tess with ten yards
to spare. He heard the shouting of the watchers
behind the barricade, but ignored them as he
turned to watch Pavda cross the finish line.

But there was no rider on Pavda's back.

Tess lay crumpled in the sand three yards from
the finish line, her red *carobel* shattered and lying
in splinters, her body still.

Panic raced through Tess as she gasped helplessly
for air. She hadn't expected to hit the ground so
hard, and the impact had knocked the breath from
her body.

She could hear Galen saying something, his
voice oddly husky above her, but she was too
dazed to make out the words. She dimly felt him
loosen the straps of the broken *carobel* and jerk
it off her. Then his hands were running down her
limbs.

"Is she hurt?" Sacha's voice, Sacha's concerned
face, hovered behind Galen.

"I don't know," Galen said hoarsely. "She
hasn't moved."

"Not—hurt," she gasped. "Can't—breathe."

"Thank God," Sacha breathed. "I told you it
was dangerous, imp."

Galen shot him a fierce glance. "But you still
helped her in this madness, didn't you? She
couldn't have done it alone."

"You underestimate her," Sacha said. "I think
she could have managed without me." He nodded. "But yes, I gave her my *carobel* and showed

her where to hide in the brush to wait for the riders to pass."

"And damn near got her killed," Galen said harshly. "Why?"

"She was persuasive." Sacha shrugged. "And you always knew I detested Hakim."

"Not—Sacha's fault." Tess struggled to a sitting position in the sand. "I had to—"

"Kill yourself?" Galen demanded. "Two men died racing in the last *carobel*."

"Had to show . . . Hakim." Tess was at last able to draw a deep breath. She was immediately sorry as the stench of perfume nearly overpowered her. Dear heaven, she stank. "Not . . . an animal." She stiffened as she saw Hakim riding toward her.

The old man halted before her and smiled down at her with malicious satisfaction. "You see what happens when women forget their place and try to mimic men? They end up kneeling humbly in the dust." He turned to Galen and demanded, "You will punish her?"

"Be assured, you will hear her scream," Galen said grimly. "There should be time before we meet for the final vote this afternoon."

"Good." The old man turned his horse and rode away toward the tents of El Kabbar.

Sacha stepped forward. "Galen, I know you're angry, but you have to admit she had justification, and she wasn't as self-indulgent as you might bel—"

"Go find Viane and tell her to heat water for

a bath." Galen wrinkled his nose. "Dear Lord, she
stinks." He turned to Tess and asked coldly, "Can
you walk?"

"Of course." She struggled to her knees and
then to her feet. "I told you I wasn't hurt."

"Then go to the tent and wait for me there."
He turned and took Pavda's and Selik's reins and
started for the enclosure. "Pavda deserves more
care than you do. You could have killed her on
that fourth jump."

"I knew she could make it. I would never do
anything to endanger Pavda."

He neither answered nor glanced at her as he
stalked toward the enclosure.

Sacha gave a low whistle. "Be careful, imp.
I've never seen him like this."

Tess was out of the bath, and Viane was wrapping
her in a long length of toweling when Galen came
into the tent. He carried a short riding whip.

"Leave us, Viane."

Viane gazed in horror at the whip. "Would not
a small stick do as well?"

Galen smiled grimly. "The whip was sent by
Hakim as a gesture of goodwill and a reminder of
how a woman should be disciplined. Wasn't it
kind of him?"

Viane hesitated. "I'm sure she didn't mean to
cause trouble, Galen. Couldn't you—"

"She meant to cause the furor she did,"
Galen said curtly. "Leave us, and tell your servant
to start packing. I've told Kalim he's to form an

escort and take you back to Zalandan this afternoon."

"But truly, Galen, she meant no harm. Could you not forgive her?"

"No, it's gone too far. If I don't punish her, I lose Hakim's vote for unity."

"That vile old man. What do you care—?"

"He's right, Viane," Tess said quietly. "I must be punished. It's the only way. Leave us."

Viane gave her a worried glance and reluctantly left the tent.

"I didn't expect you to be so understanding," Galen said without expression. "Was humiliating Hakim in the race worth it?"

She lifted her chin. "Yes."

"I disagree." He started toward her. "Nothing would be worth what I felt when I saw you—" He broke off as he stopped before her. "I thought you were dead when you fell off Pavda."

"I didn't fall off Pavda," she said indignantly. "I don't fall off horses."

He went still. "What?"

"Well, I did, but only because I wanted to fall." She frowned. "But I didn't know the ground would jar me so badly. I haven't taken a fall since I was a child, and I thought the sand would be softer."

"Would you care to explain?" Galen asked carefully.

"I told you, I fell deliberately." She shrugged. "I didn't wish to enrage Hakim or any of the other sheikhs by a total victory. That would have dis-

rupted the council and your chance for unity. I
thought if I took a fall and broke the *carobel*, it
would be enough to soothe their wounded pride."
She met his gaze fiercely. "But he had to be punished. He had to know a woman could best him."

"But you didn't best him. You gave up your
victory just as you had it in your grasp."

"It was enough." She scowled. "No, it wasn't.
I hated lying in the sand with him smirking down
at me. Next time I'll—" She stopped and drew a
shaky breath. "But it was enough for now." She
looked at the whip again. "Do you wish me to
kneel?"

"No, just turn around."

She turned her back.

"Now drop the towel."

She unwrapped the towel and let it fall to the
carpet. She waited, bracing herself for the first
blow.

Then, incredibly, she felt not the lash but a
warm brushing in the hollow of her spine.

She looked over her shoulder to see Galen
kneeling on the carpet, his lips moving across the
flesh of her lower back. The whip lay on the rug
beside him. She felt a wild leap of joy.

"You're not going to punish me?" she whispered.

"I didn't say I'd punish you, I said I'd make
you scream." His hands cupped her buttocks and
began to knead. "And I fully intend to keep my
word."

His hands encircled her waist, and he pulled
her down to her knees.

"I thought you were angry with me."

"I am," he said thickly. He pushed her down on the carpet, his hands searching, petting, arousing. "Dear God, you frightened me. You deserve to be punished—but not with a whip."

She should be fighting him, she realized hazily as hot shivers began to race through her. She had been prepared for a beating, not his lust, and he had caught her off guard.

He parted her thighs, and three fingers plunged deep and then began a jerky rhythm that brought a cry to her lips, and her body arched upward in a delirium of pleasure.

He spread her limbs, and his hand left her. He bent closer until his warm breath teased the flesh of her inner thigh. "There are other, more delicate torments." His tongue flicked out, and shock convulsed her. "You see?"

His palms slid beneath her buttocks; lifting her, he drew closer. "I'll have no difficulty making you scream for all to hear."

Only a few minutes later his prophecy proved true.

*His mouth . . .*

She whimpered and screamed and whimpered again as he drew her from valley to peak and would not let her go. He permitted her to descend for not more than a moment before he began again. She was not conscious how long it went on. She was aware only of arousal and release, arousal and release. When he finally lifted his head and moved between her thighs, she was trembling so badly she could do nothing but cling to him.

His dark eyes glittered fiercely down at her, his chest moved in and out with the harshness of his breathing. "Never again," he said hoarsely. "You will never take a risk like that again." He punctuated each word with a bold thrust. "I—will—not—bear—it."

He plunged deep, thrust fast and furiously, and only moments later obtained his own pleasure.

She felt a tiny stirring of hope through the haze of exhaustion enfolding her. "It was necessary. There was no danger. You know I ride well."

He flexed within her. "Even better on me than on Pavda."

"Admit I did well."

He smiled down at her and gently brushed a lock of hair from her face. "When I wasn't tempted to stop and beat you, I was very proud."

"Truly?"

"Truly." He moved off her and reached over to retrieve the toweling she had dropped at his command. "And now I believe that our purpose has been accomplished, and sufficient time has passed for me to go to the council."

The heat rushed to Tess's cheeks. "You think they heard me?"

"Without doubt. At one point I was sure your cries would carry to Zalandan."

Her flush deepened. "I was . . . surprised."

Galen finished adjusting his clothing. "You won't

won't be any longer, will you?" He moved toward the entrance of the tent. "Stay here in the tent until the council is over." He glanced back at her lying on the carpet as he untied the flaps of the tent. "You look entirely too satisfied and are notably lacking in bruises. I'll give orders that no one is to come to you but Said."

"I do have a bruise." She touched a faint blue mark where his thumb had grasped her hip. She chuckled. "But I suppose that doesn't count?" She lifted herself on one elbow to look at him. "You believe they're going to cast their votes for unity, don't you?"

"I don't know what to believe. I'm so close. . . ." His hand closed on the flap of the tent. "Perhaps I'm afraid to hope."

She knew she should distance herself from him again, but she could not do it now when he looked so alone. "Then I'll hope for you."

"Will you, *kilen*?" A brilliant smile lit his face. "Then all will be sure to go as it should. How could fate deem otherwise?"

She knew the result as soon as he walked into the tent.

"Unity!" She ran across the tent and threw herself into his arms. "Who reigns?"

"My humble self." He swung her in a circle. "But we're still very far from our goal. A system of laws has to be hammered out, and there's bound to be an uproar at the first dispute. Now

that the union is formed, I have to find a way to
hold the alliance together."

"You'll do it. Who else could accomplish so
much as you have already? You won't let all that
go."

"No." He pulled her down on the cushions,
cradling her in his arms, his face boyish with eagerness. "Dear God, unity." He rocked her back
and forth. "It's happened, Tess!"

"Hakim?"

"Voted with the rest. Unity."

"What next?"

"We go back to Zalandan, and I make plans
for how to shape the laws to my satisfaction and
not Hakim's. The sheikhs meet there in a month's
time."

"Viane departed with her escort this afternoon.
She said to tell you farewell." She nodded at the
cage in the corner. "She left Alexander with me.
I didn't know where we would have to go after the
council, and I thought Viane and I could exchange
messages."

"I don't care if she left you every bird in her
entire aviary. I don't care about anything." He
gave the bird in its wicker cage only a passing
glance as his arms tightened about her. "Unity!"

She loved him.

No inner arguments, no self-deception. The
knowledge was there before her, stark and inevita-
ble as it had been from the beginning. He was a
man worth loving, and she loved him. So simple.

No, not so simple. She desperately wanted freedom in a land that offered none to women, and this joy she was privileged to share with him might well signal the end for them. Unity meant his need for her was enormously lessened.

A child. He still wanted a child. She grasped desperately at the hope. A child in his image that she could love. . .

"You're very quiet." His lips caressed her ear.

She was no fool. She could find a way to work out their difficulties. She tilted her head to look up at him lovingly. "I believe we should have a celebration."

"Indeed?"

She nodded as she began to unfasten the ribbon that bound his queue. She pulled it free and tossed it on the cushions. "A very special celebration. You promised to teach me the manner in which *kadines* give pleasure."

"Then I must certainly do so." He laid her back on the cushions of the divan. "You're right, I believe that would constitute a splendid celebration."

She ran her fingers through his dark mane of loosened hair. The expression on his face held both tenderness and sensual savagery. "I thought you'd agree," she whispered.

A child . . .

# Chapter 11

Several times during the night Tess wakened to the sound of horses' hooves and the creak of wagon wheels. By dawn the festival encampment was nearly deserted, and the only tents remaining were those of the El Zalan.

Sacha's brows lifted quizzically as Tess came out of the tent. "What a springy step, what glowing cheeks. You appear remarkably fit, considering your horrendous ordeal."

She smiled serenely. "I recover quickly."

"But you must have some aftereffects of your experience." He brought the back of his hand to his forehead in mock horror. "What screams, what cries of distress."

Tess's cheeks flushed. "You heard?"

"How could I help it? I was about to come to your rescue when I realized—"

"What?"

He grinned. "That I had heard just that kind of scream before and hoped to hear it many times again before I reach my dotage."

She quickly changed the subject. "What are you doing here?"

"Galen sent me to make sure you were ready to go. A messenger just rode in from one of the hill tribes, and he's talking to him now."

Her gaze flew to his face. "Trouble?"

Sacha shrugged. "We'll have to ask Galen." He nodded to Galen's approaching figure. "But he doesn't look pleased."

"No." On the contrary, Galen's expression was exceptionally grim. "Tamar?"

Galen shook his head. "A troop of men wearing Tamrovian colors was sighted heading toward Zalandan."

"My father?"

"Presumably. Who else?"

"How far away?"

"Perhaps two days' journey."

She felt an instinctive shiver of fear, and suddenly she was a child again, trembling before the wrath of her father. "Then we must go and meet him." She straightened her shoulders. "I'm ready."

He shook his head. "Not you." He turned to Sacha. "Will you come with me? Your presence may help, but it will mean publicly aligning your-self against the royal family."

"Would I miss a chance of tweaking my dear uncle's august nose?"

"I'm not afraid to face him," Tess lied.

"Your presence would only complicate things and add fuel to the fire," Galen said. "You'll stay here under Yusef's protection until I send for you. Your father would be foolish to launch an attack on Zalandan with only a token force. It will be a matter of threats, not battle."

"Then why hide me here? I can't—"

"No," he said sharply. "I won't risk you being taken from me."

She was bursting with happiness. There was no doubt about the possessiveness of his manner. "Very well, I'll stay here."

Sacha chuckled. "Such meekness. The chastis-ing you gave her must have robbed her of spirit, Galen. Perhaps old Hakim had the right of it."

Galen ignored him as he stepped closer and gently brushed the hair back from Tess's face. "I'll send for you as soon as I deem it safe. I'll prepare a welcome for your father that will illus-trate both Zalandan's military power and wealth." He smiled. "Don't worry, dealing with the reign-ing head of a country is entirely different from confronting the sheikh of one tribe. We'll come to an agreement."

"By paving Axel's journey back to Tamrovia with gold?" Sacha asked dryly.

"Without a doubt. It will be worth it." Galen

dropped a kiss on Tess's forehead. "I'll leave Yusef a full troop of men for your protection. Promise me you won't be foolish."

"I'm never foolish." But his expression was grave with concern, and Tess again felt a burst of golden happiness. "I promise."

Sacha shook his head mournfully. "She's just a crushed flower, a ghost of the Tess I knew."

"Be silent, Sacha," Tess said without looking at him. "I'm only being sensible."

"Is that what it is? I thought it—"

"Come along, Sacha." Galen turned and walked toward the enclosure where Said was saddling the horses.

Sacha lifted his hand in farewell to Tess. "God watch over you, imp." His grin disappeared. "And heaven knows we'll do our part to keep you safe."

"It will be difficult for you to return to Tamrovia after this."

He shrugged. "No loss. Life at court seldom amused me anyway. They didn't appreciate either my amazing intellect or keen humor."

It was only a few hours later that Kalim rode into the encampment.

His arrival set off cries of alarm that brought Tess running out of the tent to gaze at him in horror. A rough bloody bandage encircled Kalim's head, fresh blood stained the shoulder of his white shirt. He appeared barely able to stay in the saddle.

She saw Yusef, half running beside Kalim's horse, speaking urgently, but Kalim only shook his head as he walked his horse up to Tess and stopped.

"Kalim," she whispered. "Viane?"

"Leave us," Kalim ordered Yusef as he dismounted. As he touched ground, his knees buckled and he clung to the saddle.

Yusef stepped forward. "Kalim, you're hurt. Let me get you—"

"Leave us." Kalim pulled himself up straighter and released the saddle. "I must speak to the *majira.*"

Yusef muttered something beneath his breath before reluctantly turning and walking away.

"What happened?" Tess asked.

"Tamar. He attacked the escort in force when we were only four miles into the hills. We had no chance. They were double our strength."

"Viane?"

"Captured. They're all dead or captured."

Tess inhaled sharply. "How did you get away?"

"I didn't." Kalim smiled bitterly. "Tamar let me go to bring a message back here to the encampment."

"To Galen? He's not here. He rode out this morning for Zalandan."

"I know. Tamar also knows. He had men watching the encampment." Kalim paused. "The message is for you."

"Me?"

He nodded. "Tamar doesn't want Viane. He wants you. He feels you're the most likely weapon that can be turned against Galen." His expression was wooden as he gazed straight ahead. "He'll trade Viane for you. I'm to bring you to him, and he promised to release her and let me take her back to Zalandan."

"Sweet Mary," Tess whispered.

"If you don't come, he'll give Viane to his men and then kill her." Kalim's voice was still without expression. "He said to tell you this."

Tess dazedly shook her head. "Where is he?"

"In the hills."

"Perhaps you could ride to Zalandan and tell Galen where he is, and he could surprise him."

"Tamar's an experienced raider and no fool. He'll move camp every night. There will be no way for Galen to find him." He looked somewhere past her shoulder. "He said the exchange must take place by noon or not at all."

She drew a deep, shaky breath. "You're saying I have to go."

He closed his eyes for a moment, and when he opened them they held such pain they struck her like a blow. "I'm saying Tamar will keep his word."

"There has to be something we can do." She distractedly ran her fingers through her hair, trying to think. Tamar had threatened he would make Galen break the alliance. Even if Galen didn't love her, he felt a strong sense of possession, and she knew he would come after her. After persuading the El Sabir not to attack Tamar, he would invalidate his own position if he sought vengeance himself. "It's not only me, it's the alliance. Galen mustn't be forced into a tribal war now."

Kalim was silent.

"*Help* me," Tess said in exasperation. "What can I do?"

"I cannot help you. You must make your own decision."

"How can I when—"

"I cannot help you," Kalim's tone was fierce. "Don't you understand? He will kill her, and it will be my fault. I failed to protect her. Tamar took her from me as if I were a sniveling old man. She will die. I won't tell you not to go, even if it means breaking faith with the *majiron*."

"No." She felt a ripple of sympathy blend with her sense of helplessness as she stared at his tortured expression. She had not dreamed stiff, stern Kalim could feel so deeply. "You cannot tell me not to go." She shrugged wearily. "And there is no question I will not go. Viane is no match for that slithering snake."

"No. She—she was very frightened. She realizes what he is. She's known Tamar since childhood."

Tess was also frightened, but she must not let it cloud her thinking. "Then we must get her away at once." She turned. "Come inside the tent and let me look at your wounds while I try to think of a way to—"

"No."

She glanced back at him. "What?"

"I will not let you tend me. I have no right to your kindness."

She gazed at him in exasperation. "Will you stand there and bleed to death, then? What help will you be to Viane dead?" She took his arm and pulled him toward the tent. Her brow wrinkled in thought, as she pushed him toward the divan, she said, "I believe the first thing to do is make sure the trade is done without trickery. We'll take Yusef and the rest of the men to protect Viane after the exchange, and then you can escort her safely back to Zalandan to tell Galen—"

"He will not forgive me." Kalim's words were almost inaudible. "He's closer to me than anyone but Viane, and I have acted without—"

"*Merde*, will you be silent?" She pushed him down on the cushions. "You could do nothing else. You had to save her."

"What of you?"

"I'm not like Viane." Tess began to untie the cloth tied about his head. "You care very much for her?"

"I would give my life for her," he said simply. "I have already given my honor by this act."

"I didn't know. . . ."

"From the time I was a wild boy down from the hills, I have loved her," he said. "I'm not good with words. I do not have your cousin's winning ways. I am only a soldier with—" He broke off, his hands clenching into fists. "She cannot die."

"Of course she won't die." Tess examined the

cut on his temple. "This doesn't look too bad. Is the wound on your shoulder worse?"

"A mere scratch."

"Good. Though you're probably lying." She moved toward the entrance of the tent. "I'll get Yusef to bandage your wounds and give you some laudanum. I'm better with a horse's than a human's ailments." She stopped at the entrance. "And I wish you'd stop looking at me as if I were going to march into a tomb. I have no intention of allowing Tamar to best Galen. I just must think of a way to prevent it. It should not be so difficult."

Fine, bold words, she thought wearily as she left the tent, but how was she to save herself from Tamar and Galen from a tribal war? She would have difficulty escaping by herself if Tamar's force was as large as Kalim said, so she must rely on Galen. If Tamar changed his camp each day, though, how could Galen find him?

Weapons. There must be some weapon she could wield against Tamar. Perhaps she had one advantage that could be used. It was clear that Tamar, like Hakim, regarded her as only a mindless, highborn pawn in Galen's scheme. Maybe she would be able to— She stopped short, her eyes widening. "Sweet Mary, I wonder if I could?"

She turned and ran back into the tent to Kalim. "I think I have it!"

\*    \*    \*

Tamar took one look at Tess sitting straight and proud on her horse and threw back his head and shouted with laughter. "Allah be merciful, what have we here? Did you bring all the goods of the entire encampment with you?"

"I see nothing amusing." Tess lifted her chin haughtily as her gaze traveled from Tamar to the grinning tribesmen mounted behind him. "I could hardly travel without a few necessities. Who knows to whom you'll decide to ransom me, or how long it will take?"

"Necessities?" Tamar's gaze went from the band of emeralds encircling Tess's throat to the gold cloth parasol she carried in her left hand. Her horse's mane was braided with matching gold cloth ribbons, and the horse on lead behind her that was heavily burdened with trunks, valises, and even a beribboned wicker cage containing a bird. "A peacock. Galen's wed a peacock!"

"He's wed a princess of Tamrovia," Tess said. "Which he would never have done if I'd known of the barbarism to which I'd be subjected when I came here." She pouted. "In Belajo I would never have suffered these indignities." She turned to Kalim and said impatiently, "Let's get on with it. Take the girl and go, so that I can get off this abominable horse. The heat is insufferable."

Kalim looked inquiringly at Tamar.

Tamar's gaze was still fixed in bemusement on Tess. "You dislike our country?"

"Zalandan is pleasant enough, but the desert country is unbearable." She wiped her brow with

a perfume-drenched handkerchief and said pointedly, "You're keeping me waiting."

"My apologies, Your Highness." Tamar swept
her a mocking bow. He snapped his fingers, and
the riders behind him parted to reveal a small
figure toward the rear of the column. "Viane!"

Viane rode forward toward Tess. The young
girl's face was white and set, her eyes dark with
pain. Tess felt a flare of anger at Tamar that she
knew was reflected in her face, and deliberately
turned it to Viane. "You foolish girl, you've caused
me a great deal of trouble."

"I'm sorry," Viane whispered.

Tess shrugged. "Perhaps it's for the best. If
he's sensible, this brigand and I may deal very
well together. It may be fate that brought us
together."

Tamar lifted his brow. "Indeed?"

"Later." Tess gestured haughtily to Kalim.
"Take her and leave."

"Tess." Viane stopped her horse beside Pavda.
"I'm sorry, I would not have—"

"If you're sorry, then leave so I can get off this
animal. You know I detest horses."

Viane's eyes widened in shock. "But, Tess, I
don't—"

"Come, Viane." Kalim quickly took the reins
of Viane's horse and led her away.

Would Tamar let them go? Tess held her
breath as she saw the sheikh's speculative gaze
follow Kalim and Viane. She had no faith he would
honor the exchange if it suited him to do other-

wise. Galen had said he was a man who acted on whim.

Distraction. She swiftly nudged Pavda forward, blocking Tamar's view of Kalim and Viane. "Now, I have a proposition for you."

His gaze shifted back to her. "A proposition?"

She nodded. "Why else would I have consented to this exchange? It was my opportunity to leave this dreadful country. If you wish to hold me ransom, why not ransom me to my father in Tamrovia?" She wiped her brow again and said peevishly, "Why do you keep me here in this heat? Is there no shade anywhere in this country? Come, we will go back to your encampment."

"Oh, will we?" Tamar's lips twisted. "I think not, Your Highness. We've broken camp, and we'll have a long ride before we stop." He glanced at Kalim and Viane, who were almost out of sight, hesitated, and then turned back to Tess. "And I will decide when you will be permitted to rest. You'll find I'm not Galen Ben Raschid. He was always soft where women were concerned. It was that bitch of a mother who ruined him for the pleas—" His eyes suddenly widened, and he started to laugh again. "Damn!" He slapped his thigh. "Of course, why not?" He turned his horse. "Come along, Your Royal Haughtiness, I've just had a wonderful thought. Let's get on our way."

"My proposition," Tess protested, shooting a sidewise glance at the curve of the road. She breathed a sigh of relief as she realized Kalim and

Viane had rounded the curve and joined Yusef and the waiting escort.

"Be sure I'll listen." Tamar laughed. "You're proving to be more amusing than I thought. I'll let you speak all you wish as long as you continue to amuse me. After all"—he shot her a malicious glance—"we must have something to do . . . between."

Tess kept her expression pettish. "You're as crude as my husband. I will not tolerate this treatment any longer. I'll be glad to be home in a civilized country again, where gentlemen speak sweetly and courteously."

Tamar gazed at her in astonishment as if she were some startling new animal he had discovered. "Don't you understand what I'm going to do to—" He stopped and began to laugh again. "Impossible!" He was still laughing as he put spurs to his horse. "I could almost pity Galen. What he must have suffered, dragging you from tribe to tribe these last two months. He should reward me, for I'm truly saving him from himself."

"Dear God, you *left* her with him?" Galen had the odd feeling he was breaking apart inside. "You gave her to him?"

Kalim flinched. "It was wrong, but I didn't know what else to do. Viane was—"

Sacha stepped forward. "How is Viane? Did he hurt her?"

"No, she's just weary and frightened. She

scarcely spoke to me on the road back to Zalandan," Kalim said hoarsely. "As soon as she reached
the palace, she went to her chamber, and I came
here."

Galen moved across the chamber toward the
door. "Where did the exchange take place?"

"In the hills above the *carobel* encampment."

"Gather the men. We leave at once."

"He's wounded, Galen," Sacha reminded him
quietly.

Galen whirled to face them. He could feel the
anger, raging, flaming, devouring him. "Do you
think I care? If he can ride, he goes. Everyone
goes. He's fortunate I don't *strangle* him. We're
going to get her back."

Sacha shook his head. "We can't ride out
blindly. You know Tamar. He's like a shadow. We
could be searching those hills for days."

"Then that's what we'll do."

"No," Kalim said.

"No?" Galen said silkily, his glance a barbed
sword as he turned on Kalim. "Perhaps you wish
to leave her with Tamar? You certainly gave her
into his tender care with great alacrity."

Kalim turned pale. "I could not—" He swallowed. "I deserve your anger, but it was the *majira*
who said you were to wait here."

"Wait! She doesn't know what Tamar—"

"She knows," Kalim interrupted. "She said she
will get word to you where she is."

"And how will she do that?"

"Alexander. She took him with her. She said

she would send you word where she was. She also had a plan to render Tamar and his men helpless."

Galen stared at him in astonishment and then felt a leap of hope. He didn't see how Tess, a lone woman, could possibly hope to defeat Tamar's band, but the pigeon might prove her salvation. "How long since you left her?"

"Noon."

Galen glanced at the sky. "It's nearing sunset. They'll be stopping at dusk to camp." He turned and strode toward the door. "Have the horses saddled and the men ready to ride, Sacha. Kalim, come with me and tell me about this plan. I'm going to Viane's chamber and wait for Alexander."

Terror clutched at him, turning him sick and cold. Such a slim hope. Yet it was the only hope he had to free her.

Dear God, Tess had said the blasted pigeon wasn't even overbright. Even if she got a chance to release him, what if the pigeon failed to come back to Zalandan?

Dear Heaven, let him not go to Said Ababa again.

Tess watched Alexander's wings lift as he wheeled away from the tower and flew toward the west. Said Ababa?

As she heard a step on the spiral stone staircase, she hurriedly turned away from the window, kicked Alexander's empty cage into the shadows, and was walking toward her open trunk across the room when Tamar flung open the door and strode into the chamber.

"I can't find my jewel box," she complained. "I knew those louts would misplace it."

"On the contrary, they placed it exactly where I told them." He grinned. "It's in my saddlebag."

"You cannot steal my jewels." Tess glared at him. "What else have I gotten from this marriage? Sand, heat, quarrels, and insults . . . and . . . and *freckles*." She glanced around her. "And now you bring me to this filthy tower. Why are we here?"

"I came here once a long time ago with Galen." Tamar's gaze went to the curtained bed across the chamber. "It was convenient, and I thought it fitting."

*Tamar killed one of the whores in a drunken rage.*

Tess hid a shiver as she remembered Galen's words about that horrible night that had changed his life.

Tamar was still staring at the bed. "Besides, Galen would not think of coming here. His memories of the tower are not as pleasant as mine."

"My proposition," Tess started. "I wish to—"

"Not now," Tamar said abstractedly, his eyes glittering in his bearded face. "Do not bother me. It's good to relive the past at times."

The air was suddenly heavy, thick with malevolence.

"I'm hungry. Don't you intend to feed me?" Tess demanded.

His gaze shifted from the bed to her face. "Dear God, what a persistent shrew."

"And where is that trunk of bottles of wine I

was carrying with me? It was a very good vintage."
She scowled. "Surprising that such uncivilized
people as the El Zalan could produce such a fine
wine."

"My men told me it was quite a brew. Though
they probably don't have the palate to enjoy it
fully." He grinned. "However, I have more dis-
cerning tastes, and I shall tell you whether I agree
with them."

"Those bottles are mine! That trunk of wine
would have lasted me years after I reached
Belajo."

"I'll see if I can wrest one bottle from them
for you. Or perhaps not. I want you alert and
vigorous for the joust." He smiled mockingly.
"Will you give me your favor, Princess?"

"I don't know what you mean, and I'm sure
it's disgusting." She frowned. "But now I'm hungry, and you must feed me."

He turned away. "I'll send someone with a
bowl of stew."

"In my own silver bowl," she said quickly.

He gazed at her over his shoulder. "You're
lucky I even feed you."

"*My* bowl."

He threw back his head and laughed again.
"Your bowl."

He slammed the door behind him, and she
heard him laughing still as he ran down the steps.

She felt weak with relief as tension flowed out
of her. Sweet Mary, she was frightened. Tamar's
expression as he had looked at the bed had made

her almost ill. How could Galen have thought they were even a little bit alike? Tamar was a monster.

She turned and went back over to the window. She could only pray the wine she had deliberately ordered packed would keep Tamar and his men occupied for a time before he demanded further amusement. She hadn't realized she would be this afraid. She was not sure how long she could keep up this idiotic pretense when her knees were shaking with terror whenever he came near.

She glanced at the sky, but there was no sign of Alexander. Had he wheeled away from the west and gone east instead?

"Not Said Ababa," she whispered. "Please, Alexander. Not Said Ababa. Zalandan."

Over the last two hours the shouting and laughter in the guardroom had gradually lessened and then stopped entirely.

Tess's hands closed on the arms of the chair with white-knuckled force as she strained to listen. She could hear nothing. Had Tamar drunk the wine? Was she safe?

Then she heard unsteady footsteps on the stone staircase. Not safe yet. Her gaze wandered frantically around the room.

The silver pitcher on the table looked heavy enough to use as a weapon.

Tamar flung open the door and staggered into the chamber.

"You didn't knock," Tess said as she forced her hands to release their grip on the arms of the chair. "These discourtesies must cease." She stood up and moved swiftly toward the table that held the silver pitcher. "And you didn't bring me the stew you promised."

"All gone. The wine too." Tamar's words were slightly slurred, his eyes fastened malevolently on her. "My men found it a curiously heady brew. I found myself wondering why. . . ." He lurched toward her. "I asked myself, now why should they have grown drowsy and thickheaded so soon when they're used to much stronger draughts?"

Tess's shoulders tensed as she kept her back to him. If she could only reach the pitcher. "It was a very good wine. Anyone could see why—" She broke off as Tamar's hands fell on her shoulders and jerked her around to face him.

"What was in it?"

"I don't know what you mean. Please release—"

She gasped as Tamar's hands tightened with agonizing force on her shoulders.

"What? Poison?"

The pressure increased until she had to bite her lower lip to keep from screaming.

"What?"

"Laudanum."

"Much?"

"I don't . . . know. As much as I could find in the encampment."

"And you played the stupid highborn bitch to lure me into believing you too witless to sting me." His face was twisted with rage as his hands moved from her shoulders to her throat. "Whore!"

*Tamar killed one of the whores in a drunken rage. He strangled her.*

For an instant Tess imagined she could hear that poor strumpet's scream echoing from the walls of the room. Was she going to die here as well?

"Do you think I need you?" Tamar asked softly, his hands slowly tightening on her throat. "Your death will serve me as well. Galen cannot ignore the murder of his wife, even if he cares nothing for you. I thought to play a little with you, but you've been too clever."

His grip was cutting off her air. She reached blindly behind her to grasp the silver pitcher, but before she could reach it, he swung her away from the table. Her hands flew frantically to her throat, trying to pry his fingers away.

Pain!

She could feel the blood pounding in her ears, exploding in her temples.

Her knees gave way, sagged. Tamar was holding her upright only by the merciless grip on her throat.

She didn't hear the door open or Galen's shout, but Tamar did.

His grip loosened, but he still grasped her throat as he turned toward the door, dragging her with him.

Galen. Sacha.

"Let her go, Tamar." Galen's eyes glittered as savagely as Tamar's in the light of the candles.

*He's my mirror. He's what I could be. . . .*

Tamar cursed, released her throat, but struck her a vicious blow on the cheek that sent her reeling. He reached for the dagger at his belt.

"No!" Galen sprang forward across the chamber.

Galen's expression . . . Something was there that she had waited for. Something was there. . . .

But he was moving too slowly. Tamar already had his dagger in hand and was turning toward her.

Galen was going to be too late!

She was going to die.

No, not now. Not when she knew Galen—

Candlelight gleamed on the lifted blade of the knife.

She felt herself falling into darkness.

# Chapter 12

Galen's strong arms were carrying her. She heard the click of his boot heels on stone.

"Don't"—her throat hurt terribly as she forced the words out—"let me die."

"Hush, Tess." Galen's voice broke on the words. "Don't talk."

She opened her eyes to look up at his pale face. Didn't he understand? She had to tell him how important it was that she live and they be together. "It's important. . . ."

Cool air on her face, the glare of a hundred torches from the El Zalan riders waiting on horseback outside the tower.

Galen said hoarsely, "You're not going to die."

She was shifted to someone else's arms as Galen mounted Selik.

Sacha's arms, she identified, as she gazed up into his familiar blue eyes. "Tell him——"

"Don't be stubborn, imp," Sacha interrupted impatiently. "You've put us through quite enough without wringing our emotions with that wisp of a frog's croak."

Comfort flooded through her. Even Sacha wouldn't call her a frog if she were a dying woman. "Not my fault," she said with as much indignation as her lack of volume permitted. "I . . . couldn't do everything."

Sacha smiled down at her. "You certainly tried. Drugging Tamar's men, sending the message. You left us deplorably little scope for heroism. I suppose we should thank you for leaving Tamar to us."

"Didn't reach the pitcher in time."

"Give her to me," Galen said.

She was being transferred to Galen's arms again, wrapped in a cloak and held close. "I did do very well."

"Splendidly." Galen pulled the cloak closer and settled her comfortably across the saddle. "Now, go to sleep and let us do the rest."

"Tamar?"

She felt Galen's muscles tense against her. "Dead."

A broken mirror . . . No, that wasn't right. She had to tell Galen how wrong he had been. "Twisted. Not like you."

"Shh." He pressed her cheek into the hollow of his shoulder as he turned Selik and raised his arm to signal to the men behind him. "You can talk later."

A moment later the rhythm of Selik's gait began to lull her to drowsiness. She breathed in the scent of dew-wet grass, leather, and lemon. "We should—talk. There's much to say."

"Later."

Yes, it could all wait. Now that she had seen his face in that revealing moment, she could wait for the rest.

She nestled closer. "Later."


Sunlight was streaming into her chamber at the palace, and Viane was sitting in a chair next to the divan when Tess woke several hours later.

Viane's features were taut with strain as she leaned over to clasp Tess's hand with her own. "Do not try to talk."

Tess's hand went to her throat, flinching as she touched the bruised flesh. "Hurts."

"There are terrible bruises," Viane whispered. "I am so sorry. It is my fault—"

"Nonsense." Tess sat up and threw off the sheet. Dear heaven, she sounded like a squawking crow. "How could it be your fault? It was Tamar who choked me. Where is Galen?"

"He just left you. He's been sitting here all night."

That seemed an excellent sign to Tess, and

added to what she had seen in his expression last night . . .

"I want to see him." She stood up, swayed, and then steadied on her feet. "Will you help me dress?"

"You should rest." Viane frowned. "Besides, he can't see you. He's just received word that the Tamrovian party has been sighted a mile from the city gates."

Her father! Sweet Mary, she had almost forgotten this new threat on the horizon. Yet she found to her surprise that the news didn't bring the same fear it had when she had first heard he was coming. After facing Tamar, she found the threat posed by her father dwindled. "Is Galen in his chamber?"

Viane nodded. "Why can't you wait? Kalim is still outside in the hall. You can send a message to—"

"I hate to wait. I want to go myself." Tess's brows lifted. "Kalim has been outside all night too?"

Viane flushed and nodded. "He's been very kind, but he will not leave me. He seems to think he's done something unforgivable."

*I would die for her*, Kalim had said.

"I'm sure Sacha would have been equally—" Tess stopped and shook her head. The words felt wrong, somehow. She must think this through at a later time.

"And Galen will not forgive. He's very angry at Kalim for letting you be put in Tamar's hands."

"It wasn't Kalim's fault. I'll talk to Galen about it later." But not now, she was too impatient to put her own life in order. "Come, I want words with Galen before my father arrives." She moved across the chamber toward the dressing room. "I'll wear the emerald-green gown. While I wash and dress, will you choose a beautiful scarf to go around my neck and hide these bruises?"

She must try to speak normally as well. Galen must not be influenced by pity. Whatever his decision, whatever he told her, it must come from his heart.

"Go back to your chamber." Galen frowned as soon as she walked in his chamber. "Better still, go back to bed."

"Why? I belong here." Tess closed the door behind her and looked at him. "And I find bed very boring when interesting things are happening elsewhere."

For an instant a glimmer of humor eased the grimness of his expression. "I've noted you're not overcome with ennui when interesting things are also happening in bed." His smile faded. "I don't want you here when your father arrives. You've fought enough battles."

"But this is mine also. Where is my father?"

"He should be here soon. Sacha rode out to meet him and bring him to the palace."

"Then we'll wait together." She smiled at him. "I must be here to defend myself. After all, I'm

only a helpless woman. How will I know you won't
hand me over to him?"

"Helpless woman? You jest. All of the El Zalan
are talking of how you arranged Tamar's capture."
He frowned. "And I told you I wouldn't— Why
are you laughing?"

"I feel like laughing, I'm very happy." She
moved across the room to stand before him. "Tell
me, Galen, now that Tamar is dead, the threat to
the alliance is much less, isn't it?"

"Yes."

"And you don't really need me any longer to
secure the unity?"

He stiffened. "I didn't say that."

"Then say it. Give me the truth."

His lips tightened. "No."

She smiled. "Then I'm free. After my father
leaves, I will go to France. You will furnish an
escort, of course?"

"No!" Galen's hands closed on her shoulders
as he glared down at her. "You promised me—"

"A child? But you don't need a child now."

"I *do* need a child."

"Not for the unity."

"No, but I . . . need that child."

"But you promised you'd release me when I
was no longer needed for unity. Would you break
your promise?"

"I told you . . . I *need* you."

"It's the act of a barbarian to break his word,"
Tess said softly. "Aren't you going to be civilized
about this, Galen?"

His expression was tormented as his hands tightened on her shoulders. "No! I don't care if— You stay!"

"How long?"

"Forever!" The word exploded from him with such violence it reverberated around the room.

She beamed up at him. "Excellent." She hurled herself into his arms. "I feared you would make me ask you to let me stay, which would have been most undignified."

He stiffened in shock and pushed her away from him. "You wish to stay? Lord, I hope you know what you're saying." His big hands were unsteady as they cupped her cheeks and tilted her head so that he could look down into her face. "For I cannot let you go," he said hoarsely. "Even if it means keeping you here by force, as my father did my mother." He closed his eyes. "Dear God, what does that make me?"

"The man I love," she said simply. "And if God is good, the man who loves me."

His lids opened to reveal glittering eyes. "Oh yes," he said thickly. "I think I've loved you from the moment I saw you clinging to Apollo in that damn bog."

"That's most encouraging, considering I was dripping green slime and stank atrociously." She hurled herself back into his arms and buried her face in his chest. "It was as well we got the worse over at once. After you saw me like that, I was bound to appear to advantage in any other situation."

"Last night wasn't an improvement." His arms tightened around her. "White and still—your throat." He buried his face in her hair. "I swore if God let you live, I would let you go, but when I saw you walk into this chamber today. . . ." He whispered, "I would have risked my salvation to keep you. I'm every bit the barbarian my father was."

"No." She pulled back to look up at him. "You're not your father, and you're not Tamar. You may be a barbarian, but if you are, I love that in you as well as all your other qualities." Her brow wrinkled as she searched for words. "Can't you see? We are what we are. I am too impulsive and blunt, and I like my own way very much indeed. Do you love me less for what I am?"

"No." A faint smile tugged at his lips. "Though I earnestly hope we can modify your impulsiveness in the future."

"It may never happen, as you may die still being a bit of a barbarian. It's the struggle to be better that counts, and we'll go through life doing that together." She hugged him with all her strength. "I think it will prove very interesting."

"Even if I can't promise you the freedom you wish here in Sedikhan?"

"You'll give me what you can, and the rest will be my battle." Her jaw set determinedly. "And that will be interesting, too, don't you think?"

He gave a mock shiver. "Dear God, what fate awaits us all? Poor Hakim."

"He deserves it." She waved an airy hand. "And so do the rest of you."

He threw back his head and laughed, his expression suddenly joyously boyish. "Poor Galen."

"No." She stood on tiptoe to brush a loving kiss on his lips. "I'll protect and love you forever and ever. You'll have no chance to pity yourself."

"Forever and ever," he repeated, his gaze holding her own.

It was a vow, and the knowledge filled her with such exhilaration, she felt as if she were going to explode into a million sunlit splinters of joy. "I could almost be grateful to Tamar, if he made you realize you loved me."

"I realized before last night. I knew when you fell off Pavda during the race and I thought you dead."

"I didn't fall off Pavda. You know I purposely—" She frowned. "You did? Why didn't you tell me?"

"Why didn't you tell me you didn't intend to leave me?"

"The bargain. I was afraid that—"

"So was I." As he saw her eyes widen with surprise, he continued in a low voice, "I've never been more afraid in my life. I couldn't believe you wouldn't leave me, if I didn't force you to stay."

As his mother had tried to leave him.

"I'll never leave you." She gave him a quick, loving kiss and then backed away from him. "That's all I wanted to say. Now, I'll sit down in the chair over there and be very meek and let you and my father have your discussion about— Stop laughing." But the next moment she was laughing too. "Well, truly I'll try to keep silent."

They broke off as Sacha strode into the chamber without knocking.

"What the devil is wrong, Sacha?"

Tess turned to face her cousin and instantly realized what had prompted Galen's question. Sacha's face was pale, his expression dazed. She asked quickly, "What did he say? Was he very angry with you?"

"Who?"

She looked at him, puzzled. "My father."

"Axel?" Sacha shook his head. "I don't know whether he is or not. He's not here."

She looked at him, stunned. "Not here? Did he send an envoy then?"

"Yes, an envoy. Axel couldn't leave Tamrovia at the moment."

"Sacha, what the hell is wrong with you?" Galen asked.

His roughness jarred Sacha from his abstraction. "They're dead. They're both dead."

"Who?"

"My father and my brother. They were both drowned. Their boat overturned on the river Zandor, and they were swept away by the rapids before anyone could reach them. It happened two days after I left Tamrovia. Axel is acting regent." He lifted his head to look at them. "Regent for

me in my absence. I'm now the king of Tamrovia."
He suddenly started to laugh. "Dear God, isn't
that ridiculous? Me!"

"You're sure?" Galen asked.

"Count Mazlek assures me both the court and
the populace are eagerly awaiting my arrival in
Belajo." He smiled bitterly. "It's the first time
anyone has ever showed any eagerness to see me
at court." He paused. "I suppose I should feel
sorry they're dead, shouldn't I?" He shrugged. "I
refuse to be a hypocrite. I had neither respect nor
liking for either of them in life, and I will not
grieve for them in death."

"What now?" Tess asked.

Sacha looked at her blankly. "I suppose I have
to return to Tamrovia at once." He stood up and
moved toward the door. "I'll have to order my
valises packed." He didn't look at her as he
opened the door. "I'll also order your maid to pack
your trunks, Tess. I'll meet you in the courtyard
in four hours."

She stiffened. "Mine?"

His expression was stern as he glanced back
over his shoulder. "Well, as king of Tamrovia, it's
my duty to assure your marriage to Tamrovian
aristocracy."

Her eyes widened. "Sacha!"

His light eyes were as icy as his tone as he
said, "I'm sorry, but the deaths in the royal family
dictate the family line must be strengthened. This
marriage will be dissolved, and within the year
we'll have you wed to a nobleman of the realm."

"What!" Tess felt Galen's arm slide protectively around her waist.

"Well, we can't have a Tamrovian royal princess married to a barbarian sheikh like—" Sacha broke off, dissolving in laughter. "Dear heaven, your *face*, imp!" He collapsed back against the door, his entire body shaking with laughter. "You believed me!"

"Wretch." She smiled grudgingly. "You caught me off guard for a moment."

"I thought I mimicked my father exceptionally well." Sacha shuddered. "What a ghastly thought." He grinned slyly. "And I almost had Galen reaching for his dagger to stab the wicked villain and keep you by his side."

"I was not amused," Galen admitted, his arm tightening about Tess's waist. "Your first act as monarch would have plunged Tamrovia into a war."

Sacha's eyes widened in shock. "*Merde*, I forgot I must start thinking about those boring kinds of repercussions. What a depressing thought." He uneasily shifted his shoulders as he turned toward the door. "I don't believe I'm going to like this business. I'm not at all suited for majesty."

Four hours later Tess stood on the steps with Galen and watched Sacha mount his stallion in the courtyard below.

"I'll miss him," she murmured huskily.

"He's not gone forever," Galen said.

But they both knew Sacha's road was taking a

new curve that was leading him away from them. In spite of Sacha's apprehensions she thought she could already see signs of new power and authority in his bearing as he turned to Count Mazlek and gestured impatiently for him to mount. "He's going to change."

"So are we all." Galen gently brushed his lips on her temple. "Life would be very dull if we stayed the same. You wouldn't like that either, my love." He released her and nudged her forward. "Now, go and tell him farewell."

She started down the steps. "Aren't you coming?"

"I went to his chamber earlier to say good-bye. I have no liking for prolonged farewells."

Sacha smiled down at Tess as she crossed the courtyard toward him. "Don't look so forlorn, imp. Zalandan isn't a world away from Belajo, and I'll remember the way back."

"Did you tell Viane good-bye?"

"Yes." His smile faded. "As well as I could with Kalim hovering in the background. She was very . . . courteous." He sighed. "It made me feel melancholy."

"Nonsense."

His eyes widened. "I thought you'd have more sympathy for my suit."

"At first, I thought you should have Viane merely because you wanted her." Tess met his gaze. "But now I realize she wouldn't do for you at all. You and I are a great deal alike, Sacha. You wanted her only because she represented a safety and sanctuary neither of us have ever had. She would have driven you mad in three months. She's much better off with Kalim. He told me once he'd give his life for her."

He frowned. "I'm not without valor."

"Valor has nothing to do with it." She gestured impatiently. "That's why she's wrong for you. You'd *enjoy* risking your life for her, but what then? You'd go away and search for a new challenge to face. Tell me, why are you leaving Sedikhan so meekly after six years?"

"It could be because no one has offered me a throne before," he suggested dryly.

She shook her head.

"No?" He lifted his brows. "Then I'm sure you're going to tell me."

"You have no desire to be a king. You're leaving because, though the struggle here will continue, the unrest and danger is gone now that we have unity. Don't you see? You don't need a sanctuary. You need an adventure, a great adventure. Viane wasn't your great adventure, Sacha."

His expression softened as he looked down into her earnest face. "And is Galen your great adventure, imp?"

"Oh yes," she said softly.

"No following in Marco Polo's footsteps?"

"Perhaps someday." She grinned. "But you can be sure I'll take Galen with me. *Kadines* are much too well-accepted in Sedikhan for my liking." She reached up and affectionately squeezed his hand resting on the reins before stepping back. "Go with God, Sacha, and return when you can."

"I will." He smiled down at her. "And come to Belajo in a year or two, and you may see a few changes at court." He turned his horse and rode forward to join Count Mazlek and his escort. "I've always thought it needed a bit of livening."

She chuckled as she watched him ride out of the courtyard, his hair blazing in the sunlight, his bearing indomitable yet insouciant. She had a sudden mental picture of him lolling on the Tamrovian throne, bejeweled crown slightly askew on his curly red head, his blue eyes shining with deviltry.

"Lord help them," she murmured.

"Tess?" Galen called.

She turned to see Galen waiting on the steps, his dark hair lifting in the breeze, his expression a little impatient but very loving. Galen was a complicated man, one she might never know completely, one who would change and grow with every passing day. She could hardly wait to see what interesting challenge he would offer her next.

She smiled. "Coming."

She started across the courtyard toward her own great adventure.

## About the Author

IRIS JOHANSEN, who has more than eight million copies of her books in print, has won many awards for her achievements in writing. She lives near Atlanta, Georgia, where she is currently at work on a new novel.

Iris Johansen returns with a novel of even more shattering suspense . . . a chilling tale of murderous greed and deadly passions.

# LONG AFTER MIDNIGHT

At twenty-nine, Kate Denby believes she's finally carved out a safe and secure life for herself and her nine-year-old son. But the gifted scientist couldn't be more wrong. . . . Deep in a research laboratory, Kate is very close to achieving a major medical breakthrough. But there is someone who will stop at nothing to make sure she never finishes her work. Someone not interested in holding out hope, but in buying and selling death. Now Kate is waking up to a nightmare world where a dangerously unpredictable killer is stalking her . . . where the people closest to her are considered expendable . . . and where the research to which she has devoted her life is the same research that could get her killed. Her only hope is to put her trust in a stranger, a man whose intentions are nearly impossible to fathom, a survivor used to putting his neck on the line. For no matter what happens, Kate must find a way to protect her son, and make that breakthrough. Because destroying her enemy could mean saving millions of lives . . . including the lives of those who mean the most to her.

Turn the page for an exciting preview of this thrilling new novel.

The rays of the late afternoon sunlight dappled the path in front of Ishmaru as he ran swiftly through the woods. He always chose a motel that opened onto a wooded area. It was necessary for the preparation for the kill.

He ran faster. His heart was pumping with fierce pleasure.

He was fleet as a deer.

He was unstoppable.

He was warrior.

But warriors should not be guided by fools like Ogden. The kill should be made in a burst of glory, not cool calculation. He had lain awake a long time last night thinking of the kill tonight, the disturbance growing within him.

He reached the summit and stood there, gasping for breath. Below him spread a subdivision with neat, small houses like the one in which Kate Denby lived. If he shaded his eyes, he could see her subdivision just on the horizon. He had been pleased that her house was so close to the others in the neighborhood. It was an exciting challenge for him to move like a shadow among these sheep, to strike boldly.

But Ogden did not want him to strike boldly. Ogden wanted him to hide the act behind lies and deception.

Since it disturbed Ishmaru, there must be a reason. His instincts had told him from the first moment that Kate Denby might be special. Was she Emily sent to challenge him? He would meditate and wait for a sign.

He fell to his knees and dipped his finger into the dirt of the path and painted streaks on his cheeks and forehead. Then he threw out his arms. "Guide me," he whispered. "Let it become clear."

The ancient ones used to pray to the Great Spirit, but he was wiser. He knew the Great Spirit was within himself. He was both the Giver of Glory and the Punisher.

He stayed kneeling, arms thrown wide for one hour, two, three.

The rays of the sun paled. Shadows lengthened.

He would have to give up soon. With no sign he would have to submit to Ogden's will.

Then he heard a giggle in the shrubbery to his right.

Joy tore through him.

He didn't move. He kept his head facing straight ahead, but he slanted a glance toward the bushes from the corner of his eye.

A small girl was watching him. She was no more than seven or eight, wearing a plaid dress and carrying a backpack. His joy increased as he realized she had fair hair. Not the same ash blond as Kate Denby's but pale yellow like Emily Santos's. It could be no coincidence; his power must have pulled the child to him.

She was the bearer of the sign. If he could count coup on her, then that must mean he could ignore Ogden and follow the true path.

He slowly stood up and turned to the little girl.

She was still giggling. "You have a dirty face. What are you—" She broke off and her eyes widened. She took a step back.

She felt his power, Ishmaru exalted.

She whimpered, "I didn't mean— Don't—"

She whirled and ran down the path.

He started after her.

It would do no good for her to run.

He was fleet as a deer.

He was unstoppable.

He was warrior.


"Did you pack my laptop and my video games?" Joshua asked.

"They went in the trunk right after your bat and

catcher's mitt," Phyliss said. "And don't ask us to stuff one more toy in this car. There's barely enough room for the suitcases."

"All we've got in there are clothes," Joshua said. "Who needs clothes for sleeping? We could take out my pajamas and—"

"No," Kate said firmly and shut the trunk. "Now go into the house and take your bath. I'll be in as soon as I check the tires and oil, and you'd better be in bed."

"Okay." Joshua made a face at her before loping toward the front door.

"He's perking up," Phyliss said. "I think this trip will be good for him."

"I hope so. Will you hold the flashlight for me? It's getting too dark to see."

"Sure." Phyliss took a step closer and aimed the beam of the flashlight as Kate opened the hood and took out the oil stick.

"It's a quart low. We'd better stop at a gas station before we get on the road tomorrow."

"You made up your mind in a hurry," Phylliss observed. "It's not like you."

Kate grinned at her. "Slow, boring, methodical Kate?"

"You said it, I didn't."

"I have a right to an impulsive moment now and then."

"Maybe." Phyliss paused. "And it's not like you to run scared just because some young hoodlum decided to rob us."

"I thought we'd all had enough."

Phyliss's gaze searched Kate's expression. "Is something wrong, Kate?"

She should have known Phyliss was too perceptive not to be aware of Kate's tension. "Of course there's something wrong. We're a house of mourning." She knelt and began checking the air in the left front tire. "Will you go in and see if you can keep Joshua from smuggling his tennis racquet into his pillowcase? He was entirely too sentimental about taking his very own pillow along."

"I thought so too." Phyliss chuckled. "What a schemer." She went into the house.

Joshua was always a good distraction, Kate thought. Or maybe Phyliss had merely allowed herself to be distracted. She had a great respect for personal privacy, both her own and—

"What you got there?"

Kate's heart leaped to her throat and then quieted when she looked up and saw the man who had spoken wore a blue police uniform. She hadn't seen the police car draw up to the curb, but there it was.

"I didn't mean to scare you." He smiled. "I'm Caleb Brunwick. You're Dr. Denby?"

She felt foolish. No one could look less frightening. Caleb Brunwick was a heavyset man, with gray-flecked dark hair and a lined face. She nodded. "You weren't the one on duty last night."

"No. I just got back from vacation. I took my grandkids to the Grand Tetons. Beautiful country, Wyoming. I've been thinking of retiring there." He squatted beside her and took the tire gauge. "I'll finish this for you."

"Thank you." She stood up and wiped her hands on her jeans. "That's very kind of you. May I see your ID?"

"Oh, sure." He handed her his badge. "Here's my shield. Smart of you to check."

"I'll return this to you after I call the precinct."

"No problem." He moved to the next tire. "Sorry I'm late. There's a little girl missing from the Eagle Rock subdivision about ten miles from here. Since I was going to pass it on the way here, they asked me to stop and make out the report."

"A little girl?"

He nodded. "She missed the school bus."

My God, what a terrible world when a child could be put in danger because she missed a bus. It came too close to home. Joshua took a bus from school everyday. "Why didn't one of the teachers take her home?"

"She didn't ask. The subdivision where she lives is right over the hill from the school." He glanced at her. "I know how you feel, but they're searching for her now. She might have just gone to a friend's house. You know how kids are."

Yes, she knew how kids were. Thoughtless. Trusting. Impulsive. Defenseless.

"You taking a trip?" he asked.

She nodded. "Tomorrow morning."

"Where are you going?"

"I haven't decided."

"You ought to try Wyoming." He bent his head over the tire. "Great country . . ."

"Maybe I will." She smiled and held up his badge. "I'll bring this back in a minute."

It took more like ten minutes to check with the precinct and return his badge to him.

Joshua was in his pajamas and looking extremely disgusted when she entered his room. "I need my tennis racquet."

"You're taking enough equipment to open a sports store."

"My tennis racquet goes wherever I go."

"I'll make you a deal. Leave your baseball glove and you can take the tennis racquet."

Joshua's eyes widened in horror. "Mom!"

She had known he would never leave that treasured beat-up glove. "No? Then give it up, kid."

He studied her and then nodded. "Okay, now I'll make a deal with *you*. If I need a tennis racquet, we'll go to a store and you can buy—"

She threw a pillow at him. "Brat."

He grinned. "I had to give it a try." He hopped into bed. "Grandma says we have to get up at five."

"Grandma's right . . . as usual." She drew the covers over him and brushed her lips on his forehead before straightening. "Joshua, what would you do if you missed the school bus that brings you home?"

"Go back in the school and call Grandma."

"You know we wouldn't be mad at you. You *would* call us?"

He frowned. "Sure, I told you I would. What's wrong?"

"Nothing." She prayed for the sake of that little girl's parents that she spoke the truth. "Good night, Joshua."

"Mom?"

She turned back to him.

"Will you stick around for a while?"

"You can't put off—" She broke off as she saw his expression. "What's wrong?"

"I don't know— I feel— will you stick around for a while?"

"Why not?" She sat down on the edge of the bed. "You've been through a lot. It's natural to be a little nervous."

"I'm *not* nervous."

"Okay, sorry." She took his hand. "Do you mind if I say that I'm nervous?"

"Not if it's true."

"It's true."

"It's not that I'm scared. I just feel kind of . . . creepy."

"Do you want to talk about the funeral now?"

His brow immediately furrowed. "I *told* you I wasn't thinking about that anymore."

She backed off. It was clearly still too soon to approach him. It was just as well. She was probably too raw herself to maintain any degree of control. All he needed was to see her break down. "I was only asking."

"Just stick around for a while. Okay?"

"As long as you want me."


She didn't look like a warrior, sitting there on the boy's bed, Ishmaru thought in disappointment. She looked soft and womanly, without spirit or worth.

He peered through the narrow slit afforded by the venetian blinds covering the window of the boy's room.

*Look at me. Let me see your spirit.*

She didn't look at him. Didn't she know he was there, or was she scorning his threat to her?

Yes, that must be it. His power was so great tonight, he felt as if the stars themselves must feel it. Coup always brought added strength and exultation in its wake. The little girl had felt his power even before his hands had closed around her throat. The woman must be taunting him by pretending she was not aware he was watching her.

His hands tightened on the glass cutter in his hand. He could cut through the glass and show her he could not be ignored.

No, that was what she wanted. Even though he was quick, he would be at a disadvantage. She sought to lure him to his destruction as a clever warrior should do.

But he could be clever too. He would wait for the moment and then strike boldly in full view of these sheep with whom she surrounded herself.

And before she died, she would admit how great was his power.


Joshua remained awake for almost an hour, and even after his eyes finally closed, he slept fitfully.

It was just as well they were going away for a while, Kate thought. Joshua wasn't a high-strung child, but what he'd gone through was enough to unsettle anyone.

Phyliss's door was closed, Kate noted when she reached the hall. She should probably get to bed too. Not that she'd be able to sleep. She hadn't lied to Joshua; she was nervous and uneasy . . . and bitterly resentful. This was her home, it was supposed to be a haven. She didn't like to think of it as a fortress.

But, like it or not, it was a fortress at the moment and she'd better make sure the soldiers were on the battlements. She checked the lock on the front door before she moved quickly toward the living room. She would see the black-and-white from the picture window.

Phylliss, as usual, had drawn the drapes over the window before she went to bed. The cave instinct, Kate thought as she reached for the cord. Close out the outside world and make your own. She and Phyliss were in complete agree—

*He was standing outside the window, so close they were separated only by a quarter of an inch of glass.*

Oh God. High concave cheekbones, long black

straight hair drawn back in a queue, beaded necklace. It was him . . . Todd Campbell . . . Ishmaru . . .

And he was smiling at her.

His lips moved and he was so near she could hear the words through the glass. "You weren't supposed to see me before I got in, Kate." He held her gaze as he showed her the glass cutter in his hand. "But it's all right. I'm almost finished and I like it better this way."

She couldn't move. She stared at him, mesmerized.

"You might as well let me in. You can't stop me."

She jerked the drape shut, closing him out.

Barricading herself inside with only a fragment of glass, a scrap of material . . .

She heard the sound of blade on glass.

She backed away from the window, stumbled on the hassock, almost fell, righted herself.

Oh God. Where was that policeman? The porch light was out, but surely he could see Ishmaru.

Maybe the policeman wasn't there.

*Didn't Michael tell you about bribery in the ranks?*

The drape was moving.

"Phyliss!" She ran down the hall. "Wake up." She threw open Joshua's door, flew across the room, and jerked him out of bed.

"Mom?"

"Shh, be very quiet. Just do what I tell you, okay?"

"What's wrong?" Phyliss was standing in the doorway. "Is Joshua sick?"

"I want you to leave here." She pushed Joshua toward her. "There's someone outside." She hoped he was still outside. Christ, he could be in the living room by now. "I want you to take Joshua out the back door and over to the Brocklemans."

Phyliss instantly took Joshua's hand and moved toward the kitchen door. "What about you?"

She heard a sound in the living room. "*Go.* I'll be right behind you."

Phyliss and Joshua flew out the back door.

"Are you waiting for me, Kate?"

He sounded so close, too close. Phyliss and Joshua

could not have reached the fence yet. No time to run. Stop him.

She saw him, a shadow in the doorway leading to the hall.

Where was the gun?

In her handbag on the living room table. She couldn't get past him. She backed toward the stove. Phyliss usually left a frying pan out to cook breakfast in the morning. . . .

"I told you I was coming in. No one can stop me tonight. I had a sign."

She didn't see a weapon but the darkness was lit only by moonlight streaming through the window.

"Give up, Kate."

Her hand closed on the handle of the frying pan. "Leave me *alone*." She leaped forward and struck out at his head with all her strength.

He moved too fast but she connected with a glancing blow.

He was falling. . . .

She streaked past him down the hall. Get to the purse, the gun.

She heard him behind her.

She snatched up the handbag, lunged for the door, and threw the bolt.

Get to the policeman in the black-and-white.

She fumbled with the catch on her purse as she streaked down the driveway toward the black-and-white. Her hand closed on the gun and she threw the purse aside.

"He's not there, Kate," Ishmaru said behind her. "It's just the two of us."

No one was in the driver's seat of the police car.

She whirled and raised the gun.

Too late.

He was on her, knocking the gun from her grip, sending it flying. How had he moved so quickly?

She was on the ground, struggling wildly.

She couldn't breathe. His thumbs were digging into her throat.

"Mom." Joshua's agonized scream pierced the night. What was Joshua doing here? He was supposed to be— "Go away, Josh—" Ishmaru's hands tightened, cut off speech. She was dying. She had to move. The gun. She had dropped it. On the ground . . .

She reached out blindly. The metal of the gun hilt was cool and wet from the grass.

She wasn't going to make it. Everything was going black.

She tried to knee him in the groin.

"Stop fighting," he whispered. "I've gone to a great deal of trouble to give you a warrior's death."

Crazy bastard. The hell she'd stop fighting.

She raised the gun and pressed the trigger.

She cold feel the impact ripple through his body as the bullet struck him.

His grip loosened around her throat. She heaved upward, slid out from under him and struggled to her knees.

He was lying on his back on the ground. Had she killed him? she wondered numbly.

"He hurt you." Joshua was beside her, tears running down his face. "I was too far away. I couldn't stop him. I couldn't—"

"Shh." She slid an arm arund him. "I know." She started coughing. "Where's Phyliss?"

"She's using the Brocklemans' phone. I ran out of the house—"

"You shouldn't have done that."

"And you should have come with us," Joshua said fiercely. "He *hurt* you."

She could hardly deny that when she couldn't muster more than a croak. "It's not as bad as it—"

"It's bad enough." She turned at the voice to see a lean, darkhaired man running up the driveway.

She instinctively raised the gun and pointed it at him.

"Easy." He held up his hands. "Noah Smith sent me."

"How do I know that?" How could she believe anything? she wondered dazedly.

"You don't. Just keep the gun pointed at me and you'll feel better. I'm Seth Drakin."

Seth. Noah had mentioned a Seth. "What are you doing here?"

"I told you, Noah thought you might need some help.

I was protecting you." He added, "Though I seem to be a little late." He turned Ishmaru's body over with his foot. "This was the same man who was here last night?"

She nodded.

"I don't think there's any doubt it's Ishmaru."

"Is he dead?"

He bent down and examined the wound. "No. Nasty flesh wound in the right side. It doesn't look like you've cut an artery. Extremely painful but not serious. Pity. Do you want me to finish him?"

"What?" she asked, shocked.

"Just a thought." He turned to Joshua. "Go get your grandmother, son."

Joshua looked at Kate.

She nodded. "Tell her to call an ambulance."

Joshua streaked across the lawn.

"An ambulance for a man who just tried to kill you?" Drakin asked.

"No, for me. I don't want to be responsible for killing a man if I can help it."

"Noble," he said. "I'm afraid I wouldn't be as generous." He glanced away, his gaze raking the dark houses along the block. "Nice supportive neighbors you have. Someone must have heard that shot."

"Most of them know how Michael died, and they've seen a police car here for the last two nights. Naturally they're afraid." She shuddered. "I would be too."

He studied her and then smiled. "But I don't think you'd be hiding behind closed doors if you thought a neighbor was in trouble. I'll be right back." He disappeared into the house and returned with a length of drapery cord. He swiftly tied Ishmaru's hands behind him.

"What are you doing? He's helpless."

"You won't let me kill him. I need to make sure of him. Ishmaru has the reputation of being always more than expected." He pulled her to her feet. "Come on, we have to get out of here before the police and ambulance come."

"Run away?" She shook her head.

"You just shot a man."

"It was self-defense. They won't hold me."

"Maybe not for an extended time, but do you want to leave your son alone and unprotected while you make explanations down at the police department?"

"He's safe now."

"Really? And where's the officer who was supposed to be protecting you?"

She glanced at the black-and-white. "I don't know."

"Probably somewhere spending Ogden's money. Suppose the police send your officer to protect Joshua while they're holding you?"

"Stop it. I'm not going anywhere with you. You could be lying. I don't even know you." She ran her fingers through her hair. She couldn't think. "And you're confusing me."

"You don't have to go with me. Go to Noah at the motel. Now's not the time to make a mistake. You wouldn't be the one to pay for it."

Joshua would pay. Joshua must be protected. Maybe Drakin was right. At any rate, she needed time to sort things out. She nodded jerkily. "I'll go to the motel."

"Good. I'll phone Noah and tell him you're coming. Do you need anything from the house?"

"No."

"Don't change your mind." His gaze searched her face. "Don't get halfway there and decide to take off. You need all the help you can get."

"I'll go to the motel," she repeated. She turned and watched Joshua and Phyliss coming across the lawn toward her. She was still clutching the gun, she realized. She picked up her purse and stuffed the weapon inside. "That's all I'll promise."

"Hurry. You've got to move fast." He glanced at Ishmaru. "And don't untie him. I have a hunch he's playing possum. Are you sure you don't want me to send him to the happy hunting grounds?"

So casual. So cool. What kind of a man was he? She shivered. "I told you no."

"Just asking." He hesitated. "I don't want to leave you alone. Suppose I wait until you take off before I go."

"And what will you do to him after I leave? Kill him? You go first. I don't trust you."

He nodded approvingly. "Good, you shouldn't."

"Leave."

"Promise you won't untie him."

"I promise," she said through clenched teeth.

"Then I'm on my way." He strode down the driveway.

She stared after him. The appearance of this stranger had been as bewildering as everything else this evening. Bewildering and terrifying. He had seemed to know just what buttons to push to get her to do what he wanted.

"Emily . . ."

At the whisper she went rigid and then swung around to look at the man on the ground.

His eyes were open and he was staring directly at her. How long had he been conscious?

"I knew it was you, Emily."

"My name is Kate."

"Yes, that too." He smiled. "You're . . . wonderful, Kate. You did . . . well."

A chill went through her. He was lying there with a wound she'd inflicted and there was genuine admiration in his voice. Noah was right, the man had to be insane. "Why did you do this?" she whispered.

"Coup . . . I will have three when you are all dead." He closed his eyes. "But you alone will bring me great honor, Kate. I can hardly . . . wait."

She took a step back before she realized what she'd done. There was no reason to be afraid. He was no threat. He was wounded, bound, and soon the police would be here. She could hear the sirens now. She would call Alan from the motel and tell him what happened, and he would make sure this scum was kept in jail, away from them.

She turned her back on him and went to meet Phyliss and Joshua.


Ishmaru opened his eyes and watched the taillights of the Honda move down the street away from him.

Happiness flooded him, warming him. The woman had brought him down but he felt no shame. The women were always the coldest, the fiercest. That's why warriors always gave their prisoners to the women for torture. This wound she had given him was great torture. Every breath he took was pain, and she had known it. When the man had asked if he should finish him, she had said no and the man had thought her merciful.

Ishmaru knew better. She had wanted him to suffer. She wanted him to lie here and know she had done this to him. He had been right about the strength he had sensed in her.

Sirens . . . far away . . .

It made no difference what she had said. She had called an ambulance to heal him so that he would be well enough to face her again. She had realized that he was her destiny.

But the police would also come. A gauntlet for him to run before he could get to her.

*Clever, Kate.* She was testing him to see if he was worthy of meeting her again.

He was worthy.

He rolled over and began to crawl up the driveway toward the open front door. He would get a shard of glass from the window he'd cut and slice through these bonds, then go out the back door and lose himself in this suburban wilderness of tract houses.

He was bleeding and each movement was agony. It didn't matter. He was used to pain, he welcomed it.

He was in the shadows at the side of the house.

The sirens were closer.

He must move faster. He pressed his back against the brick wall and pulled himself up to a standing position.

Dizziness swamped him and he swayed.

He fought it back and staggered toward the front door.

*You see, Kate. I'm coming.*
*I'm worthy of you.*

LOOK FOR IRIS JOHANSEN'S NEW

NOVEL OF SUSPENSE

**AND THEN YOU DIE . . .**

A BANTAM HARDCOVER ON SALE

JANUARY 1998


TURN THE PAGE FOR A SNEAK

PREVIEW.

## September 19

Danzar, Croatia

The dogs were howling.
Sweet Jesus, Bess wished they'd stop.
*Focus.*
*Shoot.*
*Move on.*

Dark here. Adjust the light.

The babies . . .

Oh, God, why?

Don't think about it. Just take the picture.

*Focus.*

*Shoot.*

She needed more film.

Her hands were shaking as she opened the camera, took out the used roll, and inserted a new one.

"We have to leave, Ms. Grady." Sergeant Brock stood in the doorway behind her. His words were polite but his expression was full of revulsion as he stared at her. "They're right outside the village. You shouldn't be here."

*Focus.*

*Shoot.*

Blood. So much blood.

"We have to go."

Another room.

The camera was knocked out of her hand. Sergeant Brock now stood in front of her, his face white. "What are you? Some sort of ghoul? How can you do this?"

She couldn't do it. Not anymore. She was exploding inside.

She had to do it. She bent down and picked up the camera. "Wait in the jeep for me. I won't be long."

She scarcely heard his curse as he turned on his heel and left her alone.

No, not alone.

The babies . . .

*Focus.*

*Shoot.*

She could get through this.

No, she couldn't.

She leaned against the wall and closed her eyes. Closed out the babies.

The dogs continued their howling.

She couldn't shut them out.

Monsters. The world was full of monsters.

*So do your job. Let everyone see the monsters.*

She opened her eyes and lurched toward the last room.

Don't think. Don't listen to the dogs.

*Just focus.*

*Shoot.*

*Move on.*

## January 21

Mexico

She just might murder her.

"You see? I told you so," Emily said, beaming. "This is working out just fine."

Bess braced herself as the jeep drove into yet another pothole. "I hate people who say I told you so. And will you stop being so damn cheerful?"

"No, I'm happy. You will be, too, when you admit that I was entirely right to persuade you to bring me with you." Emily turned to the driver in the seat next to her. "How far, Rico?"

"Six, maybe seven hours." The boy's cheerful smile lit his dark face. "But we should stop and set up camp for the night. I'll need to see the road. From here it gets a little rough." Another bone-jarring bump punctuated the sentence.

"This isn't rough?" Bess asked dryly.

Rico shook his head. "The government takes good care of this road. No one repairs the one into Tenajo. Not enough people to matter."

"How many is that?"

"Maybe a hundred. When I left a few years ago, there were more. But most of the young people are gone now, like me. Who wants to live in a village that doesn't even have a movie theater?" He glanced over his shoulder at Bess, who was sitting in the back. "I don't think you will find anything interesting about Tenajo to photograph. There's nothing there. No ruins. No important people. Why bother?"

"It's for a series of articles I'm doing for *Traveler* on undiscovered destinations in Mexico," Bess explained. "And there better be something in Tenajo, or the Condé Nast people won't be happy."

"We'll find something for you," Emily said. "Practically every Mexican town has a plaza and a church. We'll go from there."

"Oh, will we? Are you directing my shoots now?"

Emily smiled. "Just this one. I approve of this assignment. I like the idea of you shooting nice, pretty scenery instead of having crazy idiots shoot at you."

"I enjoy my work."

"For God's sake, you ended up in a hospital after Danzar. What you're doing isn't good for you. You should have finished medical school and gone into pediatrics surgery with me."

"I'm not tough enough. I knew it the night that kid died in the emergency room. I don't know how you do it."

"I suppose Somalia was easy and Sarajevo was a

piece of cake. And what about Danzar? When are you going to tell me what happened at Danzar?"

Bess stiffened. "Stay out of my job, Emily. I mean it. I don't need supervision. I'm almost thirty."

"You're also exhausted and drained, and still you have an obsession with your camera. You haven't taken it off your neck since we started this trip."

Bess's hand instinctively went up to cup the camera. She *needed* her camera. It was part of her. After all these years, being without it would be like being blind. But it was no use trying to explain to Emily.

Emily had always seen things in black and white; she had absolute confidence that she knew right from wrong. And she had always tried to guide Bess into doing what she thought was right. Most of the time Bess could handle it. But Danzar had shattered her, and that had alerted all of Emily's protective instincts. Bess should have stayed away, but she hadn't seen Emily in a long time.

Now Emily's older-sister mode was in full bloom. Time to change the subject before she became any more dictatorial.

"Emily, why don't you try to get Tom on the cellular? Rico said we'll be out of range of any tower pretty soon."

Emily was immediately distracted as Bess knew she would be. Her husband, Tom, and their ten-year-old daughter, Julie, were the center of Emily's existence. "Good idea," she said, pulling out her portable and dialing the number. "It may be my last chance. They're taking off at dawn for Canada to do that wilderness thing. No telephone, no TV, no radio. Just Tom passing on his survival expertise to his heir." Holding the receiver to her ear, she listened intently, then scowled. "Too late. Nothing but static. Why couldn't you choose a civilized little village to bring me to?"

"I didn't choose, I was sent here on assignment. And *you* weren't invited."

Ignoring the jab, Emily turned to Rico, who had been politely ignoring the discussion between the sisters. "We can stop now. It's getting dark."

"As soon as I find a stretch of flat ground to set up camp," Rico said.

Emily nodded, then looked at Bess. "Don't think I've said all I want to say. Our conversation isn't over yet."

Bess closed her eyes. "Oh, my God."

"They've stopped for the night. They're setting up camp." Kaldak lowered the binoculars. "But there's no doubt they're on their way to Tenajo. What do you want to do?"

Colonel Rafael Esteban frowned. "This is most unfortunate. It could cause complications. When do you expect the report from Mexico City?"

"An hour or two more. I sent the order as soon as we caught sight of them this morning. We already know the license plates are registered to Laropez Travel. Finding out who the hell they are and what they're doing here is what's taking time."

"Unfortunate," Esteban murmured. "I detest complications. And everything was going so well."

"Then remove the complication. Isn't that why you brought me here?"

"Yes." Esteban smiled. "You came highly recommended in that area. What is your suggestion?"

"Put them down. Disposal should be no problem out here. It'll take me no more than an hour and your problem is solved."

"But what if they're not innocent tourists? What if they have awkward ties?"

Kaldak shrugged.

"That's the problem with people of your ilk," Esteban said. "Too bloodthirsty. It's no wonder Habin was willing to let you go."

"I'm not bloodthirsty. You wanted a solution. I gave it to you. And Habin has no objection to blood. He sent me to you because he felt uncomfortable around me."

"Why?"

"His fortune-teller told him I'd be the death of him."

Esteban burst out laughing. "Stupid ox." His laughter faded as he stared at Kaldak. That face . . . If the Dark Beast could be personified, it would have a face like Kaldak's. He could see why a superstitious fool like Habin would be uneasy. "I don't use fortune-tellers, Kaldak, and I've put down better men than you."

"If you say so." He lifted the binoculars to his eyes again. "They're spreading out their sleeping bags. Now would be the time."

"I said we'll wait." He hadn't said any such thing, but he wouldn't have Kaldak pushing him. "Go back to camp and bring me the report when it comes in."

Kaldak started toward the jeep parked a few yards away. His instant obedience should have reassured Esteban, but it didn't. Indifference, not fear, spurred that obedience, and Esteban was not accustomed to indifference. He instinctively moved to assert his superiority. "If you must kill someone, Galvez has offended me. It wouldn't displease me to see him dead when I return to camp."

"He's your lieutenant. He may still have his uses." Kaldak started the jeep. "You're sure?"

"I'm sure."

"Then I'll take care of it."

"Aren't you curious what he did to offend me?"

"No."

"I'll tell you anyway." He said softly, "He's a very stupid man. He asked me what was going to happen at Tenajo. He's been entirely too curious. Don't make the same mistake."

"Why should I?" Kaldak met his gaze. "When I don't give a damn."

Esteban felt a ripple of frustration as he watched the jeep bounce down the hill. Son of a bitch. Having Kaldak obey his command to kill should have brought the familiar flush of triumph. But it didn't.

Kaldak would have to go the way of Galvez when it was convenient. At the moment he needed the entire team to complete this phase of the job.

But after Tenajo . . .

"Are you awake?" Emily whispered.

Bess was tempted not to answer, but she knew that wouldn't do any good. She turned over in her sleeping bag to face her sister. "I'm awake."

Emily was silent a moment, and then she said, "Have I ever done anything that wasn't for your good?"

Bess sighed. "No. But it's still my life. I want to

make my own mistakes. You've never understood that."

"And I never will."

"Because we're not the same. It took me a long time to find out what I wanted to do. You've always known you wanted to be a doctor, and you've never wavered."

"No job is worth going through what you did. Why the hell do you do it?"

Bess was silent.

"Can't you see I'm worried about you?" Emily continued. "I've never seen you like this. Why won't you talk to me?"

Emily wasn't going to leave it alone and Bess was too exhausted to fight her. She said haltingly, "It's . . . the monsters."

"What?"

"There are so many monsters in the world. When I was a kid, I thought monsters existed only in the movies, but they're all around us. Sometimes they're hiding, but give them an opportunity and they'll crawl out from under their rocks and rip you apa—"

*Blood. So much blood.*

*The babies . . .*

"Bess?"

She was starting to shake again. *Don't think about it.* "We stop the monsters when we can," she said unsteadily. "But most of us get bored and lazy and too busy. So when the monsters do crawl out, it has to be someone's job to expose them."

"My God," Emily whispered. "Who the hell appointed you Joan of Arc?"

Bess could feel the flush burn her cheeks. "That's not fair. I know I sound like an ass. And some Joan of Arc I make. I'm scared all the time."

She tried to make her sister understand. "It's not as if I go around looking for monsters, but in my job it happens. And when it does, I can do something about it. You save lives every day. I could never do that, but I can point out the monsters."

"And I can try to save you from yourself. Let's talk this out and see what—"

"Don't do this to me, Emily. Please. Not now. I'm too tired."

Emily reached out and gently touched her cheek. "Because of your job. You're too impulsive, and you're always rushing in and getting hurt. That trip to Danzar was almost as disastrous as your marriage to that good-for-nothing Kramer."

"Good night, Emily."

Emily made a face. "Oh, well, I have two weeks to do the job." She turned her back and drew her sleeping bag around her. "I'm sure you'll be much more mellow after Tenajo."

Bess closed her eyes and tried to relax. She was tired and sore from that jarring ride and should have no trouble sleeping.

She was wide awake.

She was raw and hurting and she didn't need additional pressure from Emily. So she had made a few mistakes. A bad marriage, a few false career starts. Her personal life might still be a disaster, but now she was in a profession she loved, she made a good living, and was respected by her peers. If there were thorns that ripped at her from time to time, that was something she just had to accept. Danzar was the exception, not the rule. She might never know another horror like the one she had faced there.

All she needed were two peaceful weeks taking boring photos of town squares and cantinas, and she'd be ready to go back into the fray.

The trucks and equipment had arrived when Kaldak got back to camp. Galvez was directing the distribution of the equipment among the men.

Kaldak silently watched until Galvez finished and turned toward him.

Galvez smiled maliciously. "You'd better grab some of this crap yourself unless you think you can do without it. Can you walk on water, Kaldak?"

"I'll get mine later."

"You know what it is?"

"I've seen it before."

"But you didn't know you'd need it here. Esteban tried to keep it such a big secret, but I knew it was coming."

Esteban was right, Kaldak thought. Galvez was stupid to run off at the mouth. "Esteban sent me to check on the report from Mexico City."

Galvez shook his head. "Nothing. I checked the fax machine fifteen minutes ago. Only two from Habin and one from Morrisey."

"Morrisey?"

"He's always getting phone calls and faxes from Morrisey." Galvez raised his eyebrows. "You don't know about Morrisey? Maybe they don't think so much of you after all."

"Maybe not. Esteban really wants the report. Will you check again?"

Galvez shrugged and went into the tent. Kaldak followed him to the fax machine.

"Nothing," Galvez said.

"Are you sure? Maybe it's out of paper. Check the memory."

Galvez bent over the machine. "I told you, there's nothing here. Now, leave me—"

Kaldak's arm went around Galvez's throat. It took only a quick twist to break his neck.


# Tenajo

January 22


*Holy Virgin, help them. Their immortal souls are writhing in Satan's fire.*

Father Juan knelt at the altar, his gaze fixed desperately on the golden crucifix above him.

He had been in Tenajo for forty-four years and his flock had always listened before. Why would they not listen to him now in this supreme test?

He could hear them in the square outside the church, shouting, singing, laughing. He had gone out and told them they should be in their homes at this time of night, but it had done no good. They had only offered to share the evil with him.

He would not take it. He would stay inside the church.

And he would pray that Tenajo would survive.


"You slept well," Emily told Bess. "You look more rested."

"I'll be even more rested by the time we leave here." She met Emily's gaze. "I'm fine. So back off."

Emily smiled. "Eat your breakfast. Rico is already packing up the jeep."

"I'll go help him."

"It's going to be all right, isn't it? We're going to have a good time here."

"If you can keep yourself from—" Oh, what the hell. She wouldn't let this time be spoiled. "You bet. We're going to have a great time."

"And you're glad I came," Emily prompted.

"I'm glad you came."

Emily winked. "Gotcha."

Bess couldn't help but smile.

"Now," Emily said, "with any luck we'll be in Tenajo by two and I'll be swinging in a hammock by four. I can't wait. I'm sure it's paradise on earth."

Tenajo was not paradise.

It was just a small town baking in the afternoon sun. From the hilltop overlooking the town Bess could see a picturesque fountain in the center of the wide cobblestone plaza bordered on three sides by adobe buildings. At the far end of the plaza was a small church.

"Pretty, isn't it?" Emily stood up in the jeep. "Where's the local inn, Rico?"

He pointed at a street off the main thoroughfare. "It's very small but clean."

Emily sighed blissfully. "My hammock is almost in view, Bess."

"I doubt if you could nap with all that caterwauling," Bess said dryly. "You didn't mention the coyotes, Rico. I didn't think that—" She stiffened. Oh, God, no. Not coyotes.

Dogs.

She had heard that sound before.

Those were dogs howling. Dozens of dogs. And their mournful wail was coming from the streets below.

Bess started to shake.

"What is it?" Emily asked. "What's wrong?"

"Nothing." It couldn't be. It was her imagination. How many times had she awakened in the middle of the night to the howling of phantom dogs?

"Don't tell me nothing. Are you sick?" Emily demanded.

It wasn't her imagination.

"Danzar." She moistened her lips. "It's crazy but— We have to hurry. *Hurry*, Rico."

Rico stomped on the accelerator, and the jeep careened down the road toward the village.

They didn't see the first body until they were inside the town.